The Golem of Hampstead and Other Stories

03.28.17

To Redfern Astle,
From the Land
of Klowns—
Clown Love!!

01.98.7

TO WORTHY COUPLE
FROM THE MAN
OF GIANT
CLAW LOVE!!

THE GOLEM OF HAMPSTEAD AND OTHER STORIES

With a foreword by David Gow

J. Jacob Potashnik

Penny-a-Page Press
Washington, D.C.

A shortened version of "Stalking the Mastodon" appeared in *The Last Honest Man, an Oral Biography of Mordecai Richler*, edited and copyright by Michael Posner, McClelland & Stewart (March 29 2005), reprinted here by permission.

"Sedalia, Missouri" appeared in the February 15, 2015, issue of the on-line journal, *JONAHmagazine*.

The Golem of Hampstead and Other Stories
Copyright © 2017 by J. Jacob Potashnik
All Rights Reserved

Published by Penny-A-Page Press
Washington, DC

ISBN-13: 9780692762141
ISBN-10: 0692762140
BISAC: Fiction / Jewish

987654321

Dedication

My late father and mother, Joseph and Paula, were great storytellers who relished the human drama of the theatre of life. From their relative idyll in pre-WWII Oströg in Poland's Wolyn province, they fled across the border through Mother Russia by train ahead of the Nazis' advance. For two years they lived amidst Tajiks and Uzbeks in Leninabad, Tajikistan and then married during a post-war sojourn in a Jewish Agency collective farm near Bayreuth, Germany. Their stories of survival and those of their friends have informed my vision of this world.

These stories are dedicated to those who inspired them.

Do your utmost and let Providence do the rest!

--Henry Miller

Perfection has one grave defect: it is apt to be dull.

--W. Somerset Maugham

Homo sum, humani nihil a me alienum puto.

--Terence

Table of Contents

Foreword · xi
Acknowledgements · xiii
Preface · xv

King Kong versus Yukon Eric · 1
The Oracle of the Soo · 7
Sedalia, Missouri · 47
The Revelation of John Mullen · 57
Snowdon Story · 103
Elegy for a Hit and Run · 115
Stalking the Mastodon · 141
The Golem of Hampstead · 153

Glossary of Yiddish terms and words · · · · · · · · · · · · · · · · 229
About the Author · 233

Foreword

by David Gow

THE CLARITY, PRECISION, PASSION AND attention to detail that are the constants in Jacob Potashnik's writing call to mind the phrase "G-d is in the details." The phrase is, in fact, a favourite of the author -- in theory, in practice, in his writing, in how he conducts a friendship and in the way he cooks and presents a meal.

In reading Potashnik's work, I often stop and read a sentence again, and then the paragraph once more. He has an uncanny ability to capture mood -- that of the characters, as well as of the happenings and the day itself -- in physical and metaphysical terms, which is to say what might lie in store by virtue of fate.

Haunting in every sense are the encounters Potashnik creates between his characters. One has a sense of them witnessing critical moments in one another's lives. There is a stillness as they seem to soberly drink in the gravity of the moment or the actuality of passing each other by in the continuum of time and personal/political history. His writing is informed by being the son of Holocaust survivors and a first-generation Canadian. The writing may be more political than Political, but the history of nations, of Canada and Québec, is constantly there as an underpinning, backdrop and starry sky above, dropping salt and pepper onto the feast.

The one thing we are left wanting of Potashnik is more. I invite you to walk in, sit down and enjoy the meal, savoury and sweet, which can only be called *Potashnikian*.

Actor David Gow is the award-winning playwright of Cherry Docs, Relative Good, *and* Bea's Niece, *among others. His plays have been translated and produced internationally.*

Acknowledgements

My family and friends have been a constant support and the necessary corrective for literary excess: Carole, David, Pierro, Yona, Tony, Rosie, Jean and the late Steven Goldmann. Years ago, Denys Arcand, suggested I might have a book in me and the popular espionage author Robert Landori showed me how it could be done. I must also send a fond salute to the late and wise Dr. Frantisek Daniel and Samson Raphaelson for revealing the DNA beneath the well-made story.

It is my pleasure to acknowledge the extraordinary work of my friends Ruth Beloff and Larissa Andrusyshyn who proofread the galleys and the resourceful and enthusiastic support of publishers Larry Jarvik and Pierro Hirsch, without whom this book would still be a fantasy.

When I was 49 and resigned to bachelorhood, the fates put out a diminutive, size five, woman's foot and tripped me up. Pascale Landry saved my life, and for that I am forever in her debt.

I was born with the aspect of the confessor in my face and, as such, dozens of people, family, friends and strangers, have, for their own reasons, opened themselves up and laid their burdens down on me. Sometimes, their stories, their confessions and admissions were so heavy, so staggering I did not know what to do with them. Though I might have see them again, at other times in different contexts, these moments of complicity were seldom acknowledged, the confessor secure in the tacit pact between us. Yet, I remember. And so, these little acts of treason.

Preface

What does one do when a story, full, complete, dimensional, with characters, setting, even dialogue drops into one's consciousness? If you commit the time and energy to getting such gifts down on paper, you have to believe that your talents as writer are up to the challenge, even when dozens of rejections from literary journals tell you something different.

Or do you believe your friends, strangers and workshop colleagues who endorse your work, enjoy your stories and congratulate you and encourage your talent, such as it is?

The paradigm has shifted. There is no longer any reason (perhaps there never was?) to stand cap in hand before the gatekeepers, waiting for a chance to be let into the inner circle. More "un-consecrated" work has found its way into more readers' hands in the last ten years than in the hundreds of years before that – much to the chagrin and confusion of traditional publishers. If this is vanity, it is also sincere.

"The Oracle of the Soo" was inspired the stories of a travelling salesman who worked small towns all across Canada in the 1960s. "Elegy for a Hit and Run" is based on an actual meeting when I was location hunting as was "Stalking the Mastodon," a true-life brush-up against Mordecai Richler. "King Kong vs Yukon Eric" is based on an event in my youth. The elements of "Snowdon Story" were told to me by my then-optometrist. "The Revelation of John Mullen" came to me sitting at Wilensky's deli one late afternoon in the 1980s. "Sedalia, Missouri" was born whole cloth after witnessing the opening moments on a train platform in France.

I recited the basic story of "The Golem of Hampstead" to my great friend Pierro Hirsch after we visited Rabbi Löw's grave in Prague. I am unable to resist such gifts and only try to do them justice.

Montreal, August 18, 2016

The Golem of Hampstead and Other Stories

KING KONG VERSUS YUKON ERIC

———

IT STILL EXISTS, BUT LIKE so much in Montreal, it's no longer there. Then it was called Sir Arthur Currie School. Now it has been renamed "Les Enfants du Monde" and serves a student population far more ethnically mixed and religiously diverse than my former teachers, the revered and never-to-be-forgotten Mrs. Hood, Mrs. Granda, Mrs. Ball and Mrs. Dorence, could have ever predicted.

Back then it was still relatively new, a neighbourhood elementary school, a Canadian school with the obligatory Neilson's Chocolate wall maps and classrooms smelling of tears, vomit and plasticine. In the corner, high on the wall, the Red Ensign hung limply. When we pledged allegiance in the morning, we were supposed to salute on the lines, "…to *this* flag, and to the dominion for which it stands." Lawrence Harrison, never one to do things by half measures, saluted with his entire body, the clear highlight of his day aside from eating paper and glue. Our teachers were mostly drawn from the same socioeconomic class; terylene-suited, middle-aged WASP women with husbands serving conspicuously in the Canadian Navy and therefore never around.

My schoolmates were all sweet, innocent. The gentile kids were very white and freckled, some moon-faced, others wan and thin. Their mothers made them waffles in the morning and macaroni and cheese casseroles for supper and looked like Queen Elizabeth. The fathers were managers, paint colourists, draftsmen and insurance clerks and played golf at Meadowbrook or the municipal course north of Fleet Road in

Cote-St-Luc. Though they came from every corner of the Empire, my immigrant Jewish mother referred to them collectively as "English."

There was another less innocent group at Sir Arthur Currie. They came from The Gardens or from Walkley Avenue, housing estates that had been thrown up quickly after the war to accommodate returning soldiers and their war brides. As the ex-soldier families moved on, the underclasses moved in. Poor excuses for slums, but they were all we had. Their lives were different from ours: broken homes, alcohol abuse, precocious sexual activity, a certain mixing of the races, French, English, White, Black, the dirty and the clean. They were tough, insolent and foul-mouthed. They smoked Export "A" and had terrible dental hygiene and didn't give a shit.

The most terrible of these creatures was King Kong. No one knew his real name. He stood a head taller than most of the teachers, six feet at least, and well over two hundred pounds. Who knows how many grades he had flunked, how old he was, but he had a full five o'clock shadow and was still in seventh grade. He had chocolate brown hair, pale, spotted skin and smoked incessantly. Even in winter his uniform never changed: black, hard leather, lace-up boots, jeans, jean jacket and T-shirt. I remember his hands, those fists, huge, always curled and menacing like the ape, his namesake.

I was either terrified of him or fascinated, usually at the same time. Why? Why? He just seemed so terrible, so indestructible. What was he doing there? Why was he so angry? Who was he going to hurt next? I knew about nature, believe me, I'd read enough *National Geographic*, had seen lots of National Film Board documentaries on Friday afternoons. I knew about the jackals that trailed the lion. I trailed King Kong, drawn by his power but frightened of what it meant.

In those years there was a kind of logic to delinquency. Kong seldom picked on the straight and narrow kids. They didn't have anything he wanted and were likely to go to the principal if bullied. Kong went after the other delinquents in the school, the Paul Bachons, the Harold Dikes of the world. They had money lifted from drunk mommy's wallet, they had cigarettes fished out of the machine they turned upside-down at the bowling alley in the Cote St-Luc Shopping Centre. They had switchblades and pornography. So Kong terrorised them.

The budding social anthropologist in me was fascinated by the tribal rituals by which Kong kept his court in line. The quick, open-handed cuff to the head was his best and most common move. If that didn't get your attention, it would be followed by the short, sharp punch to the guts. You'd go down on your knees, and some smart-ass would time you to see how long it would take for you to breathe again. A teacher would push through the circle of onlookers, put his hand on the back of your head and ask you what had happened. What happened? And out of the corner of your eye you would see Kong waiting there on the periphery, waiting to hear if you were breaking the code of the schoolyard. If you would tell. Squeal. But you wouldn't.

It was King Kong's last winter at Sir Arthur Currie School when his power, his rule, was challenged. Yukon Eric was as tall as Kong but slighter, with blonde hair, Slavic features and restless green eyes. He said he came from Whitehorse, and Paul Bachon snorted sceptically. The next thing we knew, Paul's face had disappeared in a flurry of pale, reddened fists, and then there was blood on the snow and Paul was running out of the yard towards Walkley. Yukon Eric stood alone, his two fists wet with Paul's blood, his own pale, sallow face red and wet with sweat. He was laughing, bouncing on the balls of his feet, talking a mile a minute and looking for more.

So it was only natural, only a matter of time before the two met. It was a snowball fight in late winter that triggered the final showdown. And it was also me. I was supposed to get to Hebrew school by four o'clock. Sir Arthur Currie let out at three-thirty. So we hung around the schoolyard, throwing snowballs at the roof, at the trees, at each other. What started as a mild skirmish developed into open war. At one point we found ourselves up against the wall of the school, my group of straight and narrow kids pinned down by Kong and a few of his delinquent creeps. Their aim was not good, as they all wore leather-soled shoes on the hard-packed snow and therefore slipped all the time, making their projectiles pitch wildly. And we were rallying, laughing, as we sent back several well-aimed barrages that caught Harold Dike in the stomach, knocking him onto his back.

Kong was laughing at his lieutenant when I heard a sharp whistling sound and saw a bolt of white streak by my head and land with a sickening slap on the side of Gordon Gills' face. I had never seen a snowball thrown so fast, land so hard and do so much damage. Gordon was down on his knees, keening, then crying, holding the side of his head. Between his gloved fingers a small trickle of blood slipped through, followed by the stone, the grey and bloodied rock that had been at the core of the missile. And then that sarcastic laugh.

Yukon Eric had the high ground, a small hill of ploughed snow on the edge between the schoolyard and the wild fields beyond. He was alone, and in a second my eyes took in the entire situation: his dominating position, the pile of carefully made snowballs at his feet, his sadistic, over-heated delight in catching Gordon in the face, and his arm extended in a follow-through, and the tiny white dot now hurtling towards my own head faster, much, much faster, than our own pre-adolescent arms could throw. My knees gave way almost instantaneously, bringing my head down the few precious inches to avoid getting hit full on. Instead, Yukon Eric's stone-laden snowball just grazed the top of my head, pulling off my tuque, shattering against the very top of my forehead, the rock inside missing my flesh entirely.

There was a roar from across the yard as I went down, but I was able to focus my eyes quickly enough to see King Kong turn his massive head toward Yukon Eric, another rock-filled snowball curled in his hand like a major league pitcher on the mound. Kong's then turned back to me, and our eyes met across the distance. He didn't give a shit about me; I was nothing but a jackal who trailed him. It was the rage at the usurper taking advantage of prey already cornered, the hyena pulling away a hind quarter while the lion was distracted. It was inevitable, and it happened before our eyes. As Kong lumbered up the hill, his black leather boots sliding as they sought purchase, Yukon whipped volley after volley, catching King Kong in the chest and the head with wet, slapping thuds until Kong was close enough to bring his huge arms crashing down on his shoulders. They tumbled off the hill, end over end, arms flailing, landing, legs scrambling.

Once on level ground they squared off like tavern fighters, shoulders hunched forward, fists up, and blood already drawn. Yukon Eric's nose was dripping, an odd orange stain. His wild Slavic face was twisted with fear and spite. King Kong was all business, brushing off Yukon Eric's blows, shaking the rattle from his brain and bearing down relentlessly. We had never seen fighting like this outside of the movies. They were punching towards the head and face, trying to choke each other at the same time. Gordon and the rest of the kids ran for it, but I couldn't. I was tied to King Kong. To run would be to betray him.

Yukon Eric realised, as did I, that he was outclassed and made a break for it. He ran for the front of the school, towards the entrance on Chester Avenue. King Kong caught him at the door and smashed his back with both fists, forcing Yukon Eric to his knees. As I caught up to them, Kong put his hands on either side of Eric's head and started twisting. Eric cried out in pain, a strangled almost feminine squeal that shook me, almost bringing thrilled, empathetic tears to my eyes. Again, Kong applied twisting, wrenching force to Eric's head as though attempting to torque it off.

I never noticed the janitor, Mr. Lemaine, coming through the door. Lemaine was old, at least sixty-five, and lame in one leg. He was a drunk, thin and leathery and stank of booze and cigarettes, but they said he saw action with the VanDoos. He shouldered himself between King Kong and the door, trying to get his knee between them. Kong was totally calm, totally accommodating with the old man but absolutely unrelenting in punishing the bleeding, squealing boy on his knees.

Lemaine pushed himself more deeply between them, telling Kong, "That's enough. That's enough, now ..." Out of the corner of his eye, King Kong spotted me standing on the sidewalk, watching. He held my eyes for a second, long enough for the silent message. I don't know what he saw in my eyes. I know what I saw in his. This was nothing. This violence was nothing. It was just another day.

Abruptly Kong dropped Yukon Eric's head and backed away, leaving Mr. Lemaine to hustle the weeping, bleeding boy inside. Kong brushed past me and sauntered down Chester Avenue towards Walkley. I looked back at the door and saw Eric's blood, orange against the snow. I was now late for Hebrew school.

King Kong and Yukon Eric never came back to school. Eric was barely missed. His entire stay had been only a matter of a few months, but there was rampant schoolyard speculation as to the fate of King Kong. Gordon Gills said he went west to Calgary and was a featured rodeo rider at the Stampede. Lawrence Harrison said he fought under a mask on the weekly Maple Leaf Wrestling Show. Someone said he went to Vietnam and was killed in action. They never knew.

I knew but never told them that King Kong ended up delivering groceries from the back of the sea-green Steinberg's van. I knew this because one day the doorbell rang and there he was, struggling under the weight of my mother's Passover order. As he put the boxes down in the hall, I had a chance to look him over. He was much thinner. The late adolescent hormonal bloat was off him, leaving him diminished in bulk but more sharply defined. His hair was still chocolate brown, but he had let it grow and had also grown a moustache. There was a name tag pinned to his olive green bomber jacket: Willis. As he straightened up, waiting as my mother fished in her purse for some small change, I felt that weird, flushing, guilty excitement standing in his negative glow. Our eyes met, and again that silent signal, that message. This is nothing. Just another day.

THE ORACLE OF THE SOO

———◆———

THE TRAVELER HAD A WAY with the swatches that was hypnotic except, of course, that Nathan was too wary, too sharp to be hypnotized. The Traveler worked the sample pieces, twelve inches square, folding and unfolding them rhythmically, one after another, forming the symmetric delta of a snug Windsor knot so that Nathan could evaluate the pattern, the waft and warp of the fabric, the texture and sheen and finish.

It was an old routine. The Traveler was an old traveler. His line of ties weren't the best, not the worst either but popularly priced, polyester, some silk blends for the carriage trade. He knew better than to pull out the cashmere or the pure silks in Nathan's store.

In this game, the Traveler played jester to Nathan's king. He made his way to the Soo twice a year, Nathan being his most important account in Northern Ontario. He had sold to Sam, Nathan's father. He had seen the store change from an overladen dry goods emporium to Nathan's slick modern operation. He kept the best swatches off the counter this day. The loggers and mill workers wouldn't know silk from rayon, so the Traveler wouldn't insult Nathan's knowledge of his market by trying to push them on him.

In Montreal, the Traveler was known as a natty dresser, but on the road one had to know the rules to make the sale, and the one thing the Traveler knew better than his line were the rules. Nathan expected a certain deference, unspoken and subtle, so the Traveler always dressed down when he came to the Soo. He was content in his terylene and flannel. Nathan could wear the Scotch wool and Egyptian cotton and the calf-skin tassel loafers. The Traveler folded another limp, ersatz, regimental stripe into the clever triangle and waited.

With each move, Nathan would say simply, "Yes" or "No" ... there was no selling to Nathan. You couldn't. How could you sell to the man whose business it was to sell? Nathan was the king of selling, so one didn't sell to Nathan. You submitted to him in the twice-yearly rite. You courted his favour like a spring-blown virgin, and G-d help you if you missed a step. Display the goods, polished and exact in manner and tone. You held the fuss to a minimum, you folded and unfolded, and when he said no, it was no, and when he said yes, you dog-eared the swatch and carried on.

You were allowed to hesitate, but. You could linger on a swatch as though to say, "Your Regal Majesty, you've just turned down my mock, jacquard-knit, high-rolling, runaway smash hit, the toast of three continents and camp shops from coast to coast, are you sure you wouldn't like to reconsider? Yes? Well done, Sir, a cunning choice."

Of course, the Traveler kept his own tally. He moved thoughtfully, methodically, as though the sordid act of selling was the farthest thing from his mind, yet he was calculating to the nearest percentile his break-even point. It was coming inexorably slow this year. Nathan was saying "No," more than he was saying "Yes," but as long as he didn't run out of samples, the Traveler had a chance at a good season.

And after? After, there would be a steak sandwich next door at Griffin's, a couple of scotch and waters, the King would sign the decree announcing the recent acquisition of neck ties, suitable for gentlemen of the city in popular colours and prints for every taste and budget, etc., etc., and another year would pass.

"Yes ... yes ... no ... no ... no ... no ... yes ... no ... ," Nathan kept his tally, too. Long ago, very long ago, he had given up counting the pennies, the mangled, dusty, dollar bills held in trembling farmer's fingers or the blunt, nail-less mitts of the mill workers. Nathan didn't need to count because he was King, and when you are King everything flows through you, and you just know.

So he stood there saying "No" more often than "Yes" because this year hadn't been a good year and so feeling his way through, he knew to buy less but to look as though he was buying just the same. As long as he bought and sold, he was the King.

Nathan was a man who had achieved in his life what few men achieve but so many men aspire to. In his life, in his place and time, he had grown beyond the four walls of his ambition and ability. He had slipped out of the quotidian world of this followed by that followed by this again. Nathan had mastered his world with such complete comprehension that he now ceased to be discernable from it. Groman's Clothing Store was no longer seen to be a separate corporate entity. Nathan was the store, and the store was Nathan. His very senses, his perception and personality in organic extension infused every inch, every molecule of the world he inhabited.

Nothing moved but that he was aware of it. His lungs ventilated the selling floor, his blood was the capital flow-through. The Traveler surreptitiously hoping for the break-even point; the girl at the cash miscounting MacCormick's change … There was nothing, nothing of which Nathan was unaware, and that also made him the King.

As for the Soo, no one ever thought of the store without thinking of Nathan. You couldn't. It was not possible. They were the same, not separable, not distinguishable. Even his presence on the streets of the Soo away from the Levis and the Sans-A-Belt pants, the work shirts and the fleece-lined union suits could not be perceived without the Kingdom in the background. It was always there, always. His face implied power and wealth and authority that were unquestioned. He was a part of the town the way the mill was part of it, the way the river was a part, the air and the woods and the winter night sky. If you grew up in the Soo, he was part of what you knew of the world as a fact, a reality as sure as gravity.

Nathan was trim at sixty-five, his stomach flat from his morning routine with the gut buster. He didn't look Jewish, which worked well for him. It confused the citizenry, his subjects. Just six feet tall, neatly formed with sharp gentile features, with his jet-black hair, blue eyes, thin lips, he resembled a naughty, Irish altar boy. His speech was broad Ontarian, northern Canadian, his voice nasal and high, coloured by gales of old scotch and ginger ale.

He was slight and trim and hard. He played scratch golf. He wore expensive suits that were cut in an everyman style; ostentation would have struck a discordant note and separated him from the clientele. There was nothing to spare on him, no outward sign to betray the affluence, the wealth that he and the rest of the dwindling Jewish community tried so hard to hide.

It was a credo drilled into him since childhood. Hide from the farmers, the miners, the steel workers from Algoma. Let them shake in their pants when they walk in the store from what they could only imagine and not from what they could ever know. It had been a constant refrain from the time he first stocked the shelves on his little boy legs his father's voice would boom down from Olympus, "They must never know how much, how much, how much!"

Insinuate, incorporate the body public and the body politic, assimilate but not quite. To that end, he was on the city planning commission and developed and chaired the first Parking Authority as a response to the growing commercial requirements of the town. Army service had connected him with the Masons, then the Shriners, the playground of the Masonic movement. He golfed, he drank, he drank some more, his oval, leprechaun kisser shining like a full moon.

And then the crowning achievement, the *ne plus ultra* of gentile acceptance: an invitation to join the Lake View Curling Club, where he could sacrifice on the altar of single malt, tobacco-stained conformity. There he was, broom in his hand, tam o'shanter tipped rakishly over his brow, his breath coming hoarse and hacking in the chill rink air, flinging polished stones at other polished stones while crowds of dissipated old money (really, no money) Scotch-English has-beens teetered slobbering, cheering him on. The son, yes, but not the father. Not the old man.

And when the old man passed on the mantle, Nathan was there to shroud himself with it and partake of the special knowledge gleaned from his father's lifetime of service to the community. The old man had given him the running start, but it was Nathan who had built his life and his success into a philosophy. A philosophy that had the strength of a religion and would have become his religion if not for the sobering fear of the G-d of the Old Testament. And it was a philosophy that had become the man himself so that the two were as one, and you couldn't talk to one without getting the benefit of the other. And the secret was "Never sell."

Nathan never sold because he knew when the good people of the Soo stepped in through his door, they were already sold. When they stepped into his domain, they weren't looking for clothes or underwear or work gloves. They were looking for sanctification.

Imagine, no need to haul out the wares, no need to convince, cajole, seduce. When you dared enter the castle, you did so because you had business with the King. What, how much, how many? Details for his handmaidens. You were there to get the King's benediction, and with that in hand, with his blessing, you could take your place in the world, assured that you were well dressed, well shod, in good taste, with everything matching perfectly. You could slick back your hair on any Saturday night, slip on the King's clothing and answer with a brave face that you got it all at Groman's.

How many of the Traveler's ties had the King sold? The Traveler could count them on the necks of the good men of the town. He could tell the age and social rank of almost every man in town by the tie he was wearing, and he could know with absolute certainty that the tie had been bought at Groman's.

"Howdja do this year?" Nathan inquired, to break the monotony.

"Shit," replied the Traveler. "Kamloops wasn't bad, Medicine Hat and Moose Jaw ... Moose Jaw fer chrissake," he moaned, shaking his head. "Brandon bought a few, Kenora, Thunder Bay wasn't bad..."

Nathan fished a roll of butterscotch Lifesavers from his pocket, his favourite. He offered the roll to the Traveler.

"No thanks," replied the Traveler, looking longingly at the candy.

Nathan raised an eyebrow.

"I got sugar. Doctor says ..." His voice trailed off as he followed Nathan's gaze, followed as Nathan's eyes followed the uniformed man into the store.

Buddy Lake looked very impressive in his chief constable's uniform. Blonde, tall and ruddy-faced, Buddy was the adopted son of Joe and Esperanza Lake. Joe Lake and Nathan were old friends; they had served together in Italy during World War II. When they got their walking papers after VE Day, Nathan returned to Sault Ste Marie to take over the store; but Joe, who had always suffered from wanderlust, went on an extended and debauched tour of Central and South America, which culminated one morning when the young and no longer innocent small-town Jew awoke to find himself curled up in a cramped hammock swaying in the sea breeze in a small coastal town in Bahia. Rubbing the sea salt from his eyes, Joe was surprised to find himself not alone. Wrapped around him was the beautiful Esperanza, the seventeen-year-old daughter of a local worthy. She waved a paper in front of his confused face which, when he was able to decipher it, appeared to be, to his horror, a certificate of marriage.

When he tried to protest, Esperanza suddenly manifested several older, beefy-looking brothers. Resigned to fate, Joe returned with his bride to the Soo, where Esperanza was duly converted to Reform Judaism and where she remained stubbornly without child, an advantage in her previous vocation but hardly a quality valued by someone looking to make a patriarch of her husband. So they adopted.

It was rumoured that Buddy's real father had been a member of the wartime O.S.S. who had impregnated his mother while passing through the Soo in search of a U-boat crew rumoured to have penetrated the Great Lakes and to be hiding out in the tall timber surrounding the city. Buddy grew up blonde, blue-eyed and pretty beefy himself and, despite the advantages of a Jewish upbringing, fulfilled his genetic patterning and was drawn to police work where, through diligence and craft, he rose to the position of chief constable.

"Howyerdoin', Jesse?" drawled Buddy to the Traveler.

"I got sugar, how are you?" replied the Traveler, impatiently flicking his sample squares but otherwise poker-faced.

"Unc? Can you come down to the station? I got a call. We got stranger, a holy roller."

Nathan looked up, squinting, smiling.

"A religious, uh, a Hassid, an Orthodox," fumbled Buddy, his cheeks going even redder that their normal rosy color.

"Yeah, so?" laughed Nathan, already on the move to get his coat.

The King was being called to civic duty. No one trifled with his time or patience. When they called him, it was always a matter of the highest importance.

Buddy continued his explanation to the Traveler.

"The morning patrol found him at the bus station, cold, broke and wandering around. He's got a piece of paper with a Toronto address, only speaks Yiddish."

"Well, why didn't you call Marty Halpern, ferchrissake? I can barely understand it, let alone speak!" Nathan fired off, agitated as he struggled into his vicuna overcoat.

"The Halperns are in Florida, Maidy's visiting her brother in Sudbury, the Katzes are in Las Vegas on the junket with your brother. I was in the area when I got the call. Are ya comin'?" whined Buddy, sighing much as he did when he was a little, round, red-faced boy. Nathan followed him out of the store, reaching up to tousle the hair of his ruddy, husky little nephew.

There is nothing so pitiful, thought Nathan, as a confused, lost and lonely old Jew. Multiply that ten times when the Jew is Hassidic. The man was old, older than seventy-five but younger than ninety. He was old. He wore a heavy black gabardine overcoat, a heavy, round, black wide-brimmed hat, heavy-looking black shoes and carried a small black leather satchel. He was quite small, frail and had a full white beard. His sidelocks were wound behind his ears, but the gait, the furtive milky-blue eyes, the fine pink fingers with their trimmed blunt nails, delicate yet well-formed, were the give-away. A man of the Book.

He sat under the police station's harsh green fluorescent lighting on a zinc-plated chair that was old when it was new. His feet barely touched the floor, giving him the aspect of a truant schoolboy awaiting the principal. His face was laced with emotions, none of them particularly positive: fear, mistrust, hurt, confusion. This was a frightened old man.

A Hassidic Jew in the Soo. A cat in the hat. About as likely. Sault Ste Marie had the occasional Mennonite perhaps, even Hutterites but no, he was definitely a Hassid with a crumpled piece of paper in his hand and a searching, somewhat puzzled yearning look on his face.

As Buddy checked in at the front desk, Nathan went over to the man, holding his breath, his stomach suddenly jumpy. He extended his hand, twisting his lips into a Cupid's bow smile. He screwed up his courage and offered one of the few Yiddish phrases he could manage with any degree of accurate pronunciation.

"Voos machkst a Yid?"

The old man looked up with a start, as though pricked in a tender part of his body. He strained his face towards Nathan, holding his breath in a silent plea.

Nathan repeated the phrase more slowly, this time getting the sounds absolutely right and all wrong at the same time, and a dark sky split open to reveal a blinding yellow sun. The old man rose feebly, painfully, reaching out to grasp Nathan's hand, his scotch drinking, curling, crap shooting, ham-eating hand between his own two white-skinned, blue-veined, scholar's hands and to hug that hand to his chest while he heaved and moaned in gratitude. Behind the police desk, the silence was deafening.

The Traveler watched, with heavy-lidded interest, as Nathan led the old man into the store and towards the counter where he was still tallying up Nathan's order.

"Maybe he was left over from a mission," kidded the Traveler.

It wasn't altogether impossible. Nathan was on every Jewish charity list in the country. And lately, as though to confirm a place at the table, that long table at the end of it all, he had started making substantial and not all that anonymous contributions to Chabad Lubavitch, those zealots of inebriated and joyously musical observance of the Old Testament. Eventually they had sent out a contingent of young vigorous Hassids to see just who was this great Jew of the North who was almost single-handedly underwriting their yeshiva. They would enter the store and create havoc trying on bush jackets and hob-nailed boots, pose for pictures in beaver hats, decline the invitation to stay for supper, and then be gone with a freshly inked cheque in their hands.

It was possible that this old man had been on a bus, a bus mission through northern Ontario. Maybe he had gotten separated?

The Traveler reached out for the crumpled note in the old man's hand while Nathan drew him away from the front cash and back over to the tie counter where it was quiet. The salesgirls skittered around trying to crane a look without being too obvious. Nathan was aware of the picture he and this old Hassid created, and it was an image he wasn't comfortable with. It's not that he was ashamed of being a Jew, far from it. He just wasn't comfortable with it being waved in the faces of his staff or his clients. No need to remind them, no need to underline it.

"Fon vonnet kimst du?" asked the Traveler in faltering Yiddish.

"Oi, barouch Hashem, du bist Yidden? Oi, ich daft dir zugen, ich chob gemaint as ich vill starben in dem studt. Alayn, alayn..."

He grabbed the Traveler's hand, shaking it weakly, gratefully.

"Chob nisht kin moira, du bist mitt freunts. Nu, zug mir, fon vonnet kimst du?"

Nathan had pulled up a chair for the old man to sit on. The Hassid removed his hat, revealing a worn yarmulke beneath. As he spoke, he ran his hand around and around the hat brim, like a nervous child confessing a misdeed. The Traveler listened carefully to the sing-song tale.

"I don't believe this," said the Traveler, gazing across to Nathan. "He's been traveling from Victoria, by bus! Visiting someone, I'm not sure who. He's run out of money and this address, Nate, it's a Toronto address here, Thornhill. You know this street?"

Nathan glanced at the note. It was a piece of paper like one would find in a primary school notebook. It had been torn raggedly from a larger piece. The address in Thornhill was written with a soft pencil. It was quite faint but still legible.

The Traveler continued. "He's run out of money, but he has this address of his brother ... Oh, I get it, that's his brother's address in Toronto."

Nathan held out his hand, and the old man struggled to rise.

"Ich bin Nathan Groman," he said his Yiddish, sounding distinctly Gaelic.

"Langleben," replied the old man, allowing Nathan to shake his hand.

Nathan turned to the Traveler as he put his hand into his pocket and drew out his wallet.

"Ask him how much he needs, and tell him we'll take him to lunch and wherever he wants to go, if he wants to spend the night."

The Traveler turned to Langleben, who appeared to be trying to follow the meaning of Nathan's words. The old man grew sullen and appeared uncomfortable as the Traveler spoke. He turned away from the Traveler even as Nathan extended his billfold.

Nathan noted the change in Langleben's demeanour before the Traveler.

"What's wrong? What did you say to him?"

"Just what you said," replied the Traveler defensively.

Nathan moved sideways, cornering the old man, his wallet still extended.

"How much do you need?" he asked and then, "Uh, gelt..."

Nathan looked back to the Traveler, who attempted once again to explain to the old man, but Langleben cut him short. Drawing the Traveler aside, he spoke in quiet, sharply hushed tones, and then drew away, sitting back down in the chair and crossing his arms.

The Traveler drew close to Nathan, his eyes downcast.

"We've insulted him," whispered the Traveler, looking back over his shoulder. "I think he understands a little English."

"Where's the insult?" replied Nathan incredulously. "He needs some money. I'm going to give it to him. What's he upset about?"

The Traveler lowered his voice, drawing Nathan away so that their backs were to Langleben, who continued to sit staring straight ahead.

"He told me he's not a shnorer and he's not a bum. He just miscalculated his traveling money, and all he wants to do is buy a ticket for the train to Toronto and go. Now!"

The Traveler drew back, nodding his head affirmatively as though to say, "There! You with the fastest wallet in the Soo, that'll show you!"

Nathan drew back confused. "Did you tell him I'm offering the money to him, a gift? I don't understand!"

The Traveler pulled back, shaking his head, puzzled.

"I don't, either. I think he didn't like the way you pushed your wallet under his nose. He's a little proud this one." The Traveler smiled wryly. "He asked me if you were really Jewish."

"Oh, come on, I ain't got the time for this," moaned Nathan in exasperation. He calmed himself. "Okay, ask him, politely, what he would like me to do."

The two men walked slowly back to Langleben, who was quietly observing life in the Soo through the windows of its most famous store. The Traveler very quietly and gently inquired of the old man if there was any way that they could help him get to Toronto.

Langleben thought for a moment and then reluctantly, as though coming to an inexorable conclusion himself, started speaking rapidly and with some energy to Nathan, pausing every few words so that the Traveler could translate.

"He doesn't want you to give him money, that's not why he came. He says he's just happy to find Jews in such a far-off town."

"Does he want to come home? I've got to tell Bella."

"No, wait," said the Traveler, listening once again to the old man.

The two exchanged some more words, the Traveler becoming progressively more and more quiet and mystified. Finally he turned to Nathan.

"He doesn't want you to give him money. He wants you to *lend* him money."

Nathan gazed at the Traveler for a second and then turned back to Langleben, who had suddenly taken on the air of a man about to propose a deal. The hair on Nathan's neck prickled. This was talk that Nathan knew only too well.

"How much does he want?" he asked a little archly, a sly Cupid's grin crinkling his choirboy face.

"He wants to borrow three hundred dollars. Canadian," the Traveler said flatly.

Once again, and this time without a trace of a flourish, Nathan slipped out his billfold and started counting. The Traveler stopped him.

"And he wants to leave you with collateral."

The old man started speaking.

"He says you lend him the three hundred Canadian dollars ..."

The old man reached deep into an inner pocket and withdrew a small black velvet box.

"... and he'll give you this to hold. When he gets to Toronto, his brother will send you back the three hundred dollars and you send back this."

The Traveler reached out but, still chatting away, Langleben managed to avoid being separated from the small black velvet box.

"He says that this thing is worth more than the three hundred dollars but that he feels that you are a good Jew and that it's safe with you."

Nathan put away his billfold and slowly reached for the black velvet box. Langleben stopped talking and allowed him to take it. Nathan turned the box, searching for the side that opened. The Traveler moved closer as Nathan pried open the surprisingly tight lid.

Nathan had never seen a diamond like that before, so he could be excused for reacting as he did. The Traveler, on the other hand, knew exactly what he was looking at, so there was no excuse for the long slow whistle. As Langleben beamed proudly from his chair, Nathan reached inside the box and drew the stone out into light.

Even without knowing anything about diamonds, it was clear to Nathan that this was something special and the more he looked at it, the more he held it against the light, the more he watched as it caught the light and split it into a myriad of coloured shards of crystal and air, the more it began to appreciate in his mind and imagination. This wasn't a piece of stone, this was like holding something holy.

Nathan caught himself and put it hastily back into its custom box and handed it back to the old man. He pulled a wad of money from his wallet and tried to put it into the old man's hands.

"Listen, you don't have to leave me nothing, O.K.? Nisht gut, nisht gut," he said. Turning to the Traveler, "Will you help me here for chrissake! Tell him it's not necessary. He can take the money, here's my card. Tell your brother to send it to me whenever he wants."

Nathan gently helped the old man to his feet and tried to lead him to the door. But Langleben turned away once more and appealed to the Traveler. They spoke in Yiddish again, rapidly. The Traveler turned helplessly to Nathan.

"What the hell's wrong with you, for godsake? Why are you acting like this?" cried the Traveler angrily.

"What did I do?" replied Nathan, laughing defensively. "Just tell him it's not necessary, I don't need security. Tell him to take the money."

The old man pushed Nathan's money into the Traveler's hand, put his black velvet box back into a deep inside pocket and started towards the front door. Outside, the early afternoon sky had darkened, threatening snow. Indeed, a few flakes had already fallen.

The Traveler turned to Nathan.

"He's leaving, for chrissake,"

"What did I do?" protested Nathan, shrugging his shoulders. He smiled his leprechaun grin, but the Traveler was having none of it.

"You treated him like a thief, for godssake. What is it with you? An old man stumbles in, he wants to borrow a lousy three hundred bucks, and you treat him like he's a goddamned thief."

The old man was almost at the front door. He looked ten times smaller and one hundred times more frail than when he walked in.

"I don't want the diamond," pleaded Nathan again.

"He's a proud man, what would it hurt? You hang onto it for a few days, his brother sends you the money, you send it back. Why hurt his feelings?"

"And what if I lose it?" countered Nathan, raising a finger under the Traveler's nose. "Ah?"

"Oh, please," snorted the Traveler. "Give me the three hundred. If you won't do this, I will."

"Use your own money," said Nathan.

The Traveler reached into his wallet and looked up in frustration.

"I don't carry a lot when I'm on the road, I use my credit cards. Just give me the money, I'll go to a bank machine. No wait, cash me a cheque."

Nathan watched the old man at the front door. Langleben was craning his head up towards the sky, watching as the snow started to fall in earnest. Nathan walked towards him. The Traveler followed.

"Ask him where he got it from," said Nathan. "Politely."

The old man turned, his face once more stricken with fear and angst.

"Fon vonnet kimst tsu dir der shtayndel?" the Traveler asked gently.

Langleben drew back his shoulders and faced the two men squarely.

"Ich chob geharbet aff zeben-unt-fertzick fur drei-unt-fertzick yor. Ich chob gehandelt mit stein ven die chot noch bapished dine hoisen. Ich chob gechat efsher funf stein azoi. Dist is der latste."

"He's from Forty-Seventh street, New York. He says he was in the business for thirty-four years and that he dealt in stones when we were still peeing in our pants. He must be retired now ... Anyway, he says he had a few stones left and that this is the last."

The old man drew closer and with one hand on his hip, he shook his finger at Nathan as though he were a friendly uncle admonishing a favourite nephew.

"Az er nemp nisht der stein fer halten, ich nempt nisht ir gelt fer borgen."

He then smiled again, his pale blue eyes catching the light.

"He says if you don't take his stone to hold, he won't take your money to borrow." The Traveler felt Nathan melt. "Take the stone and let's go for lunch already."

Nathan had been going to Griffin's ever since he could remember. It had always been the store restaurant during his father's day and now during his own tenure. It was a comfortable family restaurant with middle-class pretensions. The menu was small but always creative. The steak sandwich was Nathan's weakness, rare, with baked potato and a crisp toasted slice of garlic bread. He ate there so often, sometimes alone, sometimes with his wife Bella or a traveler, that the manager, a ruddy-faced Englishman named Kelly, would hold a favoured booth till two o'clock. If by chance Nathan was late and some absent-minded waitress had seated someone in his booth, Kelly would discreetly ask them if they wouldn't mind moving, offering drinks on the house to ease any hurt feelings. The King's patronage was of the utmost importance to Griffin's.

They had convinced Langleben to come along with them under vigorous protest and only after the office girl Denise had confirmed that the next train to Toronto was the night milk run, leaving the Soo at seven-twenty and changing at Sudbury for Toronto. When faced with the logic of staying with friends until then, the old man agreed and allowed himself to be seated between Nathan and the Traveler.

Kelly took their drink order himself, not trusting his young gentile staff to do so without gawking. Gin and tonic for the Traveler, scotch for Nathan, and soda water in a disposable paper cup for Langleben. Nathan took a moment to surreptitiously slip a nitro pill under his tongue. The pain was dull, not debilitating, but enough to pay attention to. His triple by-pass was several years old and though he was in excellent shape, Nathan was acutely aware of any stress on the coronary muscle. He carried the nitro in the same small, flat, gold pill container in which he kept his saccharine. When he was nervous or anxious, tired or breathless, he'd take a nitro and feel better.

Nathan had also noticed an interesting side-effect related to his medication. Everyone he dealt with knew about his by-pass, and everyone was always sure to inquire about his health. So when the gold pillbox emerged from his pocket, whether it was during a parking commission meeting or in tough negotiations with the Levi's jeans salesman, it was a sign, a signal, that the King was nearing the limits of his patience, that a deal had to be struck and quick. Because one could never tell from his smiling face what Nathan was thinking, but he would let you know, if you paid attention. The pillbox was a tell.

"I think I understand something," said the Traveler across the Old Man's back. "I don't think he's eaten anything. I mean, where do you find kosher on the road?".

Nathan was shocked at himself for not guessing.

"Ask him," he demanded. He waited impatiently for a response.

"He had food with him," the Traveler said finally. "When he left Victoria, they packed him a bag. But it ran out just yesterday."

"That's why he wants to go tonight, he's gotta be starving. Tell him we could go to my home. Bella's got kosher meat in the freezer. Tell him we get it sent up from Toronto."

The Traveler and the old man put their heads together again, talking in low tones. Finally the Traveler raised his eyes, shaking his head.

"He's scared of insulting you, but he won't eat at your home. It's simply not his style of kosher. He'll take some vegetables and fruit here as long as they don't put it in a dish, just on a piece of paper, and a glass of tea."

Nathan shook his head and motioned to Kelly. And so as Nathan tucked into his bloody rare steak sandwich and the Traveler wolfed down his seafood salad, Langleben sat stiffly between them, taking tentative sips from his tea and chewing quietly, but with appetite, on a few carrot sticks, some celery, and some peeled apple. With every old man bite he took, Nathan felt a little more ashamed and a little better.

The snow was falling lightly but steadily as the three men entered the store. The Traveler made himself busy filling out his order forms while Nathan sat Langleben down in a chair in his office. The offices were all at the back of the store, raised high so that Bella and Denise could look over a small partition and keep an eye on the floor. There was also a back door near the offices which opened onto the rear parking lot. Denise peered in as Nathan made the old man comfortable. Langleben raised his arm, revealing an old gold Marvin watch.

"Iz balt shpaat, ich daft gehen zu mineh breeder," he said indicating his watch.

Nathan caught the meaning and looked up at Denise.

"What time does the train leave for Sudbury?"

"Seven-thirty, but he should be there a little early," Denise replied.

She didn't leave but indicated with her eyes that she had more to say. Nathan walked over to the door, where the girl spoke in a hushed voice.

"The one-way fare is one hundred and ten dollars," she whispered as though revealing a closely guarded secret.

"You don't say," whispered Nathan teasing, his eyes narrowing.

The girl nodded and, lowering her eyes and casting a quick glance at the old man, withdrew. Nathan watched her for a moment, then poked his head into the corridor.

"Thank you, Denise," he said, still whispering.

The girl was still walking softly backwards. "Just thought you should know," she whispered back, which drew Bella out from behind her desk and into the corridor. "What's goin' on," she whispered, unaware of why she was whispering.

Bella was a short woman and plump and petty and bossy and kind and hard, and soft and mean and sweet; a holy terror and instant refuge for all manner of lost souls. She had the air and manner of a great *balabuste*, a woman of means and ability. She took shit from no man and ran the office and sales staff with a no-nonsense, razor-sharp wit and rapier tongue. She could spit vitriol and honey in the same breath.

Bella was more than conscious of her position in the world of the Soo and took the deference accorded her by the citizenry as her due but no more. She was a princess grown past the stage of queen to the role of Empress-of-all-she-surveyed. To hear her was to obey, or G-d help you.

Nathan drew her to the window that looked onto his office. There sat Langleben, nervously twirling his side locks, checking his watch.

"He walked in from the bus station. He's stranded. I think he got on the wrong bus or he got off, I don't know."

"Well give him some money, Nate, and I'll have Bruce drive him to the station. What's he doing in your office? Why is he sitting there? Is he after a hand-out?" Bella demanded, her voice rising exponentially.

"Bell," Nathan cried, cutting her off and leading her towards her office. "That's exactly what I'm doing, but the train don't leave till seven-thirty and it's cold and snowing!"

"When did it start snowing?" Bella snorted, charging towards the sales floor. "Are the awnings still out? Where's Bruce?"

"Bell!" moaned Nathan. "Bell! I'll take him myself. Just let me take care of it, will you?"

Bella moved back towards her desk, eyeing Nathan suspiciously. She turned her head and barked out just in time to catch a tall young man scurrying towards the back door with an awning pole in his hand.

"Bruce! It's snowing!" she practically shrieked.

"Yes, Mrs. Groman, I'm going to close the awnings," Bruce mumbled, grabbing his winter parka.

"And hurry!" Bella called after him. "And don't you be such a softy, Nate. Send him on his way."

She shot Nathan another side-winder glance and then made a dignified, tactical, retreat.

Nathan rubbed his brow. Then, tightening his jaw, he re-entered his office. Langleben was on his feet, pacing. Nathan held out his own watch.

"Zeeben..uh..zeeben und driesick, the train...umm...," he tried in his creaking Yiddish.

"Zebehn dreisich? Der tram geht zebehn dreisich?" repeated the old man, trying to understand.

"Ya, zeeben dreisich, and here's the three hundred dollars."

"Drei hundret Kanadien," the old man interrupted.

Nathan took a deep breath. "Drei hundred Canadian, and you don't have to give me anything to hold. You can…"

But the old man was already thrusting the black velvet box into his hands. Nathan gently pushed it back, but the old man was not to be denied. He continued speaking rapidly, insistently in Yiddish Nathan couldn't hope to understand, and it was a push-me-pull-you scene that the Traveler came upon, his purchase order ready for Nathan's signature.

Nathan looked up, laughing. "I can't get him to take no for an answer."

The Traveler seated himself behind Nathan's desk and started to check his addition with an adding machine. He addressed the old man absent-mindedly.

"Ehr vill ist nisht nehmen fon dir, du dafts nisht," he tried.

Suddenly the old man stopped and walked up to the desk. He spoke rapidly to the Traveler, who stopped his calculating and listened attentively, a stubby pencil waving from his lips. He glanced at Nathan furtively as the old man spoke. He then interrupted.

"Ober ich zug dir as ehr vill ist nisht," he said, almost whining.

The old man gestured towards Nathan and then, strangely, gestured towards the hallway towards Bella's office. The Traveler looked in Nathan's direction then back at the old man, a smile curling the corners of his mouth.

"Fraig ihm, nu?" said the old man, turning to Nathan.

"What?" said Nathan, intrigued.

The Traveler pushed himself away from the desk and folded his hands. He shook his head, smiling.

"He's asking me to tell you that he thinks you're a fine man and he would like to take your money, but he won't take it if you won't take the diamond to hold. But you're a fine man and you won't take the diamond, so what he's saying," the Traveler drew a breath, "is maybe you want to buy it?"

The Traveler leaned his elbows on the desk and cradled his chin in the palm of his hand. The tug of war had left the small black box on Nathan's side of the court as it were, and even as he protested, his hands were opening it.

"I have no use for a diamond," he laughed. "Why would I want to buy it?"

"For your wife," replied the Traveler smugly. Nathan caught him in a cold stare.

"It's what he said," cried the Traveler defensively, returning to his order pad.

Perhaps the light was better in Nathan's office. He had recently got rid of the fluorescent strip lighting and had installed a track light unit with halogen bulbs. And, though it was snowing, the sky was bright outside, and blue white light was seeping through between the vertical blinds. For whatever the reason, this time, when Nathan looked down at the open box, even though he let the stone sit in its moulded plush setting, he could see clearly that it was perfect.

"What's it to you?" said the Traveler, rising from behind the desk.

There was something in the Traveler's tone that tickled something in Nathan. Was that a dare? Was this a challenge? Was the jester mocking the King? What's it to you, indeed!

"I don't want it. But," said Nathan slowly, still caught by the purity, the color.

Langleben sat back down, folded his hands and started talking.

"He had a few stones left when he sold his business. This is the last." The Traveler came up behind Nathan, still listening to the old man.

"He says he's an honest man, and this is an honest stone. It's a first-quality, blue-white. A ... a... oh, he says it is a rare shape. Asscher... Asscher cut. Almost flawless," continued the Traveler.

Langleben rose and joined the other two, his face now closer, his voice lower.

"A diment lib hobn dos iz shats fertsik toyznt tullars bay der gas. Gebn mir tsen toyznt," said the old man.

The Traveler coughed suddenly and then caught himself.

"He says it's worth forty thousand. Give him ten ..." said the Traveler, his voice drying.

"Amerikan," whispered the old man.

"... and it's yours."

Nathan held up the stone again and eyed the Traveler.

"I don't need this. I don't want it," he said, smiling, once again closing the box and handing it toward the old man.

"So, don't buy it," said the Traveler quickly. Nathan thought too quickly.

He felt rather than saw Bella at the window. He caught her through the vertical blinds, her eyes were fixed on his in a way he had never seen. She never flinched, never blinked, and the message was clear.

"I'll be right back," he muttered, leaving the Traveler and Langleben alone.

Bella backed towards her office as Nathan left his.

"What's going on, Nate?" she spat, her eyes boring into his skull.

"Bell, I don't know anything, I just..." he tried, but it was no use. She had seen it.

"How much does he want?" she said through gritted teeth.

"I don't know anything about it, Bell ... it could be, it might be ..." he left the thought hang.

Bella walked towards him like the force of nature she was.

"You take him right down to Hub and you show it to Bernerd. How can you just say no, Nate? How much does he want?"

Nathan rubbed his brow again, his chest tightening by degrees.

"Ten thousand. American," he muttered, not able to meet his wife's eyes.

Bella backed towards her office, a finger extended, pointing.

"I want that stone, Nate," she said, and was gone.

Nathan took a second to slip a nitro pill under his tongue. He calmed immediately under its oxygenating effects. He smoothed his hair and walked back to his office.

"Do you know anything about this stuff, stones?" Nathan asked as the Traveler picked up his coat and hat.

"A little," he replied, shrugging. "I've seen a few, and that one ..."

Nathan looked at the old man, still smiling.

"Tell him to come with me," said Nathan firmly.

The Traveler spoke a few words with Langleben, who rose to go with Nathan.

"Mind if I make a few calls, Nate?" asked the Traveler.

"Go ahead and stick around. We'll be back soon."

Hub Jewellers was what passed for prestige in the Soo and, to be sure, they did carry a full line of fine watches, engagement rings and wedding bands to please the cognoscenti. The store had been founded in the 1930s by Bernerd Bentley, an Englishman who still worked the front counter and was now aided by his son Chris who, having passed through an accredited gemology school in London, was looking forward to taking the family business to new heights.

That day, however, it was Eric and not Bernerd who greeted their much-valued client Nathan Groman and the odd little Hebrew fellow in tow.

"Hi, Eric, where's your Dad?" asked Nathan with a wry smile, just enough to hide the giddy nerves he was starting to feel. He slipped another pill under his tongue.

"Hi, Mr. Gorman. Dad's up at Soo General."

"What happened?" inquired Nathan with genuine concern.

"Nothing serious. He broke his hand over the weekend and didn't know about it," said the young Bentley somewhat sheepishly.

"He didn't know! How could he not know?" cried Nathan, incredulous at this goyish shenanigan.

"Oh, he cracked it against the shift knob in his car, and Mom kept insisting it wasn't broken until this morning it swelled up and started turning blue," chuckled Eric.

"Is he all right?"

"Oh, sure. He just phoned. It's a small fracture; won't even need a cast. He'll be back in about an hour. Was there something you needed?"

Nathan hesitated. He really wanted to see the father; but glancing over at Langleben, who was starting to show renewed interest in his wristwatch, he decided the son would have to do.

He pushed the closed black velvet box over the counter towards Eric.

"Look at this, will you?" said Nathan, and he watched as Eric carefully opened the case. His deadpan joke was well rewarded. The young man nearly dropped the diamond, case and all.

"Holy! That's quite the stone, isn't it?" gasped the young jeweller, raising the gem to the light.

"Ever seen one like it?" asked Nathan, teasing.

"Just at school. But even then, nothing like this," replied Eric clearly in awe.

Nathan leaned in, lowering his voice.

"I need an evaluation on it, pronto," he whispered, motioning with his eyes towards Langleben, who was now busy looking over a tray of earrings.

Eric straightened up, winking slyly at Nathan.

"Just give me a moment, I'll have to take it in back. Take a sec." said the young man, his voice deepening and his demeanour becoming business-like.

He disappeared just as the old man approached Nathan. He gestured towards the cases filled with the best the Soo could offer.

"Is in ganse dreck," squeaked the old man. "Ist vort goornisht!"

For some reason, he seemed delighted with his assessment. He turned again to Nathan. "Nu?" he said, holding up his palms.

Young Eric Bentley returned, beads of sweat now faceting his forehead. He carefully put the diamond back into its box, closed the lid and handed it to Langleben. Motioning to Nathan, he moved slightly down towards the back of the store.

"A stone like that," he began nervously. But then catching himself, he started again. "That's an Asscher cut. A carat for sure. They don't do that anymore because it wastes too much of the stone. It's practically flawless, and the colour… This type of stone should really go to Toronto for a precise evaluation. I mean insurance companies will insist."

Nathan cut him short.

"It's not for insurance. I just got to know, is it a real diamond?"

The Bentley boy nodded his head affirmatively.

"How much is it worth?" asked Nathan quietly, looking the boy dead in the eyes under avuncular lids.

Eric swallowed, swaying slightly on his feet. He chewed his lip as his young jeweller's mind did back flips of calculations. Nathan prodded gently.

"Just an idea, Eric, a ballpark..."

Eric sighed then swallowed deeply, his Adam's apple bobbing.

Nathan took the stairs up to his office two at a time, pushing Langleben before him. The Traveler emerged, his coat on and hat in hand. Nathan checked his watch, it was five o'clock.

"Well?" asked the Traveler.

Nathan pushed the old man towards his office and turned towards the Traveler.

"Forty to fifty thousand," he hissed, his face cracked with smiling. "Maybe more."

"You gonna buy it?" demanded the Traveler, putting down his hat.

Nathan hesitated, looking around the floor of the store. Quiet for a Thursday. He barely heard the Traveler for the ringing in his ears.

"'Cause if you won't, I will," said the Traveler.

"What!" snapped Nathan. "Before you didn't have a lousy three hundred bucks to give him. Where are you gonna get ten thousand? American, no less!"

The Traveler looked offended. The jester tweaked the King.

"For that stone? I'd find a way." The Traveler put his hat on his head, pulling down the brim. "Maybe I can drive him to Toronto?"

The floor of the corridor shook as Bella called from her office.

"Nathan!!"

Her voice said it all. Nathan took a few steps in the direction of his wife's office before turning his gaze on the Traveler, who shrugged in reply.

Nathan screwed his face up as though smelling dog shit. He slipped into his office before the second "Nathan!" rang through the store. He held out his hand and, without hesitating, the old man placed the black velvet box in his palm. His eyes twinkled as the third "Nathan!" shook the windows.

Nathan slipped out of his office and down the corridor. Bella was standing behind her desk.

"Let me see it," she said, her voice as firm as concrete.

"Bell, I don't want it, we don't need it," he moaned, but it was no use.

Bella's clever little hand grabbed the box from his fingers and pried open the lid. She popped out the stone as though gutting a fish and examined its perfection as though reading entrails.

"Bella, listen," Nathan started, but she was having none of it.

"How much, Nate?" she repeated, her voice taking on a threatening tone.

Nathan sighed. He spoke with the voice of a man being pushed off a cliff.

"Chris Bentley says it's worth forty or fifty thousand. Maybe more. The old man wants ten thousand, American."

"American?" Bella snarled. "What's wrong with Canadian? He's in Canada! He'll take Canadian and he'll like it."

"No, Bell, he won't take Canadian. He wants American money only."

"Well that's too bad. I want it and that's it!"

She was already wearing it as two earrings, a pendent to die for, a brooch clustered with rubies. The Queen must be appeased.

Nathan withdrew quietly. The Traveler was waiting for him.

"Nu?" he prodded.

Nathan walked stiff-legged into his office. Langleben was beside himself with muttered fretting. He looked up as Nathan entered followed by the Traveler.

"Nu?" said the old man, holding out his hand.

Nathan turned to the window and observed the day's last light fall across the white building that faced his office window. In the near distance he could see the red and blue neon of the Ogidaki Mountain general store, his competitor for the jean trade. He was aware of the Traveler waiting at his shoulder. He could hear the rattle of the Traveler's car keys like the precautionary hissing of a bush snake. He reached out slowly, grasped the old man's hand and shook it once, firmly.

"Mazel tov," cried the old man, his cheeks flushing bright red, his pale blue eyes sparkling.

The Traveler sighed, slipped his hat on again and hefted his sample cases. "The order is on your desk, I signed it for you."

"You're leaving, now?" asked Nathan, concerned.

"I can still make Sudbury"

The Traveler stumbled out into the corridor. Nathan motioned to the old man to wait for him.

"Listen, if you want to sell it, my brother knows this Israeli guy in Montreal, the best price," kidded the Traveler. "I'll see you in May, Nate, zei gezunt."

Nathan watched the Traveler squeeze through the rear door, his sample cases banging his legs as he slipped and then caught his balance on the freshly fallen snow. He turned back to find Langleben standing at his office door. He pointed to himself.

"I'm getting the money, uh...de gelt.." he tried.

The old man nodded and drew back inside Nathan's office, closing the door behind him.

Nathan loved going down to the basement because whenever he did, he stopped being a sixty-five-year-old, small town dry-goods magnate and became once again the beloved son of a small town dry goods magnate. The basement of the store had never been changed, and it was precisely as it had been when Nathan and his brothers, little bandits every one, had terrorized his father's staff with war whoops and shrieks as they played their boyish games amidst the bales of work clothes, the crates of

Wellington boots, the stacks of shovels and tin pails and the ephemera of a hundred years of retailing.

The floor was still rough poured cement pebbled with now smoothly polished stones. The massive timbers that held up the entire building stood still like men, like living torsos, and Nathan knew and named each and every one. He could walk through the entire length of the cellar with his eyes shut, ducking under the cast iron drain stacks and ducts, skipping through the pine slat dividers following the tiny little stream of water that ran the width of the basement and that never dried up or froze. His older brother had once told him it was a buried Indian stream, and though maturity had forced him to concede that lie, he could never think of it as anything other than that.

But of all the treasures down below, of all the favourite forts and period retail effluvium, nothing sang so sweetly of his lost youth, nothing so reminded him of his long-dead father than the Penfield-Thurman Bold Boy strong box model No. 13A that stood partially concealed on the back side of the scrapped, antique, wood-burning furnace.

If you didn't know where it was, you'd miss it; and even when his father showed him where it was, for years after, he sometimes couldn't find it. But it was always there. Its massive black door and sides, its art nouveau scroll work in painted faux relief all down the sides of the door. Its number wheel, which even after all these years turned like silk on silk. The number 13A was a special designation. It indicated to those who knew that it was a trick safe, and each one in the series had its own trick mechanism.

When Nathan was thirteen, the afternoon of his bar mitzvah, his father had taken him by the hand, and the two of them stole away from the reception and had walked the few blocks to the store. The store had been closed for the occasion of Nathan's passage into manhood, so there was no one around. Father and son descended the thick timber stairs into the basement and had sought out the strong box. That afternoon, Sam revealed the safe's secrets. The combination was a simple selection of birth dates drawn from the family. The trick, however, was more subtle.

The "T" shaped handle had to be drawn towards you a slight distance and then turned back until it clicked, then a final set of numbers had to be dialled in, reverse the direction of the "T" handle, push it in clockwise, and the door riding on stainless steel ball-bearings machined in Sheffield, England, would swing open with the force of a small boy's pinkie.

Nathan squatted in front of the strong box door as his father had, and he remembered his father, saw where his father's shoes and his own had worn the rough concrete smooth. He watched his own hands as they worked the door mechanism and he noticed again, but freshly this time, how unlike his hands were from those of his father.

Sam Groman could never have been mistaken for Irish. He was a squat, square Litvak with beefy shoulders and biceps that routinely tore open the seams of his dress shirts. He was of medium height and very strong, his body tempered on the steppes of the Russian Pale. He was famous in the Soo of the teens and 1920s and '30s as a fair, tough businessman who was on the side of the working man. His honesty was legend; there was something paternal about the way the Ukrainian and Polish mill workers deferred to his honesty. Many times the steel men would crowd into the store late on Fridays, clutching their pay in their baked, reddened mitts. They would petition the honest Jew; would he please take care of their wages? Would he put them in his safe for the week-end, save them from drinking it all away, save their families from their own weakness?

And Sam Groman, the good, honest Jew of the Soo would take their pay packets from their grimy broken fingers and would put them in the strong box in the basement, sometimes doling out a few dollars of mad money to the men so that they could go to the Angel Bar down by the lakeside and drink their fevered, goyish heads into oblivion.

And Nathan remembered too the Sundays when he and his father were stock-taking or cleaning, when some big, drunk mill worker would show up at the store, bleary-eyed and stinking of whores and piss and demand his money, scream for his money so that he could go on degrading himself, go on fulfilling his potential as a dumb, shaygetz bastard. And Nathan remembered how his father Sam, the honest Jew, would shoulder aside the inebriate, push him aside with his ropey forearm against the neck, slap his red, sweating face and say, "No, Leschek! No, Chris! No, Mattek! No more money for drink! Not for you!"

And Nathan could see the wives come for their crying husbands, their children in tow, embarrassed and at the same time with mean, blue-eyed defiance. And Nathan remembered the inevitable scene the next day. A massive lumberman, his hat in his hands, eyes sober now but still wet from crying, standing, shifting his weight from one foot to the other, as the honest Jew descended into the darkness and emerged with his pay packet, safe, full, and good.

And Nathan could still see the working men of all stripes take his father's hand in theirs, he could see how they kissed his father's hand, whimpering like children, and he could hear the plaintive cries for forgiveness and the repeated blessing, "Thank you, Father, forgive me, Poppa. Forgive me..." And the next week the pantomime would begin all over again.

"Will I be famous?" thought Nathan as he eyed the stacks of American bills snug in the strong box. "Will I be famous for buying this diamond that I don't want and I don't need?" The American money sat there, gathered over decades from cross border shoppers, kept as a hedge, a safety valve, a legacy. It was mad money, maddening money. Nathan counted out ten thousand.

Coming up from the basement, Nathan felt that the store was quiet. The snow, he thought, and it was supper time. He kept only two salespeople on the floor. Bella would still be in her office, but the girl, Denise, would have already gone. Nathan glanced at the clock, five-thirty. He found himself sweating, a cold, clammy sweat that would not stop. He slipped a heart pill under his tongue and waited at the foot of the stairs leading to his office. The American money formed an obvious lump in his jacket pocket. He kept his head down, waiting for the sweating spell to end. He could see the ends of the stacks of bills peeking out from where his jacket gaped open. He could count the packets, ten packets of ten one hundred dollar bills. The sweat wouldn't stop. He took one step.

Something was odd. The door to his office was closed, and the vertical blinds had been drawn, but where the window should have been lit it was dark. He could hear Bella on the phone with a friend talking about food, cooking or something. The store was still. Nathan mounted the few steps and stood outside his own office door, listening. The muffled sounds of a conversation could be heard through the door. Nathan turned the doorknob and opened the door a few inches.

Langleben had turned off the overhead track lights and had turned on the banker's lamp on his desk. Facing south by southeast, the old man stood in the center of the room, davening, his thin legs together, a prayer book in his hands. As he recited what Nathan recognized as the afternoon prayers, he swayed vigorously from the hips and gave no indication that he knew Nathan was there.

Silently Nathan closed the door. He walked quickly down the corridor towards the back door, searching his pockets for his car keys. Once outside, unmindful of the persistent snow and wind, he walked quickly to the passenger side of his Mercury Marquis and opened the door. Bending over the dash, he opened the glove compartment and rattled about through the clutter of golf balls, Chivas miniatures and broken sunglasses before drawing out his blue velvet talis bag. It was a strategy of Jewish life in a small town. A minyan was almost impossible; there simply weren't enough adult Jewish men. But occasionally, when a traveler or a group of Chabadniks on a mission augmented the Hebrew population, there would be ten men of the Hebrew faith in town at the same time. The phone calls would fly, the prayer hall would be opened, and the songs of Mincha and Ma'ariv would fill the air. Like boy scouts, the remaining Jews of the Soo were always prepared.

Back inside, Nathan opened the talis bag and slipped on his skull cap. He was about to put on his talis too but caught himself, remembering that it was not worn for afternoon and evening prayers. Listening at the door, Nathan tried to discern where in the prayers Langleben was;

when he heard the old man finish Mincha and start Ma'ariv, the evening prayers, he opened the door.

This time Langleben heard the noise behind him. He stopped swaying but only slightly. His lips and voice were on auto pilot, the recitation of the prayers, once started, proceeded on their own. Nathan stepped into the room, then thought immediately that he should leave. It was holy, the room, suffused with holiness, and he thought that he should not be there. But as he prepared to back out of his office, Langleben made an almost imperceptible movement with his left shoulder ... or maybe he was mistaken thought Nathan. But no! There it was again, as though the old man was making room for him, as though the old man was prying open a corner of his holiness to let him in.

And so Nathan entered his own office as a stranger and stood beside the old man, and he found the right page and he read the right passages and as he davened by rote with the old man, all his fears and all his hesitations dropped as though nothing. He had stopped sweating, stopped hearing his heart, stopped feeling the money in his breast pocket.

"Magnified and sanctified," said Langleben and Nathan thought, "Yes, it's a premonition, a prediction. Magnified and sanctified, that's what I am, that is my life."

His evening devotions finished, the old man stowed his prayer book in the sleek black satchel and turned to face Nathan. He held out his hand and, without taking his eyes off the old man's face, Nathan softly placed the American money in his palm. Langleben fanned the stacks carefully, smiled and put the money in his own breast pocket. He grasped Nathan by the forearms and said, "Yashir koach, ben Groman." May your strength endure.

The train station was twenty minutes from the store. As Nathan pulled up to the passenger departure area, he noticed Langleben was becoming agitated.

"Are you all right? Did you forget, ...uh, fergessen?"

Langleben shook his head impatiently and dug out a stack of the American money, gesturing towards the station. Nathan understood immediately and reached for his billfold.

"Gebn mir dray hundert tullars. Ikh vel aroysshikn em tsurikvegs keyn' du fun mine breeder's hoyz arayn Toronto," said the old man, smiling.

Nathan smiled in return and handed over the Canadian money, along with his business card, which the old man seemed particularly happy to have.

"Och, ist shoen gut. A shainem dank, ben Groman. A shainem dank!" cried the old man, taking Nathan's hand in both of his.

A car beeped behind them. Nathan was blocking the drive-through. It had been his intention to put the old man on the train personally, but a porter was at the car as Langleben got out.

"He's going to Toronto, through Sudbury," he shouted to young Chris Kenopic.

"Oh, hi, Mr. Groman! He going to Toronto?"

"Will you see him on the train, Chris?" said Nathan, his face crinkling in a leprechaun grimace. "Hey, how's your Mom?"

"Fine Mr. G., I'll get him on the train, but you better move on," he shouted, following Langleben into the station.

More cars were beeping, so Nathan could only watch them as he drove away. The small dark figure of Langleben, followed by the lanky son of a family he had known since the parents were kids. The King in his kingdom.

When he got back, it was a quarter to eight, and miraculously the store was full. The snow had stopped, and a bunch of young people were in trying on jeans. Bella was keeping a sharp eye on the floor as Irene and Bruce helped the clients.

"Well?" asked Bella in a voice just below a fog horn.

Nathan paused at the foot of the stairs, squinting up at his wife, a droll curly smile on his lips. "I got him off, Bell, he's gone to Toronto. The Kenopic boy put him on the train."

"First thing tomorrow morning, we put it in the bank. In the meantime, you put it downstairs."

She hesitated before giving the small black velvet box to Nathan. When she spoke, her voice was almost loving, honeyed.

"Did you ever see anything so beautiful?"

They both stared at it, gazing without talking. Finally, Nathan took the box from her, snapping the lid shut, tossing her a wink.

He didn't go downstairs with the diamond. Instead, he went into his office. "Magnified and sanctified," he hummed to himself. He was about to turn on the overhead lights but left them off. He did open the vertical blinds to see the night sky.

He sat down behind the desk, the black velvet box in front of him. He felt giddy and happy and good. He opened the box again. It was beyond beautiful. It was luscious, a jewel fit for a king. He loved the way the box snapped shut, the sound of it, the weight of it ... There was a candy wrapper in his ashtray. He didn't smoke himself but it came with the desk set, the ashtray that is, and he had no candies on his desk. He reached for the wrapper. It was not crumpled, as though the candy had simply been pulled out and the wrapper tossed aside. It was a toffee wrapper, Callard and Bowser. The Traveler, when he had gone with the old man to Hub Jewelry. The Traveler ...

Nathan's insides flushed ice water. He heard his heart. Without thinking, he slipped first one and then another nitro under his tongue. The Traveler had sugar.

Bella only had time to shriek, "Nathan, where the hell are you going!?" before he was out the back door.

The sidewalks hadn't been cleared of snow, and Nathan hadn't put on his galoshes. So he slipped and slid his way along the block to Hub Jewellery. There were people on the street who hailed him. Hail to the chief! All hail the King. But he didn't hear them. He couldn't hear them for the rush of sound in his ears, the vascular rush of his heart as it beat and slowed, then beat again.

As he entered the jewellery store, Bernerd Bentley was there, his left hand wrapped in an Ace bandage but otherwise a balm. Bentley brightened seeing Nathan sweep in breathless, coatless.

"So, here's the lucky man! Congratulations! Eric told me. Jeez, I've never seen him so excited!" squeaked Bernerd. "Do you have it?"

Nathan placed the black velvet box on the counter. Bernerd creaked it open.

"Oh, my, that's beautiful. Asscher cut. Eric! Come see it!" he called to his son.

Eric came out from the back of the store and bent over the counter, smiling excitedly at Nathan.

"Couldn't wait to show it off, eh, Mr. G.?" Eric said drolly.

"I know Eric couldn't give you a precise value, but just give me a minute and we'll know better, O.K.?"

Bernerd slipped off towards the back of the store while Eric moved closer to Nathan.

"I've heard of Forty-Seventh street in New York. The diamond district in Manhattan, but I never ... you know those people do deals without paper?" he whispered, incredulous, his eyebrows raised. "No receipts, no invoices, just a handshake. Hundreds of thousands of dollars on just a handshake."

Nathan focused on the face of the younger Bentley.

"Those people." he said slowly.

Eric caught himself, but Nathan wasn't sure if it was because he suddenly realized just who he was talking to or if it was because he saw what Nathan saw in the white, shaking face of his father.

Nathan made no attempt to hide the nitro pills he was slipping under his tongue at one-minute intervals. Why bother hiding them now? There was no reason.

He sat behind his desk, his office abuzz with the comings and goings of members of the Soo's finest. Tilting in the chair in front of him,

The Oracle of the Soo

Buddy Lake consulted a growing pile of faxes, emissions from RCMP offices all across Canada.

When Nathan had made the first phone call to the police, the duty officer thought it best to throw the young constable in amongst his own, just to keep things kosher.

When Nathan arrived at the store in the morning, it was as though everyone knew what had happened. All the girls were looking at him with embarrassed eyes. The store itself seemed somewhat changed. Bella walked by, a sour, nervously defiant look on her face. She barrelled past him, glancing back over her shoulder, feeling his eyes on her. She stopped in front of the door to her office.

"Don't look at me like that," she warned, the coffee lapping the rim of her cup.

Slowly, Nathan placed a pill under his tongue. He held her eyes with his, not saying, not speaking, just looking.

"You'd think it was the end of the world," Bella muttered but not quite under her breath. "Don't just look at me, Nate," she shouted shrilly, loud and forceful. "Don't just stand there looking at me!"

Nathan looked down and walked stiffly into his office. Buddy was already there.

"Bentley says that even as a copy, it's got to be worth a couple grand, at least," yawned the blonde-haired, blue-eyed constable.

"Supposed to make me feel better?" muttered Nathan.

"Are you sure he said he was going by train?"

"Yes," sighed Nathan, rubbing his face, slicking back his hair. "The Kenopic kid put him on the train, I drove away."

"Yeah, I asked Chris. He said just as you pulled out, the old man asked him to wait, he had to go to the bathroom."

Nathan raised his head. "Asked him?"

"In English," replied Buddy grimly. "With an English accent, Chris thinks. Anyway, the train's about to leave, so Chris goes to the washroom to look for the guy, and he's not there."

"Not there," said Nathan, drifting. His eyes scanned the walls of his office, his desk, his own hands, looking, searching.

"After we checked with Chris, we chased down every bus, every car. We searched all the hotels and motels, but he simply vanished."

"Probably had a car," thought Nathan aloud.

"Figure he probably had a car," mused Buddy, looking up from his notes. "You O.K., Unc?"

Nathan slipped another nitro under his tongue, almost wishing something would burst. Buddy's team had finished with the sales floor and had moved up to the office area. They dusted for fingerprints, picked at fibers. There was, in fact, nothing to find, and Nathan knew that even before they started. He had looked for the candy wrapper. When he had left the store last night, when he had run out to Bentley's, he thought he had put it down on the desk but it was no longer there. It too had disappeared.

"You shouldn't feel bad, Unc. This guy is a professional. He's been doing this right across the country. He pulls into a small town, and he finds someone, uh, somebody..." Buddy's voice trailed off.

"Rich?" Nathan filled in, smiling.

"Don't know how this guy knows."

Nathan breathed deeply, his head starting to finally clear, the rushing sound ebbing from his ears.

"He has a list," he said firmly.

"Oh yeah?" said Buddy, attentively.

"Probably stolen or borrowed from charities, Chabad, a donors list," said Nathan, speculating.

"So he knows who the big players are in all these small towns. That's how he knows who to go after!" cried Buddy, grabbing the phone.

Nathan put his hand on top of Buddy's, letting the phone drop onto its cradle.

"Which towns?" Nathan asked quietly.

Buddy fumbled with the pile of faxes, which grew as other cops entered with more information.

"Uh, let's see, uh, we think he started in ... there's a report here from Kamloops, where he took some real estate guy there for twelve thousand.

Then there was Medicine Hat, fifteen thousand from a car dealer. He played a South African collecting for a yeshiva in Jerusalem, then Moose Jaw, only nine thousand, then Brandon ... the guy's a genius."

Buddy's men came in to dust for prints. Carl Labonte shrugged apologetically and started lightly spraying the desk with a fine silvery powder. Buddy got up to get out of the way but Nathan, resisting the intrusion, stayed seated. He watched as Buddy stood in the middle of the office swaying from side to side as large men are apt to do, studying the sheaf of faxes and reciting the growing list of Langleben's successful campaigns.

Buddy's voiced droned on, but Nathan had stopped at Brandon. He glanced over his desk, then turned to his pin board. The Traveler's yellow order form, neatly checked off and totalled, was stuck just below a small wooden plaque, a gift from another traveler who used to sell his father denim work clothes. The plaque was made of wood, and in his childhood Nathan would always notice it hanging behind his father where he stood at his cash register. It was a novelty item, a crudely carved proverb plaque of an old man leaning over a wood fence, one hand raised with a finger pointing at his own head. It was one of the first things Nathan had learned to read by himself, but it wasn't till now that he felt he really understood it deeply, with its full kitschy irony. It said, "Vee get too soon olt, unt too late shmart."

"By the way, Unc, did you know what Langleben means in Yiddish?" said Buddy, gathering his police things.

Nathan stood to see Buddy out.

"Long life," said Buddy happily, his big gentile ruddy face beaming. "Long life."

Watching Buddy go, Nathan could almost imagine the hefty blonde kid happy to have a case like this, happy to tackle a criminal mastermind as skilful and insidious as Langleben. Happy that at last something glamorous had happened in the dull gray Soo. Nathan reached into his gold pillbox and tucked another pill under his tongue, only to draw back his lips in disgust. Saccharine.

Things changed in the Soo after that, slowly at first then faster with the passing years. The mill suffered through hard times, money became tight, and the clothing wholesalers started to look elsewhere for representation. They wanted to go with winners, and more and more Groman's was starting to look its age. Sure, people still came in, but they had less money to spend, had lower expectations and looked for cheaper goods. There was a time when a young mill family would only buy Canadian, and Nathan was happy to stock it. Now with price the principal concern, goods from the Far East began to infest the racks, and those young mill families stopped asking and stopped caring.

Nathan changed, too. It wasn't noticeable at first; perhaps he didn't buy a new car every year as he used to. Then he started buying small cars. The store started to lose business to the new mall across the street. He tried to hew himself a chunk of that action by putting in a hip annex outlet, but it failed. Some of the older sales staff retired, and the place started to feel odd to him. He no longer recognized the faces of his clientele. They looked like strangers.

Bentley's closed. It was a direct result of Nathan's misfortune. Somehow the rumour got around that the young Bentley had pronounced a piece of glass to be worth thousands. The public lost confidence and gave their custom to the People's in the mall. Bernerd and his wife moved back to Dorset. Eric married a Lebanese real estate agent in Sarnia. He never worked in jewellery again.

Buddy Lake was able to wangle his investigation of the Langleben case into a fact-finding junket that took him all over North America. He was called back to the Soo when it was discovered that he had hooked up with a Vietnamese card counter in Reno and, with her help, had parlayed his per diem into a low six-figure nest egg. He eventually married the girl.

And sometimes when Nathan would take a traveler into Griffin's for a steak sandwich, he'd find people in his booth; and though Kelly would offer to move them, eventually Nathan would tell him not to bother. "It's O.K.," he would say, his leprechaun face squinting and grinning, and he would sit at another table. Finally, Kelly wouldn't move at all, and Nathan would simply take whatever table was available.

The mill failed, then was bailed out then failed again. The community itself started to wither, as young people no longer bothered to make their lives in the Sault Ste Marie but went south to Toronto or west to Alberta to cash in on the boom and the jobs. With the jobs and the young went the future and, finally, Groman's Clothing Store failed.

As for the Jewish community of the Soo, it had died years before the events of this story, long before Langleben breezed into town. There were times when Nathan, buffeted on his way to lunch, would scan the unfamiliar faces on the streets, look deeply into the weathered, reddened, wind-whipped, beaten faces of the unemployed, the disenfranchised youth of what was once a thriving, happy town, and he would feel for all his memories and all the family history and for all the benevolence he had displayed as King, as though he were a lonely Jew surrounded on all sides by strangers.

Bella kept the two thousand-dollar paste job. Before the Bentleys closed their doors, she had them mount it for her in a brooch surrounded by ruby chips in a solid silver setting. It looked great, and one evening before a trip to Toronto to visit their kids, Nathan caught her in front of her mirror in a black dress modeling it for herself. Without a word, he gently unclipped it and put it on her dresser. He did this with such quiet caution that for the first time in her life, Bella was unable to say anything.

And Nathan stopped going to the curling rink and started davening, by himself, mornings and evenings.

Sedalia, Missouri

Winter, 1990. The walk from the hovercraft to the train station was short but left me wet and thoroughly chilled to the bone. The weather, a mix of wind and pelting rain and snow, was an affront. On the platform for the train from Boulogne to Paris, Mr. Six-Four bent low and easily hoisted a limp sack of a young man out of a wheelchair and into his huge arms. A porter folded the chair and led the way. A woman, grey-haired, frail, thin, at least sixty-five, followed.

My seat on the train was across the aisle from theirs, and they were quick to smile and nod to me as they settled in. He whom I had taken for a young man was not a young man, and his story was very clear. Forty, remarkably thick dark hair falling like a wave over his forehead, thin, grey, gleaming skin, Kaposi's sarcoma, full-blown AIDS.

At the first pass of the car snack service, Six-Four ordered coffee.

"Teddy," the woman stage whispered, "will you look at that?"

It was the standard French train café filtre, a two-stage plastic unit: hot water goes in the top, filtered coffee drains into the bottom. Six-Four was so pleased he was beaming, but Teddy has seen it all before.

"Wait till you taste it," he muttered, smiling gamely.

"Well, I never," said the woman in admiration. "They make such a fuss."

"Smells heavenly," Six-Four agreed. "After the English stuff."

Teddy wasn't doing so well. Up against the window seat, his head pressed to the glass, he barely seemed able to register the passing countryside, but every once in a while he would fuss, and either Six-Four or the woman would react.

"What was that, dear?"

Sometimes he would motion with his hand, other times just smile. The woman spoke to me this time.

"We're taking my son back to Paris."

"Yes we are," Six-Four confirmed. "But this time it's just for pleasure, right Ted?"

"It was never work, anyway," Ted managed.

Clearly the confessional doors were wide open, and Ted's mother felt obliged to step right in and bring me up to date.

"Ted's made this trip many, many times before with his grade twelve students."

"Always oversubscribed," smiled Six-Four proudly. "It was the highlight of their year."

Ted objected.

"Well, it was," insisted Six-Four, brandishing his coffee cup.

Mother picked up the thread again.

"It was always his students and a couple of parents, and they did run him ragged the last few years."

"I liked doing it, Mother," Ted moaned, shaking his head at me as though to dispel that martyr status his mother was attempting to bestow. "I wouldn't have done it if I didn't."

A little silence, but the pot had been stirred.

"What part of the States are you from?" asked Mother.

"I'm not," I replied. "I'm Canadian."

Six-Four perked up.

"Canadian? Toronto?"

"Montreal," I said.

This time it was Ted who perked up, catching Six-Four's eye with sudden complicity.

"Montreal? We've been to Montreal. What a wonderful city. You are really lucky."

"Where are you from?" I asked.

"Well, we're from Sedalia, Missouri?" she replied, ending with the terminal rise. "That is, I am and Teddy was."

"Ted and I live in Princeton, New Jersey."

"I'm still in Sedalia. My husband passed on earlier this year, so it's just me."

Six-Four leaned in, his forehead wrinkling.

"But you are coming to stay with us, right?"

An odd tension stiffened Mother's spine.

"Well, we'll have to see," she said, reaching over to brush Teddy's hair off his forehead. "We'll just have to see how things go."

The snack cart came by again. Six-Four got excited.

"Have a tea, Mom," Teddy suggested. "You liked the tea in London."

Mother was scanning the service cart nervously as though looking for the item that was going to jump up and hurt someone.

"I don't know, they make such a fuss over the coffee, I dread to see what they do with the tea."

"Avez-vous le thé dans les petits sacs?"

The porter rummaged around and presented Mother with a variety of teas bundled in little gauze bags.

"Well, I never," she squealed in admiration.

"I told you," Teddy managed between clenched teeth. "Everything is better in France.

I did not see what secret sign passed between Teddy and Six-Four, but the big man was on his feet in a second, picking Teddy up like a doll and pulling him into the aisle.

"Bathroom?" he asked the porter, who motioned toward the end of the car.

They had been gone only for a moment when Mother, trailing her tea bag in her cup, spoke up again.

"He's quite sick."

"Hmm..." I replied.

"They didn't let him take the kids last year," she remarked with a tinge of bitterness. "The parents. They didn't like how it looked. When those spots started to come through."

"That must have been terrible."

Mother took a sip of tea and looked straight into my eyes.

"He was shattered. Shattered, absolutely."

They took turns going to the restaurant car. Teddy had no appetite, even though they had brought along some excellent morsels. He mostly drank Gatorade and nibbled saltines. I slipped off to eat just as Mother was returning, so I was not surprised when Six-Four joined me at my table.

Six-Four had no trouble with his appetite and was a refreshingly polite and fastidious eater. He perused the menu with care.

"I promised myself that I would always order something I never had before."

He pointed to the menu.

"Do you know what moreau is?"

"That's codfish," I replied, reading above his massive, well-manicured finger. "A filet with beurre blanc."

"Perfect," he said, pointing it out to the waiter. "What wine do you recommend?"

After the small talk and the plates had been cleared, Six-Four settled into his chair.

"How many clichés can I run in a row?" he said, smiling as the waiter uncorked a second split and I sipped my port. "Married to my childhood sweetheart, four kids, nice home. I taught American history and coached football in East Orange. Everything was good. Just good."

I lit up a small cigar and he took the box from me, helping himself to one. His first puff was deep and unpractised.

"When Teddy showed up to teach English and dramatics, that was in 1983, I can honestly say I did not know what hit me. We both had to leave that high school. The wife took the kids, took the house. We found jobs in a Princeton high school. Very middle class. People knew, but no one really seemed to care. We were discreet."

Another big glass of wine, another puff, and this time he looked to me to see that he was doing it right.

"Everything was so perfect, everything was so, like, I told myself, 'Remember this. Just remember this.' I knew he was sick almost from the beginning."

"Really?" I said.

He smiled grimly, nodding his massive head, a rueful smile on his lips.

"The fact that we didn't have sex was one big clue. He wouldn't let me. It didn't matter."

Six-Four had made it through half the second bottle of wine before winding himself down.

"The past two years he keeps fading and coming back. I knew it was now or never. You won't believe what I had to do to get Dale to come with us. He needed her to see it."

"Must be very rough for her."

Six-Four rose, taking a last long gulp.

"Dale?" he put down his glass. "Here's a clue: She had to get her very first passport for the trip."

Back in coach, Six-Four leaned his bulk against the window and promptly fell asleep. Dale had wandered off, and I could look at Teddy and Six-Four openly as they sat sleeping, opposite each other, moving with the rolling train.

I needed the bathroom and as I walked, I spotted Dale standing in the corridor of the next car, gazing out the window. When I emerged from the bathroom, she was still there.

She smiled as I approached, bending a little at the knee against the movement of the train. She looked at me for a moment, a sad defeated smile on her tired face. She looked out the window as she spoke, and her voice was low but not so low, not afraid.

"In Sedalia it's all pretty much black and white. There isn't that much to know, so we fool ourselves into thinking we know everything."

I smiled at her reflection in the window. She smiled back shyly.

"I thought I did," she said, looking out the window. "I knew about men and women. I knew about having a partner in your life. I knew how love was. But I didn't know everything."

Outside, the sky gathered grey clouds together threatening rain but so far, holding back.

"It made me angry, to be so certain and then to be so unsure. It's why I snap at him so, but I don't mean it."

"I know. I think he knows it too."

She turned to me for the first time, her eyes searching.

"Do you think so?"

I nodded.

"Do you see the way Wayne takes care of Teddy? How he looks after him?"

I nodded again. Dale moved closer to me, still keeping her face to the window, lowering her voice.

"When he came out to me, he insisted on telling me everything. And he did."

Dale looked around, making certain there was no one listening.

"I didn't want to hear it. I told him to stop it, but he wouldn't," she said shivering, as if the mere memory was still too much to bear. "I understood later that he wanted me to know, in some way, what he had run away for, what he gave it all away for, Sedalia and our family, as though it was, like it was…" she said, searching.

"Worth it?"

Dale lowered her eyes, wounded still by the notion. Her eyes wrinkled shut, the knuckles of one hand pressed against her mouth as the tears came. She caught herself, drawing a deep breath and faced me, her eyes imploring, her lips white and thin.

"They have a tenderness that I never had in all my life. I never even knew about it."

Six-Four was still sleeping, snoring rarely, delicately, like a small boy. Dale had changed places with Ted so that she had the benefit of a window to lean against. She was sleeping, exhausted by the truth and shame and by speaking of it to a stranger. Teddy was now on the aisle, easier to get him to the toilet should the need arise.

It was evening, and the train was standing still. A porter passed by brusquely in the manner of all train porters.

"Pardonnez-moi mais, c'est quoi le problème?"

The porter sighed, coming to a halt in front of me. He smelled strongly of pastis.

"C'est une manifestation, monsieur."

"Une grève?"

"Oui, une action industrielle comme on dit. Les fermières contestent les frais de transport. Une longue histoire sans arrêt."

"On va être ici pour combien de temps?"

The porter never once looked at me but spoke loudly so that everyone would get the briefing once and for all and we would all stop bothering him.

"Impossible de dire mais, normalement, on ne reste pas très longtemps. C'est l'heure de dîner, pour eux comme pour nous."

And with that he whirled away in a fog of condescension and Ricard. Ted had watched and listened to the exchange with evident amusement.

"You've got guts," he wheezed with difficulty. "I've never been able to get two words out of a French public servant without drowning in their arrogance."

I smiled in turn, doing my best imitation of the Gaelic shrug, my hands spread wide.

"Mais, c'est normale, quoi?"

Ted laughed, turning his head to me. He was close to me, and now that the other two could not hear him, and after waiting patiently in line, it was his turn.

"Where do you stay in Paris?"

"I don't have a regular place. Whatever is the cheapest."

"The kids and I, we always stayed at the same hotel, near the Place de la Concorde. Views of the Eiffel Tower, the whole cliché."

"How many years did you take this trip?"

"From 1983 to 1988."

"I don't know how you could stand it, dragging pubescent kids to the Louvre, Notre Dame."

Ted took a breath and sighed, as though my description was delicious.

"It wasn't easy, believe me. They did fuck up a lot, always some scandal somewhere. But for me it was worth it, to see Paris turn on in their dull, glassy eyes."

I smiled.

"You get the biggest fucking football slob, some son-of-a-blue-collar bum, and he's mocking everything, sneaking out for beer, getting caught in some big-haired girl's room…," he paused as though perversely savouring the memory. "And then suddenly, he's on a bateau mouche and he can't take his eyes off the Pont Neuf."

Ted leaned even closer across the aisle.

"For some, it was opening their curtains and seeing the Eiffel Tower so close you could touch it. And for others it was the first sip of a café crème or the first croissant that didn't come from Pillsbury."

His breath was very shallow and he was having trouble opening the cap of his Gatorade, so I helped him.

"Or some fresh-mouthed, tough little Jersey chick would get stuck in front of a Monet at the Musée d'Orsay. Or just catch the bend in the Seine near Notre Dame. One by one the little lights would come on, and I knew that whatever else they did in their suburban lives, whenever they would look at that single stamp in their passports, they would remember. They would have that."

We were quiet for a long moment. When he spoke, it was with a low voice, mostly breath.

"When I moved east, I knew exactly what I was doing. Sedalia was, well, you can't imagine and I can't explain, so let's not even go there."

For the first time, Teddy smiled a real smile, his face cracking in mirth.

"I knew where I was headed. I didn't hold back. Nothing could have held me back."

Teddy paused to see if either Six-Four or Dale was listening.

"I was living in Manhattan in the early 1980s," I said. "I remember."
"What?"
"The first article I read was in the *Voice*. That one about the doctors at St. Vincent's noticing this disease among the Haitians and drug users."
"Didn't mention Air Canada stewards, did it?"
I shook my head.
"When it was clear I had it, I left New York and ended up in East Orange. I had no fucking clue what I was doing, but I had this job at a high school, and on the first day, there he was."

Teddy motioned toward Six-Four profoundly asleep squashed against the side of the train car.

"Did he tell you we have never had sex?"
I squinted to see if he was trying to get to me, but he was guileless.
"That would be indiscreet."

Teddy burst out with racking laughter and coughing and I immediately felt guilty, but he waved off my concern. He turned his face to me, his eyes suddenly narrowed and deeply black. When he spoke, his voice was tinged with a kind of angry regret.

"They think they are doing me a favour, this trip. One last time to see Paris. I have to tell you that every second has been torture. My body just won't die, and there are times I'm begging to die."

I listened to him, holding his eyes in mine, listening and making myself totally open to him and his angry emotion.

"Why don't you tell them?"

Teddy rolled his head to look once again at his mother and his lover. He looked back to me. A veil was coming down, and he could only stay on the surface with great effort.

"I can't leave them with the guilt."

I nodded and unscrewed his bottle, holding it to his lips. He drank deeply, paused and cleared his throat.

"Don't tell them."

I took back the bottle, capping it and placing it in his lap.

"That would be indiscreet, too."

Teddy suppressed another bout of laughter and rolled back to gaze on his sleeping loved ones. The train suddenly started to move, almost imperceptibly at first, in the manner of quality French engineering, but then palpably.

The Revelation of John Mullen

Time, thinks John, as the customer flips through the watchband samplers. Let's talk about thirty-eight years on the job. Hustling, selling, writing it up and finessing the commission. He looked around him. It was what used to be called a five-and-dime, but his Irish burr coloured it so that it always came out "fiver-and-dime" and that's the way it came out for his wife and the kids, all of them.

"Not many like these left, are there?" he says cheerfully.

The Vietnamese customer keeps flipping. He's into the stamped calfskin with the crocodile and lizard reliefs.

"Great buy on these, I could...," John starts, but his voice drifts off.

What was the use? He knew as soon as he had walked in that this was going to be a difficult sale. One glance at the wall behind the cash would tell you why. The decade's detritus of peddlers' wares, pinned, stapled, nailed to the walls of a thousand fiver-and-dimes just like this one. The nail clippers, the pocket combs, the shitty useless miniature flashlights. All garbage now, all on faded display cards, all crap of the finest order.

And now the customers weren't plump little Jewish folks or sharp-eyed, Brylcreemed Frenchies. Now they were as likely to be Gurvinder or Tran or Achmed. Everything changes. Only I haven't changed, thinks John.

"I meant fiver-and-dimes," he says, picking up the thread of his thoughts. "It used to take me a week to hit both sides of St. Lawrence up from Dorchester, my biggest season..."

The Vietnamese doesn't listen. He's ringing up a sale. A packet of cigarettes, $5.45, pack of gum, ninety cents, the chatter between the Vietnamese and his wife ceaseless, grating to John's ear.

John slips the cheaper, vinyl, leather-look, watchbands on top of the samplers. It has been a shit season. What had once taken a week back in the 1970s now took an afternoon, and what had once set him up for the entire year financially now barely covered the gas and lunch money. But I can make this sale, he thinks.

"Will you take a look at these? Look at that...can you tell me that's not butter soft glove leather? Go on, try it..." he cajoles.

The Vietnamese's wife takes over the negotiations. Uh oh, trouble. She waves a watch band in the air, her voice rising.

"Cheap, very cheap, trop cher. You price, trop cher..."

John bends down, now the beaming Irish Uncle come to straighten out these little yellow buggers. He feels a beer burp coming and catches it just in time.

"What do you think, eh? What do you think your cost is, come on tell me, 'cause you're wrong," he says slapping the counter perhaps a little too hard. "I'll tell ya, dead wrong, go ahead..."

A little confab, wife to husband, husband to wife, then wife starts to wrap things up, closing the samplers, bands slipping out of the cases, she's pushing them out of the way, clearing them off.

"Hey, wait a minute, come on, I just asked you to name your price!"

But they do not listen. Their attention is only on the next sale, the next sale. "That's the way it goes, darling! Name your price, Uncle John will see you right, come on, no need to get huffy."

The wife's not having any of it today. She gestures to the mass of junk and shit already caving in the wall behind her like cheap-goods wood rot.

"You too much expense, vous êtes trop cher, monsieur," she says.

The volume of chatter rises. Some little heathen is pushing toward the cash, a Coke and chips clenched like a prize.

"Trop cher, monsieur, too much, too much, you go."

The wife lifts the stack of samplers, holding them out to John. Fumbling, John makes one last, gentle attempt.

"Just name your price, I'm not in the mood to say no to you."

And that's when he sees them. Funny he didn't spot them before. He usually does. First thing he looks for when he walks into a store. Was it optimism or wishful thinking? Anyway, there they were under the glass top of the counter. Right under where he had spread his wares. Him, like some day-old rube still dripping.

"Oh, I see, so he's been here, has he?"

John stoops to eye the display packets of the competition. They pay for all that hard plastic casing, he thinks.

"You pay for that, you know...all that plastic, and in this day when we're trying to conserve everything, even my wife has me into the trash separating paper and plastic and look at them, each one with enough plastic to ...to..."

But what's the use.

They look better than his stuff. His samplers are old, dusty, some even cracked. He takes off a few cents for those but still, why bother? They do a nicer line, John thinks. Their salesman comes in like the Sahib himself, slick silk suit from Petones of Kowloon, pointy shoes, sunglasses, Asian, probably speaks several languages fluently, shakes a few hands, smiles ... speaks to them in a language they understand and unloads a gross of plastic-cased watch straps all clean and sleek looking. Can't walk into a fiver-and-dime in Montreal without seeing them, thinks John. They're like a bloody infestation, and who the hell is selling these things? Not me. I haven't got the little mobile flip phone. I haven't got the cream-coloured Cabriolet. I've got this shit box Chrysler...

John stuffs the samples into his sample bag. He takes his time, slipping errant watch bands into their proper slots. He's stalling, thinking, I need this sale. O.K. So she's won round one ... O.K. ... but I've taken her best punch and I'm still standing ... even after two dogs and three beers at the Point, I've still got something. He won't be pushed, no sir, not him. No sale, O.K., but I've still got my dignity.

He doesn't hurry. There is a steady flow of customers to the cash, but John doesn't hurry because John knows what his customers like. Under the guise of making room for his stock, John carefully places a stack of number 620's on the counter. He counts off the seconds until the sharp-eyed wife....

"Hey, hey! Easy with that...it's not a toy," says John firmly.

He takes the calculator/agenda from the wife's hands. It's a hit. John said so the minute he saw them. Matte black with silver casing, heavy, substantial, sleek, shiny.

"This calculator-agenda, too? Also phone numbers? How much?" says the wife, her English improving dramatically. John slowly takes out his samplers again.

The December sun can be terribly harsh some afternoons. Blinding, hot, seeing everything. John pockets the cheque with the Vietnamese man's signature and heads for Fairmount Street. He checks his watch; three-thirty. He has just enough time.

Let's see, thinks John, figuring, calculating, juggling around the numbers like a confused knitter. They took two samplers ... three samplers, that's right, three, and a sampler of key fobs, the number 312's, Jesus Christ that was the last of them, he thought. I've lugged that card around for eight, no, ten, twelve years, and I finally unloaded the last of it ... and then a dozen calculators, the 620's, a dozen comb and pen holders, that's, wait, no, not true. I gave them the holders, shit! I gave them those ... still not so bad, there might be fifty, sixty dollars...

John doesn't stop as he rounds the corner of Fairmount and St. Lawrence. He barrels along. Any sale, good or bad, any sale, he thinks to himself. It's tight out there. Very tight. Any sale.

He whips through the door at Wilensky's deli. There are several stools free. The guy with the beard recognizes him. Ditto the white-haired woman.

"Two specials, double mustard, a dill and a cherry Coke, please," he says, his hand digging into the glass holding the karnatzels.

He pops one into his mouth, worrying it with his teeth before mashing into its spicy, piquant heart and then worrying about what his wife will say when she catches his karnatzel breath. This was forbidden food, Jewish food, spicy, garlicky, fatty, hmmmmm...

"How's business, Johnny?" a voiced mumbled.

John knows better than to look at the counter staff. They never said anything, and even if they did, it was only to complain to each other, about each other, for each other, surly bunch...

No, this voice came from behind, and John recognized it even before he turned. Mashy. It was Mashy. He had been over in the far corner looking at the used books on the shelf devoted inexplicably to the novels of Louis L'Amour. Mashy, another of the walking dead in a suit that was once luscious, cut trim and smart, but was now a mass of pleats and baggy wrinkles. Mashy Gelfand, Optimum Occasions, formal tux rentals. There was a time when Mashy bought a new Buick every six months. "As soon as it loses that new car smell," he used to brag. Now he was just another baggy-assed little Hebe with a spot of psoriasis, aching ankles and a sagging Delta 88.

"You moving anything? How was your season?" mumbles Mashy as he takes the stool next to John.

Mashy would have announced the coming of the Messiah with the same inverted mumble. John was amazed that anyone understood Mashy but supposed that was part of the old man's charm. You had to work to understand Mashy. You had to want to.

"Just made a sale," grins John as the specials are laid before him by the white-haired lady.

The dills mounted on their wax-paper doily and the drink follow, delivered by different sets of busy hands as each working member of the family lean their collective shoulder to the Sisyphean task of feeding the assembled.

"Five-fifty," proclaims the white-haired woman. It was an old routine.

"You want me to pay now? For this gristle? This tainted Hebrew meat?" cries John sternly.

The family chuckles. Same routine, same restaurant, same routine. And no tipping, if you please.

"We'll call 911 for you, how's that? Five-fifty," repeats the white-haired woman.

Now Mashy is giggling too. John feigns offense as be pays the white-haired woman.

"What's with you, meshuga?" he says, rolling the Yiddish word through his Irish palate. Thirty years of peddling. You pick up the lexicon of selling in thirty years. "Come on, have a special. Have you eaten?"

Mashy waves off the offer, still giggling. He stops, watching John tuck into the steaming specials. He starts to rumble, the gurgling in his chest catching fire, the mumble flaring into clarity.

"I eat the specials but I wouldn't drink from that fountain if you paid me a million dollars." This last aimed with a sneering pout at the bearded son behind the fountain.

"Again he's starting with the fountain," screams the bearded one behind the counter.

Mashy turns on him suddenly, now sharp, on the attack.

"Can you tell me when was the last time the pipes were cleaned in that fountain? Can you tell me?" No one can take the high moral ground better than a confused, rumbling old Yiddisher.

The white-haired lady intervenes. The rest of the family are now deep in angry debate over whether or not they should ignore Mashy or throw him onto the sidewalk. Trick ankles or no.

"Leave him alone, he's an old man," moans the younger son.

"He drives away the clientele," whines the married daughter, tossing John's second special in front of him. The "clientele," thinks John, laughing.

"Mr. Gelfand," the white-haired lady says, speaking at a level just below that of a jet plane taking off, condescension flowing from her like curdled mother's milk, "The city inspectors are here every month. You can see the certificate, it's right there on the wall. Just for the record."

The Revelation of John Mullen

This last is for John's benefit, who, caught with his mouth full of hot cold cuts and fully soured pickle, nods sagely in agreement.

Mashy waves her off. He's having none of it.

"What are you telling me, the city? The city doesn't know a damn thing. I know. My brother Isaac installed the fountain, so who should know better, you or me?" replies Mashy, his voice cutting through the afternoon traffic drone.

"That it, he's out." says the bearded one, coming around the counter and undoing the soiled apron around his bulging abdomen.

"Don't," says John quietly, munching his special.

His Irish pugilist's timing is impeccable. Impeccable because John knows very few things but what he knows, he knows extremely well. And John knows how to handle a hot temper, having the benefit of a lifetime's experience handling his own.

John knows that behind the counter, the bearded son of the white-haired woman is king. No insult is tolerated, no slight is too slight. But John caught him just as he was coming around the counter. On the cusp, you might say, of the territorial imperative. For if the land behind the counter belongs to the white-haired lady and the family, the space in front of the counter belongs to the hungry masses. And John was hungry and not to be trifled with.

And Mashy was allowed to complain if that was his wish.

The bearded one caught in mid-stride, as it were, checked himself. He glanced at John, then at his mother, still engaged with but now talking more gently with Mashy, and then he looked at John again. John straightened up and looked frankly at the bearded one as if to say, "You're not still thinking about laying that fat mitt of yours on my old friend Mashy, are you?" Instead, he reaches into his pocket and takes out a key fob, Model 113, twenty cents wholesale. He flips it to the bearded one, who takes it and the opportunity to retreat behind the counter once more. "Another special, please, double mustard." John turns to Mashy.

"Mashy, shut up and eat," says John, pushing his second special over to the older man, who regards it as though it were some artefact from some distant, yet strangely Hebraic world. "But nothing from that fountain," says Mashy, girding his partial plate for the work ahead.

Start, you whore, thinks John as he winds up the Chrysler. The old car sputters and catches, then dies, then sputters, then dies, then, dies.

"Shit in a basket," shouts John, pounding on the steering wheel.

He pries the hood open, propping it up with a rusted rod he keeps for just such occasions. He looks for the ballast for the electronic ignition, wiggling it, twisting it up and down. He gets back into the car and tries again. It sputters, it catches and roars to life. "Living, whore of Babylon," mutters John as he closes the hood. He stops.

He has to check himself. What...? Everything is quiet. He listens to the engine, is it running? Yes, yes it is ... that's odd, I can barely hear it, he thinks. John looks around. The afternoon sun cuts low over the north-central end of the city. It is uncommonly warm for December. And it is suddenly very quiet, John thinks. He has noticed moments like these before. It is a trick of the afternoon sky, he thinks, a happy coincidence of traffic lights that creates such a silence, such a profound silence, like in a Church, in the middle of a city.

John stands beside his car, looking around. A bell, not far, was tolling but the sound comes to him as though through a muffling pillow. People walk by but their heels make no noise. No noise. How odd, thinks John. He doesn't want to move, to break the spell, but he's sweating, feeling restless, and he wants to get to at least two more stores before six. Sometimes his best sales are made as store owners are closing up. Probably they just want to get rid of him. But a sale is a sale, is a sale ...

John pulls into traffic heading east. He is still sweating, so he rolls down the window and lets the cooling air riffle through the rubble in his car. He could never be mistaken for other than what he was. I am a peddler, thinks John. I am the last of my breed. I am an Irish peddler, who buys shop-soiled goods from companies that no longer exist and I sell them to fiver-and-dimes that no longer know me from a hole in the ground. John loosens his collar. Jesus, he thinks, what is this, August? From the Point, to Mile End, from Park Ex, to Parc Lafontaine, this was my turf, my peddler's turf, he thinks as the rivulets of sweat seep into his now too tight collar. A peddler's beat in a peddler's car...

Now, yes! But not always, thinks John. When I came over from Ireland in 1950, I was fresh-faced and personable and was game to try my hand at anything. So I got myself a job in the Peck building, working for a string of Jewish-owned clothing manufacturers. The shmata business, rag trade. I moved up fast. Superior Pant, Quality Quilting, Better Buttons, all benefited from my managerial panache, my quick wit and good looks. John stops to check himself in his rear view mirror. Jesus, a grey, sweaty, tired-assed face if there ever was. I look beat, just tired-ass beat. Now, maybe, but not then!

More than one garment baron dragged me along when he went to the Toronto Dominion Bank on St. Lawrence to extend that loan, to boost that overdraft. Young, Irish, John makes a good impression, thinks old, tired John. Those WASP loan officers snapped to when we clicked in wearing those butter soft alpacas and those doeskin brogues. We were all hale fellows and money, what was money? This was the fifties, time to invest in the country, in business. Jesus, just the word "business" was enough to make the moneymen salivate. Yes, sir, we were in business and we were making money, thinks John. But I wasn't happy.

"I'm working for others. I'm not my own boss, Mr. Kline," I complained one day. "I need something that is my own."

"That's it," replied Kline with finality. "I'm putting you on the road. With your personality, with your drive, the sky is the limit. Your fortune is waiting to be made!"

And so it was. Mr. Kline is as good as his word, and within a month I'm on the road, in a new Chrysler Fifth Avenue, a sample case and a sample rack installed by Bernie's White Rose, and a list of clients provided by my predecessor, a man who takes my inside job.

My cronies on the Main scratch their collective heads. "He's moving from inside to the road? What gives? Too much Irish in the boy." Meaning maybe I'm stupid, but as soon as I hit that open road I knew it was for me.

It isn't easy at first but I was a natural, thinks John, and soon Montreal, Quebec, simply aren't big enough to contain me. I drove west, Ottawa, Sudbury, Sault Ste. Marie, Thunder Bay, Winnipeg, Brandon, Regina, Saskatoon, Edmonton, Calgary ... I roared through towns making sales that the factory had trouble keeping up with. I didn't sell hundreds or thousands, I sold tens of thousands. And I started looking for other lines.

John stops the memory show. I turn here, he thinks. What street is this, he questions, straining to catch a street sign. Oh, Papineau, right turn...

"John, I'm lingerie, it's what I know, it's what I like. You want to take on another line, who am I to stop you? With sales like yours, I'd be a fool. Just do me a favour. Seeing as you're taking other lines, how about my brother-in-law? It's trinkets, leather goods, you know. Please, do me this favour, just put a case in your trunk, whatever you sell, you sell," says Kline.

And I should say, Thank you, Mr. Kline! thinks John. Because I had some good years. The house in Dorval soon filled with kids. Good, clean Irish Catholic kids and his wife, a good clean Irish Catholic wife grew round and beautiful, and they were very good years.

Jesus, thinks John, it's hot in here. I'm still sweating, in this shitty Chrysler New Yorker, still heading east, looking for a fiver-and-dime on Ontario, an old Jewish guy and his wife still run their little shop amidst all those angry Frenchies...

Good years, thinks John, shit in a basket, we killed them all. We slaughtered them. I took my line out west and out east, even made a few forays into the States. The fifties and the sixties were the years to make money. And I made it. Expo '67, I got that franchise with, now what was that bastard's name, Hartley, Paul Hartley. Every bloody trinket, every key fob, anything with the Expo logo went through us, and we made a killing. Those nights, that whole summer. The kids were just wild. I got them all jobs on the site, what a summer.

Oh, shit, missed my turn, let me see, is there a cop? I'll just pull a U ... what was I driving then ... a big Chrysler, oh, yes, that Imperial, with the leather seats that little Angela burned with the cigarette lighter, those perfect little round holes, taking after her daddy, embossed leather goods. What is this street?

John strains again to find his bearings. He pulls the big car out into traffic again, still heading east. I should take Papineau down, shouldn't I? he thinks ... but the traffic ... better stay on Laurier, then go down one of the little avenues past St. Denis.

He watches the Plateau triplexes slip by, the new doors and windows announcing, proclaiming, working as a sign, the blood of the paschal lamb marking, "Here, within these walls, the fruit of the revolution." John chuckles to himself, sweat creeping into the tiny grooves of his upper lip. These houses state, just for the record, your honour, no trinkets wanted, no key fobs, no shmatas.

I suppose the first to go was Society Slips, he remembers. Good line that was, sold a ton. Then Quality Quilting, then Superior Pant and Paragon Zipper, then, what was his name? That little round fella, Better Buttons and Holes. One by one the Peck building and a dozen like it emptied out. One by one, Kline, and Jacobovtitz, Pressman, Litner, all gone to Florida, where they pass the days watching their melanomas propagate under the harsh Miami sun.

"I've got an inside lead on these townhouse estates," Kline whispered as though bearing the word from the Mount. "Get in now, buy all you can 'cause they're gold, you hear? Gold! Everyone is buying in."

John had hesitated.

"I'll lend you the money," cried Kline teasing him. "You Irish putz, richer than God and the apostates..."

"Apostles," laughed John. "And don't you blaspheme, you Hebrew yotz."

And perhaps he might have, but that string of children, those good Catholic children. Maybe the Jews were smarter. You have one, maybe two but back-to-back. They grow up together, leave home around the same time, then you're free. Free. Free to buy a condo in Florida.

But that wasn't the way his came. There was Marc (the wife's spelling), thank Jesus a boy first out, the rest were gravy. Then Richard, then Esther (Kline's mother's name, also a great aunt. Kline was titular godfather and blushed himself to 180 over 90 ... took two pills ... under the tongue ... sssh ... don't tell...), then my sweet pearl Angela, rotten little devil, school-ducker, crib note passer, terrorist, then Milo, smarter than Einstein. Strings that he was still tied to.

So as the doors closed, as the lines dried up, as those slick little Moroccan fellers took over, that valise of leather goods from Kline's brother-in-law started coming out more and more often. Eventually it graduated to the back seat, then to the front, until it was just him and me, thought John. Oh Jesus, this traffic, this city!!

John tugs his collar, forcing the button open. He squints the sweat out of his eyes, but it's no good. The traffic is stopped. John is boxed in on all sides. Why are we stopped, for chrissake!

Jesus, it's not even five o'clock and look at all these ... come on move will ya! There is nothing stopping you, just go, screams John internally. He reaches into his inside jacket pocket. The handkerchief is there, somewhere. His arm is twisted awkwardly as he searches that now mysteriously bottomless pocket. A sharp pain in his shoulder. Ow! he shouts, a cramp ... oh I hate this. I hate this! It's 180 over 90 for sure, he thinks, but then there's that ringing, like someone has just turned to lead crystal and keeled over. A ringing, muffled by a shout.

Now what is this? The reason for the traffic jam is suddenly clear. John can see them from the car, an angry crowd of demonstrators circling, another crowd trying to push past. Police cars parked to cause the maximum constriction in the flow of traffic.

"Thank you, Montreal Police," snarls John.

He tugs the boat-like Chrysler over closer to the curb, trying to enter the slow flow that is pulsing with weary arterial movements past the blockage of the police cars. 190 over 120, thinks John, the sweat having rendered the famous alpaca a pasty, clammy cast. What are those signs? John wipes his face with the handkerchief, momentarily clearing his eyes. Oh for the love of ... an abortion clinic, is that right? asks John to himself. Yes, that's it, look at the sign, "Avortement égale Meurtre" "Every life is precious." Oh, he thinks, isn't that sweet, it's a bilingual effort.

As he slowly creeps by, the milling factions are getting more and more aggressive. The Right-to-Lifers are on the steps to the clinic, their bodies an angry impediment to the front door. The police are undermanned and people, mostly women, who are trying to get into the clinic are not making it. John's car is stopped as two cops drag a red-faced, porky-looking man off the steps and towards the open rear door of one of the squad cars.

John turns again, his attention drawn by that sound, that high-pitched tone. As he looks through the crowd, he notices, over the heads of the demonstrators, a suggestion of blonde hair and, looking more directly, he sees her, and the tone starts to ring in his ears like something breaking, horribly, twisting and giving. As he watches, fixed on her, she steps off the curb and he can see her clearly, fully. She is tallish, mannish in that delicate way certain young women have, and blonde. John can see her clearly now, in fact she is all he can see and all he can hear for the noise of the traffic and the chanting having been drowned by the persistent ringing ... what is that sound?

The blonde side-steps the front of the crowd, and it appears she has a hole to slip through, past the front line of placards and angry faces. She makes a move as though to take it but again, the side movement and without turning. She is suddenly, not there!

And suddenly nothing else matters, not the crowds not the traffic not the struggling cops not the spittle-flecked screaming lips, none of it, because John is now out of his car and racing towards her, to where she was, and suddenly all eyes are on the tall, grey, sad-faced man with the deep-set eyes and the square jaw. All mouths are suddenly still, watching as this man drunkenly loses his footing and then regains it and then loses... and then the arms of the cop are pushing him back to his car, back to the stinking, stalled Chrysler and his own voice comes to him and he realizes that he has been shouting.

Then he is being stuffed back into the car.

"Vas-y, câlisse, away!" cries the cop as the demonstrators renew their chant.

And somehow the engine catches and sputters and catches and stays caught, and John jerks the heavy car away from the curb past the intersection and down the first right turn, Mentanna Street.

And it is there that John stills the engine and rolls down the window and breathes deeply the cold, late afternoon air, like a draught of water and smoke. And it is only now that John allows himself to think of what he has just seen.

"It has been four months since my last confession," says John, which was, in fact, for the record, true. Just before cousin Norman's daughter's First Communion.

The Young Priest, in the tradition of young priests, responds non-judgmentally. After all, were they not, in fact, in the confessional? The old man with the steel grey hair and the deep-set eyes had waylaid him just as he stepped out of St. Mary's Hospital.

"I've seen something and I need to tell you about it," says John, pushing the Young Priest back into the hospital entrance. The Young Priest can see where John has left his Chrysler, parked in the doctor's reserved parking.

"Hadn't you better move your car? I mean, you can't stop there."

The logic of this observation stymies John. He lets go of the Young Priest and looks over his shoulder at his car. He straightens himself, self-consciously. He turns back to the Young Priest.

"I'll go move it," he says a little shakily, "But you have to stay here, I have to talk to you!"

The Young Priest doesn't move but looks at the old man with an indulgent smile. "I'm not going anywhere."

As soon as John goes off to move his car, the Young Priest calls to an orderly.

"I'm going to try and walk him through to emergency. Tell them I think he's had a stroke or something. I'm going to try and walk him through. He's old but he's as strong as a bull." The orderly skitters off.

John returns, his head low, sheepish. The Young Priest tries to take his arm, gently, tries to lead John in the direction of emergency but John simply doesn't follow. He straightens himself, tucking in his shirt as he eyes the Young Priest cagily.

"O.K., I've had a scare, you're smart enough to guess that, but I'm all right, I'm all right. I've seen something and I need you to tell me what it means. That's all. You have to tell me."

John and the Young Priest don't move in the vestibule. A steady trickle of people drift in and out through the revolving doors but as soon as John starts to talk, even the Young Priest doesn't want to move.

"I saw her hair first. You couldn't miss her face, though. She was beautiful, plain, but beautiful. And I think you could say she was trying to get into the clinic, even as those people were shouting in her face, screaming in her face, she tried to pass them..."

"To get into the clinic," said the Young Priest.

"I think so. That was the way it appeared to me." John glances at the Young Priest uneasily. "It was an abortion clinic."

"Was she pregnant herself?" asked the Young Priest.

John thinks before answering.

"Not that you could see, she wasn't showing anything, I mean." John thinks for a moment longer.

"And it was when I looked back that I saw it, around her head and around her shoulders, like a shawl, or like, what is that? A mantle? Is that the word?"

"A mantle," said the Young Priest, the hair on the back of his neck standing up.

"Like a mantle, or like you know, what the Jews wear, in their temple? They call it a talis. I used to call it their bib-and-tucker or tam o'shanter. You've seen them, the older ones put it on top of their heads and it drapes down their shoulders."

"Yes," replied the Young Priest, a faint nausea taking him.

"And that's what it was Father, a halo, golden, like, like ... I don't know really, but I remember thinking, So that's what they look like, not at all what you think, not like the way the artists do them, you see? More ... more natural."

"Yes," said the Young Priest.

"And I suppose when I saw it, that's when I got out of the car. I don't remember, you see, I must have stalled the car and then suddenly, there I am on the street, my eyes filled with that light, and I suppose I'm going for her because I remember thinking, I've got to tell her, she's got to know what she's carrying, she can't go into that place."

"No," says the Young Priest, the nausea passing. He smiles inwardly. O.K., he thinks, you got me. Had me going there for a moment. Ha! What a fool I am. You really had me there. Now what is the current antidote for Irish Catholic guilt? Being Portuguese, he didn't know.

"So, I suppose I have to know what it means, Father. I have to know what to do. What should I do?" asks John.

This time, the Young Priest has no problem leading John deeper into the hospital, deeper into the hallway, towards emergency.

Oona hates worry. And bother. But as soon as she sees John, she knows that the worse was over before she arrived. The Young Priest stops her from going into the examination area where John is getting dressed. His tone is only slightly condescending.

"He's going to tell you he saw a woman with a halo. Outside an abortion clinic."

"Oh no," sighs Oona.

Not that she really believes that John saw a woman with a halo in front of an abortion clinic. It's just that John is so obstinate when he thinks he has seen something. Like when he gets a price wrong in the Canadian Tire flyer and he swears up and down the price was this, but they get to the store and it's not that price at all, and the poor manager has to go find a flyer and prove to John in front of the whole store. Once he's got an idea in his head, it cannot be pried out. He'll present and represent it until either everyone in the family agrees or he eventually forgets about it.

"This is probably something for your own parish priest. May I ask which church you attend?" asks the Young Priest solicitously.

"St. Malachy's, out in Dorval," replies Oona, not taking her eyes off John for a moment.

"I'm sure he'll be able to give guidance in this." The Young Priest hesitates, but he is unable to resist asking the question. After all, curiosity isn't deadly.

"May I ask, if it's not prying ... You see, he saw this scene in front of an abortion clinic, it's been in the news. It has had a strong effect on him, this illusion he's had. If it's not prying, has someone in your family had a ... I mean..."

Oona's attention is pulled away suddenly from John. She looks up at the Young Priest and touches her chest with her hand.

"No, Father, my God, no, nothing! We're a very close family. We've nothing like that. He's just tired, he won't stop working and it's too hard. Well, look at him, Father, he's just beat. But no, we've never had anything to make him think like that," replies Oona, shaken at the very thought.

The Young Priest retreats, humbly, mincingly, away from the implication. He speaks now, softly, meekly.

"That's good. I mean, it's good that we can eliminate that possibility." The Young Priest pauses for effect.

"I've told him that this kind of thing must be thought over carefully. I told him he is not to go around insisting on what he saw when he was alone in the experience. I suggested deeper contemplation, meditation. It seemed to calm him. Medically," the Young Priest motions to a short, dark-haired, chubby intern. "Harold?"

The intern approaches, with the efficient air of someone who knows what he's doing.

"This is Mrs. Mullen, Doctor Harold Beinstock," says the Young Priest by way of introduction.

"What happened?" asks Oona.

Doctor Harold shrugs before replying.

"We're not sure. We've run a cardio and an EEG, and everything is normal. He complained of heavy sweating just before the incident and of a ringing sound. We've drawn blood for tests. Normally, I'd suggest keeping him here overnight, but it definitely wasn't a heart attack. He may have had a small stroke, but I won't be sure until I see some test results."

John notices Oona talking with Doctor Harold. Nice boy he thinks, Sy Beinstock's grandson, he chuckles. Grandson. He pulls on his sweater vest, reaching at the same time for the old alpaca coat. No reason to stay. Priest obviously hasn't got a clue ... God knows what they're telling Oona.

Of course, Oona knows whom John would appeal to. Nobody else, not anyone in the entire family would have given the time of day to such a story. Everyone, on the other hand, was more seriously concerned with the medical implications.

"He's going off the road," Marc says, using that adult tone of voice he uses when he discovers to his own amazement that Oona actually wants to hear what he has to say. "That's the beginning and the end. God knows what his pressure was like, and his eyes, and this sudden religious visitation."

"Maybe he did see something," murmurs Angela. Oona does that switchblade thing with her eyes, and Angela slinks off like an insulted cat. Oona immediately feels bad, not for hurting her young daughter's feelings but knowing that Angela will turn her hurt into sympathy for her Dad. She'll lend the ear that he needs to try and rationalize his recent experience. Better to ignore it.

"Better to ignore it," says Oona, settling down at the table.

"Uh?" says Marc.

"Everything has changed for him, understand? I told you this already. Now you see what I mean." Oona pauses for dramatic effect. "Ever since he lost the lines, he's been dragging himself around like a zombie. Well, that's it."

"It's what I said, Mother," says Marc, vindicated at long last. But he can hear the whisperings from the rec room.

"But how do you know that it was that?" says Angela, curling up beside John, knocking his glass of Jameson's.

John takes a stiff gulp, checking to see if anyone else is coming down the stairs.

"I know it because that's what I said when it happened," he says, rubbing his tired eyes with the back of his hand. "I asked myself, no, I told myself, like I already knew it and was just confirming it. I said, oh, very calm, you understand, I wasn't panicking, but very calmly I was talking to myself and I said, very clearly and calmly, I said, oh, so that's what they look like, not like the Sunday school drawings, not that circular thing, but like a ... a..."

"A shawl...?" demands Angela, settling down for a long session.

"Remember?" says John interrupting gently. "Remember Ricky Goldstein's bar mitzvah? Do you remember that? Remember the way some of the men, the old grey men, at the back, remember what they had on their heads?"

"Prayer shawl," says Angela knowingly.

"Talis they call them. It was like that but made up of light, or gold light."

John stops for a moment. His face feels light, tight, then for some reason he starts to blush. He is about to take another sip when Angela reaches up and takes the glass from his hand. Voices waft down from the kitchen, and they can hear snatches of the post-mortem.

"That's it..." "If he tries..." "... all these years and I've told him ..." "How much longer..?"

Angela unfolds herself off her father's lap, hopping up and down lightly on one foot as she gains, then loses, then regains her balance. As supple as thought, she arabesques till her lips are near John's ear.

"I believe you," she whispers. She kisses his already sleeping eye and is gone.

The only way to get out of the house quietly was to get up before everyone. As he leaves, John stops between the front door and the stoop. He half hopes Oona will hear him, not to stop him, but just to know that he will not be stopped. There is no sound from the house.

He also stops because something has changed. This day is not like the day before. This is a gray morning. In the winter half-light the mornings are gray and gray, and white. John stands still thinking, flitting thoughts, thinking. Then, of course! he thinks. I'll just go back and find her.

Nothing is the same, he thinks. The Chrysler is parked across the street from the clinic, and for a moment John thinks it's the wrong street. But no, there's the front steps, yes that's right, and there was the bus stop, I remember that, he thinks. He twists in the front seat. And she came, she seemed to come from the same direction I was driving because I only saw her when she passed the car. He twists again and reaches for the door handle.

His legs are a little shaky. He straightens himself up. Today there is only a trickle of traffic, and very few people are going in or out of the clinic. Now, there's a face, thinks John, spotting a young man at the door of the clinic. He was there, now where? Oh yes, he was trying to help another guy over the demonstrators. He was at the door when she passed through the crowd, he would have seen her, absolutely.

The young man is halfway to the curb before John catches up to him.

"Big change from yesterday," says John, with a smile that says 'I'm a smiling, avuncular old man.'

"Pardon?" Obviously the young man is French. Obviously he is a doctor, John thinks, because he has a stethoscope around his neck. John can just see it under the young man's scarf.

The young man doesn't stop but continues towards the bus stop, and John suddenly becomes another man going to the bus stop.

"The demonstration, yesterday," says John, using the time-honoured strategy employed by hundreds of thousands of Anglo-Montrealers for hundreds of years when having to deal with French Montrealers. They simply speak English.

"Yes, it was a zoo," replies the young man who, in fact, isn't French at all. He's Belgian, and not even French Belgian, he's Flemish. But John doesn't know and is oblivious to anything except what he's after.

"I was passing by," he continues. "I was right there, yesterday, you know, where the police cars were blocking the traffic? When they were taking the chubby guy off the steps, pushing him toward the police cars?"

They have reached the bus shelter, and for the first time the young man takes a good look at this overly familiar fellow transit user. And, of course, the young man recognizes John.

"You were there," he says, the scene replaying itself foggily in his mind.

"Yeah, right there, and there was this woman too," says John, trying to sidle closer.

"You're the guy who left his car, in the middle, you were the guy, and the cops told you to move your car."

"You remember me?" asks John, somewhat surprised and thrown off track.

"You were shouting at someone. Who were you shouting at?"

"Well, I was hoping you could help me with that. There was this girl, a woman, tall with blonde hair."

The young man pulls away, suspicious now, fight or flee...

"Very nice looking, she was just trying to get through the crowd on the steps."

"You were with them," says the young man sharply. He turns his head. A bus is coming. He fingers his bus pass.

"Who?" says John, now solidly off track.

"The demonstrators ... you were trying to help them." The young man moves to line himself up with the bus queue.

"No," says John, offended and showing it. "I was passing, in my car, and I saw this young woman, and if you saw me, then you must have seen her too. She was quite tall."

The bus slushes up to the curb and, as the doors opens, the queue starts to jostle forward. The young man is carried by the movement of the line. John follows, off to the side, pointing to the front of the clinic.

"I just thought that I could find her, there was so much confusion, with the traffic and the police and everything. But you must have seen her, if you saw me, remembered me, then you had to ..." But the doors are now shut, and the bus diesels past and the young man, a frown on his unlined face, is carried away from John.

How long can I sit here before someone notices? wonders John. The Chrysler is still parked across from the clinic, and except to bolt over to the nearby casse croute for a couple of steamies and a bottle of spruce beer, John hasn't taken his eyes off the front door. She didn't get in yesterday, he thinks. So she'll come today. I just have to sit here and she'll show up, and then I'll be able to...

For a second, and for a long minute afterwards, John suddenly realizes a very important issue. That he was going to try to find her was no surprise, John thinks. There was never any question. But what am I going to say to her? And he sits very still, gazing through the dipping, late-afternoon light at the door of the clinic.

And then the thought occurs to him that no matter what he says, it's not going to sound very sane; and then he thinks, very clearly now, that this is how Oona felt in the emergency room and then later at home. John feels himself, climbing out of himself like a yolk slipping through the cracked shell of a mishandled egg. He sees the events of the last twenty-four hours as though played out on a movie screen. He sees the furore in front of the clinic, sees the cops busting up the demonstrators, sees the chubby man, sees the woman, the halo, the holy halo, the holly, holy, hooly, halo, and there he is, the loutish, unkempt, Irish man, sweaty alpaca, gun-metal hair, roaring hallelujahs, after a glimpse of yellow, of gold.

"And what would I say to her?" he demands of Jimmy as Jimmy un-trays another infusion of the golden, foamy, nectar.

John looks around at the reddened, vascular faces surrounding him in the clubhouse. Now how did I get here? he wonders. The laughing, wrinkled, wheezing sons-of-bitches, hail all you Commodores and Rear Admirals of the bloody Lasalle Yacht and Sport Fishing Club, at your inebriated service.

And the faces laugh back, coughing lungs full of acrid, khaki smoke into the foul, inbred air of the clubhouse. All the Commodores, Rear Admirals, Captains all...

"What do you say? Excuse me, miss," says John, hoisting a lager, "but I must inform you, with all due respect and just for the record, that the baby you are carrying, the one you are ready to flush out into the finest sewage purification system in the Western world ... let's hear it for Johnny the Flag, gentlemen!!"

And the Captains and Stevedores and Pursers purse their lips and blow caramel-coloured raspberries into the grey-funk of the clubhouse.

"To Johnny the Flag, may his liver rot his syphilitic head!!"

"The baby, to continue gentlemen, the baby you are sheltering within that tall, slim, handsome body, your female body..."

"Hey, cut to the dirty part!" shrieks the Rear Admiral.

"The baby you are preparing to snuff, to cancel, to eradicate, to dismiss, to dissociate yourself from, forever and ever..."

"Amen," cough the Petty Officers, as they cross themselves.

"The child, the glimmer of life, that is sitting so parasitically beneath your breast ..."

"The dirty part!" scream the Boson's mates, coughing their own lungs out.

"And just for the record, I might add, sitting within your womb. This child, my dear young woman, and with all due respect, is nothing more or less, than the Messiah."

"No," cries a First Officer. "No! It's the return of Gump Worsley!!"

And the clubhouse is rocked with the dyspeptic heaving of distilled livers, rank gall-bladder, fetid guts. John turns, amazed by the reaction.

"Observe, gentlemen, and boys of the choir. Observe her Royal Navy, bloated like the corpse of a maggoty pig, observe and take heed, all you sons and heirs of the fleet."

Jimmy delivers another tray.

"How do you know?" asks Jimmy.

John looks up, his eyes sharp and clear. He bolts his hand under his chin, thrusting his cheek into the cock-eyed air.

"I saw her halo." He waits for a reaction. "I saw a golden wreath of light around her sacred, handsome head."

The press gang falls silent.

"So," says Jimmy, picking the dead soldiers off the table, "You just tell her that."

John drifts off, his placid, watery, blue eyes, sweeping past the archival photos: ice fishing on Lake Louise, summer regattas off Goose Village, the floating of the colours, a maritime flag indicating "I'm on fire."

———

Oona is so upset she's almost shrieking. Sometimes her voice does break like a confused, hurt howl. John remains silent under the collectively scrutinizing eyes of Marc and Angela. Oona is waving around the remnants of the Yellow Pages.

"If Jimmy hadn't told me, he'd still be sitting there, in his bloody car, like some pervert," cries Oona.

"Calm down, Oona," replies John meekly, still not raising his eyes.

"What were you looking for, Dad?" asks Marc.

"It's not enough I have to sit at home and worry myself blind every time he goes out. He takes his coat and that bag and he bumps his ass into that bloody car, and I have to sit and wonder what garbage he's eating and what he's drinking with those idiots at the Yacht Club, and then Jimmy phones up with this story."

Oona has almost exhausted herself with shouting and leans over the table staring right down at John, who doesn't flinch.

"I told you, I do not want an infirm old man as a husband. I told you, you had to finish with the drinking."

"Excessively," corrects Angela abstractedly. She can feel the switchblade eyes on her as her mother turns from her father.

"Excessive drinking," repeats Oona from behind gritted teeth. "And the consumption of whatever trash you and your cronies feast on whenever my back is turned."

Oona draws a breath and starts to sit down opposite her husband.

"And I told you, I want you clear-headed till the end."

Her tears are welling up, right on cue. Soon the knuckles will push into a reddened cheek, and her eyes will gaze out through the kitchen window when they will swell in fear and anxiety at the vision of a future filled with dotty clothes, soiling, infirmity, and Alzheimer's disease.

The room is quite still. Milo saunters in and comes up behind his father. He reaches across the table and takes the pieces of Yellow Pages from his mother's limp grasp. He reads them briefly.

"What were you doin', Dad?" he asks gently.

John takes the pages from Milo's hands, turning them over and over. The pages are marked with addresses crossed off, check marks, phone numbers.

"I went back to the first clinic," he begins.

Oona bolts from the table. "I don't want to hear about this!"

John watches her leave, then turns to his children.

"I had the idea that if the woman I saw, the one with the light around her ..."

"The halo," says Angela, pulling her knees up to her chin.

"Yes, the halo. I figured if she was going into the clinic, and she didn't get in, then she'd go back. So I thought I'd just go there and wait."

"He's been sitting outside of those clinics for two weeks. Two weeks! Who knows how many poor girls he's frightened!" shouts Oona from the hall.

"Then I went into the clinic, asked about her, but you know," he says, pausing for effect, "They are quite protective of the women there. Of course, I understand, I mean I could be anybody, someone's father or a boyfriend."

"Ha!" snorts Oona from the pantry.

"Anyway, I was quite impressed with the way they handled all inquiries," says John, warming up to his story as though giving a report to the Rotarians. "I was treated courteously, and most of the people at these places seemed quite sympathetic."

"Sure," says Oona, cutting through. "Did you tell them what you were looking for? Did you tell them you were after a woman with a halo? I bet you didn't!"

"I didn't have to," fires back John. "I have too much respect for them despite how I might feel about the rightness or wrongness of what they do!"

"Oh, Lord, help me," mutters Oona, now in the kitchen, rattling pots and dishes.

John turns to his audience.

"So I figured the best way was to take a very methodical approach," he says slowly.

"Scientific methodology," says Milo.

"Right. So, first, how to find these places? They are not always listed in the phone book. I mean, it was a start, but some of the clinics have subtle names, it's not always easy to spot them. After a few rejections I got a list of names by posing as a concerned father."

John pushes a pamphlet across the table to Angela, who picks it up and examines it with interest. Suddenly, Oona is behind her, snatching the pamphlet out of her hands.

"I will not have this in the house! God forbid someone should see it here and think anyone..." she says, bending low over Angela. "Anyone in this house should every have need of ..."

"And thank God for them," says John, rising to the attack.

The entire house stands still. Such a difference of opinion and so passionately expressed is unheard of ... impossible! Mother and father on opposite sides of a religious issue.

Oona walks back stiff-legged to the dining room table. Her jaw is set, her eyes, dropped in shadow by the low lamp over the table, glitter like scales.

"You mean to sit there, pontificating like someone senile ... sit there and tell me that if Angela came home and told us she was pregnant, that you would calmly and coolly hand over this?" she says, waving the pamphlet under John's nose.

John doesn't speak for a moment, and then with perfect smoothness and grace reaches up his hand and firmly removes the pamphlet from his wife's grasp. He turns his eyes on his daughter.

"If, God forbid, our Angela came home with such a problem, I would sit and talk with her; and if she asked me for information, I would give her this. Yes, I would."

"It's a sin!" snaps Oona.

"It's a sin," repeats John. "All those women, it's a sin! But I've seen their faces and I've seen their pain and I've seen how desperate they can be, and that's a sin too."

John rises from the table and heads for the basement. "That too is a sin."

"Tell me you'll stop this, John. You'll stop." Oona waits for a reply.

John stops at the door to the basement, one foot already on the first step, his left hand supporting his weight against the door frame.

"It's stopped. I didn't see anything. I didn't find her. There was no halo, there was probably no woman. There was nothing."

Those at the table can hear John's tired feet clumping down the stairs. They can hear the television come on, they can hear the play-by-play of the game. Someone has just scored.

Angela turns back to the table. The pamphlet is right where John left it. She moves to pick it up but is too late, as Oona snatches it up again and leaves the room, throwing cautionary blades at her daughter.

Father Gervais is much faster than he looks, thinks the Young Priest. In fact, on the ice, a stick in his hand, and the net only yards away, the Young Priest has as much chance of stopping Father Gervais as he has of stopping the moon.

Father O'Brian is off on the bench adjusting a problematic skate lace. Father Gervais nets the puck then, pivoting on his stumpy little legs, he pumps his thighs up the rink, intent on running down his young acolyte.

"Brother Danny," taunts Father Gervais. "Dan the man. Watch it, watch it! Here it comes, the big Jesuit line, the unstoppable line, the shock troops of the Lord!"

Father Gervais cuts right in front of young Father Daniel, unbalancing him, causing him to fall.

Father O'Brian calls from the sides, "Un-Christian!"

The three Jesuits laugh and resume the casual chasing of the puck. The snick, snick, snick of the blades against the ice of the finely groomed university rink is pleasantly reassuring to young Father Daniel. It is reassuring, and yet there is still the unsettled issue. He calls across to Father O'Brian.

"And so if someone comes to you with a vision of a miracle."

"An apparition," says Father Gervais, by way of supporting argument.

"Then you do as I did. Prescribe more thought, contemplation?"

Father O'Brian returns to the bench, his skate still not quite right. He follows the play of the other two, pacing along the boards. Father Gervais nails the Young Priest against the boards and play pauses while Father Daniel tries to catch the breath that has just been pounded out of him.

"The point is," continues Father O'Brian, "if the person is sincere, then trying to convince him that he really hasn't seen anything or trying to suggest that what he saw might not have been what he saw, is, I think, rather counterproductive. It gets you nowhere."

"And as long as the person isn't deluding himself in a dangerous direction," submits Father Gervais. "As long as he isn't likely to hurt himself or others because of what he's seen or experienced, then why patronize?"

"Precisely," says Father O'Brian.

Young Father Daniel manages to evade yet another punishing hip check thrown at him by the diminutive yet aggressive Father Gervais and starts a break-away of his own. Father Gervais, his blood up to the game, gives chase.

"Of course, he didn't really see anything. I mean he could not have seen anything," gasps the almost winded young Father Daniel as he leaves the ice momentarily via a shoulder check from the minuscule Father Gervais, who then steals the puck and lifts a wobbly to the upper right corner of the net.

Young Father Daniel doesn't bother to get off the ice this time but lies there, spread-eagled on his back as though making ice angels. Father O'Brian takes to the ice once more, tentatively trying out his new lacing. Father Gervais circles the prostrate young Father Daniel like a Shetland Terrier herding goats.

"On the other hand, he could have seen something. The greater question is, does it matter?" asks Father O'Brian meekly.

Young Father Daniel raises himself off the ice to face Father O'Brian.

"Well, yes, Brother. Truth," he replies.

"Highly over-rated," shoots Father Gervais as he whooshes past, flicking his stick like the tongue of a fer-de-lance.

"The truth," repeats young Father Daniel, insistently, "is important. I think we have to at least start with the truth. What he saw, what he thought he saw, what he actually saw, and counsel from a point of knowledge instead of ignorance."

"Belief or disbelief, you mean," says Father Gervais, cutting sharply to spray his prone brother with watery ice.

Father O'Brian waves off his sportive co-religionist.

"The point is, a Catholic person has an experience, out of the blue, a quasi-religious experience. The a priori truth of the incident is not the point, much as our lives would be made easier if it were. The point is the effect on the Catholic person. The point is what this experience means to him."

Young Father Daniel regains his footing and faces Father O'Brian.

"Then, what should I have said?" he asks, suddenly feeling even younger than his age.

The Revelation of John Mullen

"Nothing," shouts Father Gervais from the far end of the rink. "You should have listened."

Young Father Daniel looks off at the distant Father Gervais and then turns back to Father O'Brian, who is now kneeling before him, one knee on the ice, adjusting his laces again for the thirtieth time.

Now, it looks familiar, thinks John to himself, parking the big Chrysler across the road from the clinic. It is the same time of day. The same late afternoon sun catching the corners and lintels of the grey buildings and bringing them out in relief. John looks around and walks over to the spot.

I was out of the car here, he thinks, checking his bearings. Yes, and the crowd was there, the cop car was in front of me to my left and she was, where?

John turns to look at the area where the woman with the halo might have been. There are several people on the sidewalk moving to and fro. Some are men, just off a city bus, walking briskly home. Other people seem to be students. Is there a school around here? thinks John. Then a blonde girl, her hair bouncing with her girlish gait, bouncing, her hair suddenly catching a shaft of light, there! Just there! There's a point of light. John turns quickly and squints at the space between the two triplexes across the street, the sun is low, shining through the alley.

It's all done with light, thinks John. And miracles too. He walks to the spot, the exact spot on the sidewalk the girl just walked through. He raises his hand into the light, the clear shaft of late afternoon sunlight and his grey, cold hand turns gold.

It wasn't like I was particularly looking for something, thinks John, easing his tired, droopy body into the Chrysler. I wasn't looking for anything at all, he thinks. The Chrysler catches then dies, then turns and dies, then catches, then catches.

"It was a trick of light?" asks Jimmy from the bar as the Fleet imbibes the first of the late afternoon's oilings.

"Like a junk stuck in the mud of the great and noble Yangtze River."

"All hail the great yellow river of misery!" shouts the First Mate, whose cries are greeted by the feeble mumbling of so many bowels, so many colons, so many bladders.

"A trick of light falling on the unctuous, tepid flow, the yellow flow, a beam of sunlight caroming off the Earth at an angle just so, in short," says John, looking up at Jimmy. "An optical illusion."

John swaggers up to the Captain's table, resting a weathered wing tip encased in a rubber galosh on the edge. He snatches a glass from the hands of a crippled Petty Officer.

"A toast, gentlemen and proselytes, if you please, your honours, and members of the shore party," cries John.

Jimmy is about to put down another tray of draughts, but to his utter astonishment and horror, John, waves him off. The Rear Admirals, Harbour Pilots, and First Mates snap to.

"To the age of miracles! Convicted, prosecuted, sentenced, and delivered into your good and kindly hands. Gentlemen, I give you, Madonna and child!"

John starts to drink but notices that no one seems to be paying him any attention.

"A corollary, if you please," sighs the Captain of the Fleet, wheezing into his mug. The walls drop their groaning load of cheaply framed epithets and shrug and stretch.

This last is greeted by a hail of farts, burps and wheezes and the plaintive cries of the Able Seamen locked forever in the head. Someone, somewhere, is trying to roll a cigarette but keeps licking his finger instead of the gummed edge.

With a flourish, John stands, snatching up his coat and whisking it around his shoulders like a cape. All around him the creaking remnants of the Lasalle Yacht and Fishing Club, wheeze another wheeze, gulp another yard ... how much liquor and how much beer?

The Revelation of John Mullen

"How much beer, Jimmy?" asks John, turning to the bar.

"Too much," replies Jimmy. He is watching John with a somewhat surprised light in his eyes. "Hey, John, it's only six, and you haven't bought a round."

The club erupts with dog whistles, stomping of gangrened feet, the slapping of arthritic knuckles against emaciated thighs. John waltzes gracefully towards the door, twirling his coat.

"I have asked the gathered assembly to join me in a toast, and what has been the response?"

The shore party heaves another cry into the rank, brown air and sputters its collective frustration on the severance of it sustenance.

"In which case I can only fall upon your mercy," says John.

"Eat shit," cries some despondent Stoker from the bowels of the keg cellar.

"Precisely, gentlemen, your honours. And may I add, for the record, that a member in good standing prevails upon you all to raise a glass, a mug, your craniums, if you are at all able, gentlemen, to the finest woman to ever christen the muddled pate of a man..."

"Here, here!" snaps the Commodore. "That's the stuff, Johnny!"

"... the most gentle soul to ever grasp the tiller..."

"Grasp this, you recidivist!" moans an aroused Navigator.

"... the most caring, the most ... the most thorough container of dreams," says John, carefully removing a twenty dollar bill.

"Probation for the reprobate," coughs the bloated Boson's Mate.

"... the most fecund of wombs ..."

"Dirty again," shrieks the Engineer, wayward and forever lost.

"To the only and always, Oona."

"Oona!" The cry is deadening. John tosses Jimmy the crumpled twenty.

"She, who even now, awaits me, awaits my pleasure, all sails unfurled, the rudder set to compass heading North, North East, North, North East," says John, leaving the gathered to ruminate and wonder.

A week to go before Christmas. Christmas, thinks John, and if I can just unload another gross or two of this scrap. He looks down at the sample bag sitting on the stool beside him. Since it is after two o'clock, Wilensky's isn't that busy, so he can put his bag on the stool beside him. Privilege of rank. No one would dare ask him to move it, though he might move it on his own, if he thought it necessary.

A Young Man takes the stool beside the bag. The white-haired woman looks in John's direction.

"Just one, please, no mustard," sighs John.

The family behind the counter are momentarily confused. He has changed the lines in their little one act, he has departed from the routine. The white-haired woman leans across the counter as though to say something.

"And no dill, if you don't mind," John says. "And a diet Coke."

Galvanized into total stasis, the family steals glimpses over their collective shoulder, murmuring in a huddle until the inevitable cry, "For a million, if you paid me a million dollars I wouldn't drink from dat fountain!"

John makes a little room for Mashy.

"And a special for my friend," says John softly.

Somehow this act of largesse stimulates the family to action and re-establishes the equilibrium of the day. But the white-haired lady is curious.

"You're not hungry?" she nudges, offering the glass of karnatzels.

John waves off the offer.

"Promised the wife. She doesn't want a feeble husband."

"Feeble?" shouts the bearded one at the press grill. "A special is the best thing for you. The best thing. Look at Mr. Gelfand. He'll live to a hundred and twenty."

Mashy responds through a mouthful of hot deli meat.

"Dat's 'cause I don't drink from that fountain."

John giggles gently, patting the old man on the shoulder. The wounded family all scatter behind the counter, tending the high technology

The Revelation of John Mullen

that powers their empire, to wit press grill, steamer, deli meat slicer, soda fountain.

John is aware of another person laughing.

"That's some bag you got there," says the Young Fellow with an appraising air.

"You like dat bag?" asks Mashy, gazing watery-eyed at the Young Fellow. "Dat's a real sample bag, you don't see dem like dat anymore. Dey don't make 'em."

"Gimme two specials, extra mustard, a dill, and, uh, a Cola please," says the Young Fellow to the grey-haired lady.

Stepping sprightly, the white-haired woman starts to hum/sing.

"Sunrise, sunset, sunrise, sunset, dumm, da, dumm, da, da..."

The Young Fellow can't take his eyes off the bag. John notices the Young Fellow's bag: bridle leather, more modern design but a good quality piece of work. Clearly not an attaché case but thicker, sectioned. The Young Fellow also has a tiny cellular phone. The Young Fellow seems to have a lot of stuff.

"I've seen bags like that in England, at antique fairs. They make a business out of restoring old leather bags. Mail bags, bank bags, sell for a lot of money," says the Young Fellow, hefting his first special.

"This is an English bag," says John. "It came from England."

"Oh yeah?" says the Young Fellow with interest.

"They gave it to us for the line. It was custom made to hold all the samples, you know, keep them all in order," John continues.

"What's the line? What do you sell?" asks the Young Fellow.

John has finished his special and, oblivious to the frowns of the family behind the counter, he turns to the Young Fellow.

"Leather goods, novelties in leather, you know, key fobs, comb holsters."

The Young Fellow stops in mid-bite and slowly puts down his sandwich. He turns slowly towards John.

"Mind if I see?" asks the Young Fellow.

John opens the sample case. The aroma of old, brittle leather wafts up from the stool. John takes out a few, full, sample cards. Pen holsters, key wallets, watch bands.

"Nice ... nice," mutters the Young Fellow.

John is suddenly aware of being appraised. The Young Fellow knows what he's looking at, he is evaluating, not merely a tourist. He glances up to find the Young Fellow looking at him with sly, somewhat condescending eyes.

"I wondered when we'd meet. I've been following your trail for years," says the Young Fellow, hauling up his own case. "I think you've seen my lines."

And there they are. Lined up like so many sacrificial regiments, line after line of slick, plastic, cases, watch bands, grey market watches, pen and pencil sets, knock-offs, the designer series, the ersatz Rolexes.

"Something for everyone," mumbles the Young Fellow, taking the thought right out of John's mind.

"Dat's some lines you got der," gushes Mashy. "Some lines ..."

"I thought you'd be older," says John, turning away to face the back wall of the counter.

"Yeah, well, I started young. I had connections to the Far East, my dad ...."

"Taiwan?" replies John in a forced monotone.

"Taiwan, Singapore, Hong Kong, now Korea, Viet Nam, Thailand. I must have an uncle in every free trade zone in the world."

"You deal with Raiko Habari?" says John, pointing to the coffee pot. The white-haired lady notices and pours a cup.

"Raiko? Jesus, that's ancient history. We bought him out in eighty-six! Boy, do you go back," replies the Young Fellow, genuinely surprised and impressed.

"He did all our Expo '67 items, all of them," says John flatly.

"That was you? You had the concession?" cries the Young Fellow, now hot to know, hot to compare histories. "My dad tried for a whole year to get a piece of that ..."

"You wouldn't have been able to," says John, turning his seat to more fully face the excited Young Fellow. "We had the fix in the morning the fair was announced. We had a lock on it. You'd have never got a look in."

"You must have made a killing," says the Young Fellow full of awe and respect.

"Well, I had a partner," replies John, graciously taking the edge off the coup.

"Still," sighs the Young Fellow. He swigs down the dregs of his Cola. "That's what I'm waiting for, a big score, a big contract like that."

John looks the Young Fellow up and down. "Really? What would you do with all that money?

"Well, this is really not a career choice, is it?" says the Young Fellow as though confirming a fact of life that John already knows. "I mean it's hardly work for a couple of smart guys like you and me, eh?"

The Young Fellow laughs, flashing a set of shining, ivory-coloured teeth. It is only now that John notices the polyglot, blood lineage of his competitor.

"University, you see, business school. I've started at Concordia part time but next year I'm selling my lines to my cousin and it will be school full time."

A low buzzing noise intrudes. The Young Fellow reaches inside his Hong Kong tailored suit jacket and draws out his pager. He looks up at John, smiling broadly. "Business, real business. The world is my oyster."

The Young Fellow gets ready to leave, pocketing his phone, his pager, wrapping his job-lot, silk scarf tightly round his Indo-Asian neck.

"I am happy to have met you, finally!" he says with a laugh. "I hope you have a good season."

John turns back to face the counter again. His shoulders feel heavy, his hands are hot now, and clumsy. "There are no more good seasons," he mutters to no one.

John hears the door open and then steps, and the Young Fellow is standing behind him, not moving. John slowly turns to face him and finds him looking down at a business card. Sweet, he thinks, the little fellow wants to make friends. But before he can reach for it, the Young Fellow speaks.

"I don't know if you can use this. I got a call from this woman, she said she worked for a movie company and they were looking for period items, novelty items. They're making some film."

John doesn't reach for the card. He doesn't move at all except to breathe quietly, regularly, feeling the air move his lungs, his heart move his blood. He suddenly feels very, very relaxed, as though his insides were liquid, held together by a whim of will.

"I thought it was a joke, you know, who would want that stuff? I offered them my lines but ..."

The Young Fellow pulls out the small flip phone and dials, consulting the card. "It's worth a try ... eh? Anne? Mebs here. Mebs Ramtulla, remember? I think I've got something for you. I've got a friend you should meet."

And John suddenly feels as though he is a young child being led by the hand to the merry-go-round.

It is a big cheque. Signed on the spot. Thousands of dollars. The Chrysler groans as Mebs and John unload box after box of tired leather goods, sample cards, boxes and boxes.

"You've just saved me and my staff about three months of very hard work," says Anne, a small woman, round, efficient, rosy-faced. "It's getting almost impossible to find authentic period items like these anymore. I still can't believe the quality of the display cards."

"They came from England," says John, fingering the cheque guiltily.

"Beautiful. They are going to look so good on set. You know, this is what we look for, the real thing. When you have to make it up, it just doesn't have the same value, the colours and textures."

"No, it doesn't," says John, suddenly an expert. "And the name of the film again?"

"The working title is ;The Revelation,' but that might change."

Mebs approaches, wiping his hands to indicate he is done. John turns to face Anne.

"Funny about the lead character ..."

"A leather salesman," says Anne, smiling.

"You don't suppose there'd be a role for me in this movie," says John, teasing. "I wouldn't have to act, you know, I could just trip through it!"

"Well, I have your name, you know. I can always pass it on to the assistant director; they're going to need extras."

Anne is interrupted by Mebs.

"Well, all done, and I've got to be going."

Anne kisses him on both cheeks before letting him go.

"I can't thank you enough, really. This is so great of you," she says with deep sincerity.

They make for their cars. John walks with Mebs, still fingering the cheque. Mebs notices.

"You can put that in your pocket," he says, teasing.

John rounds his shoulders loosely. His neck feels like liquid rubber. He stops in his tracks, turning to face Mebs squarely.

"We'll have no nonsense now," he says, his voice coarse, deep and business-like. "Some of this is yours."

"Merry Christmas," says Mebs, shaking his head and backing away. John fishes in his coat pocket. He finds a crumpled business card.

"You might need to reach me. I'm not going to be working much ..."

"Don't spend that all in one place," says Mebs, taking the card. "I'll see you."

John watches Mebs pull his Jaguar away from the curb. He calls out after him.

"I'm a Chrysler man myself!"

And once again, that special quiet descends. The air is brisk and cold and there is a stiff, gusty breeze picking up the dust that has become Montreal snow. John walks towards his car, but he doesn't want to get in. He looks around, an idiotic grin creasing his wrinkled mug.

He looks at the Chrysler and just doesn't want to get in. He wants to walk back to Dorval. He wants to skip and leap from rooftop to rooftop, bouncing like a rubber kangaroo.

John feels light, light on his feet, so light he fears the top of his head will get blown off. So light, his shoulders feel like they're heading for the sky. He steers his feet towards the boulevard.

There is a sudden crush of people, shoppers, students, a riotous swirl and in among them is a happy man, a singing son of Eire. John fingers the cheque in his hand again. Thousands, thousands of dollars for dust, for dirt, for forgotten, unwanted ...

He wants to shout, squeal, like a dizzy child. John spots the Portuguese cafe across the street, its windows fogged and bright.

No one turns to look at him as he enters. The cafe rings with the excited, lubricated chatter of foreign tongues. The man behind the bar nods at John.

"Jameson's and a coffee," says John, watching the man to see if he's been understood and, amazingly enough, within seconds the glass of golden amber is at hand and the steaming espresso not far behind. The man behind the bar waits as John raises the glass.

"Will you drink to my retirement?" asks John.

The place goes a little quiet. But the man behind the bar pours himself a short measure and clinks his glass against John's.

"To quiet days. Quiet days and a life off the road," says John, inhaling the smooth liquor in one.

The man behind the bar does the same, and then offers his hand. John takes it as the conversation in the cafe resumes. The barman leaves John with his coffee.

There is no light but that of the lamps lining the little street. And once outside the door. The wind whips up, tugging open John's coat. He has just time enough to wrap himself in the faded alpaca when he hears her voice, "Mon chapeau ..." and, looking up, he sees the wind-blown hat, black and floppy slipping over the ground like a flat stone on a lake. The goalie's foot goes out but too late and it is one-nil for Trinity. John takes off in hot pursuit, the laughter already creasing his chin, his eyes bright, limpid blue. He hears her following at a trot.

The laughter bubbles up, exploding like a rusty wheeze as each time he nears the hat, each time he gets within range, another gust carries it further into the little park. The snow whips past, crunching as his tired brogues flap in the galoshes till finally one rubber comes loose. John presses forward almost, almost and then laughing till tears shake loose he dives and pummels the hat to the ground, and the ring announcer calls it a TKO. Mullen, a TKO!

John rolls up against the tree still laughing, trying hard to catch his breath while brushing the snow off the black floppy brim hat. Nice hat he thinks, very nice bit of millinery. He hears the footsteps approaching, sees his errant galosh in the sleek leather-gloved hand, beautiful, braided calfskin, with a shirred wrist, silk-lined $12.40 wholesale, a good mover.

"Merci, mille fois ...," she starts and, still laughing, he looks up expecting and not expecting the blonde hair, the tall handsome body, the face, that face.

And the only thing he can blurt out, the only thing that seems to make any sense, the only thing he can get beyond his lips with his stalled heart is, "You're French?"

The Portuguese cafe is less crowded but warm, steamy and made holy by the holiness of men who have stopped the day's labour. He stares for minutes on end before he is able to pry his eyes away from her face long enough to take full stock of her. She is someone's daughter, he thinks, someone's loved daughter, and someone's distraction.

They are momentarily disturbed by the barman. He is hanging up his Christmas trinkets over the bar, and on the corner of the counter is a porcelain nativity scene. The figures of the Mother Mary, the Baby Jesus, the shepherds, the three Wise men, the lowing cattle, the bleating sheep, all done in shiny, now dusty, now shiny again, creamy porcelain.

"I knew the guy that carried that line," says John suddenly. He looks over at the woman still fussing with her hat, needlessly now, but he supposes she needs something to do with her hands.

"Yes," she says in English, perfect, accented English. "They have everyone there, don't they? Mary, Jesus, is that one Joseph?"

John follows her eyes to a shepherd being given the once-over with a bar rag before being put in his place before the manger.

"I always felt sorry for Joseph," she says. She turns the small shot glass a quarter turn before drinking. It's her second. John notices this quarter turn habit and thinks it charming.

"Why is that?" he asks.

She waves for another before answering.

"All the attention on Jesus and Mary, especially these people, Latin people. She's the mother of god, isn't she? And we Catholics build her up, you know? And Jesus, of course, but what about Joseph, you know?"

"Another sad-assed little Hebe," mutters John, smiling.

"What?" She didn't catch it.

"He's like the rest of us. He didn't know any better. He just made the best of the situation, raised the child like his own, like it was his own, but knew it wasn't. Tried to give him a trade, teach him to work with his hands, didn't take, never does really." John finishes his Jameson's. "Just someone's dad."

Outside the evening sky is simply black, winter black as though the light would never cut through again, thinks John. And in this little amber yellow block of space I can ask her and she'll simply tell me.

"Why were you there?" he says quietly.

"At the clinic?" she exhales raggedly. She points to her chest. John's heart skips a beat. "Bronchitis. I was going to the clinic on the second floor. I'm not pregnant. I've never been."

The Revelation of John Mullen

She's never been ... a confession or an admission? John pulls on his coat. He's scared her enough.

"What was it that you saw?"

Her eyes follow John as he rises and as he sits down again, drawing his coat more tightly around himself. He is the kind Uncle from Ireland. He is Daddy. Everyone's father and this woman's father. With his hand, he traces a shape around her face and shoulders.

"A light, you know, like a gold light around your head, going down."

He stops himself and rises. He goes to the bar and gently takes the figure of Mary from the nativity scene. The man behind the bar watches warily. John slips back to the woman, taking the chair beside her, leaning on her conspiratorially, familiar. He holds up the figure, pointing to the halo.

"Like Mary, see? A halo. How do you say this in French?"

She hesitates searching for it. She smiles. Slowly, suddenly, she leans back on him, rocking his weight back and forth.

"Aureole," she says smiling, bringing her cool, long, fingers up to John's long, sad face.

John smiles at her, his eyes wishing and wishing, and not knowing and loving the not knowing.

"I didn't see anything,"

He stands, slipping her hand in between his two leather-worn, warm hands. He dips low, bringing her hand to his lips, pressing the white, pale skin to his lips. "I saw everything."

"Thank you for saving my hat," she murmurs.

John snaps to attention, saluting smartly as his heels clip together.

"Compliments of the fleet, season's greetings."

He turns from her, carrying the Mary figure back to the bar. He places it carefully back within the scene, within the grouping, making it whole again, reconfirming its artful design. He looks up to the barman, peeling off a twenty.

"Why isn't there a Joseph?" he asks, laying the bill carefully down on the counter.

The barman replies with what John assumes is a smile of mystery but what is in reality blank and total incomprehension.

The night air barely moves as John wrestles himself out of the still dieseling Chrysler. Finally the engine shudders and stops, giving up the ghost for another day. John crunches his way up the driveway and across the lawn. Dorval often had snow when downtown didn't, thinks John, but that was good. The snow makes him feel as though his home was cleaner somehow, removed, not of the same matter at all.

Looking up, he can just see inside the living room where Angela sits in his chair of course, twisting a strand of her precious jet black hair as she reads the paper, a foot jiggling in its droopy sock. He stops and watches her, watches the various parts of her, blessing each one, giving his benediction over the hands that forged signatures, the lips that told tales, the feet that tripped the dog, hooky-player, junk food muncher, thief of hearts, heart breaker ... he catches himself smiling, and then he sees the movement. Dark, in the shadows, familiar.

"Father?" John peers, his vision clouded by the porch light. The silhouette comes down towards him.

"I hope I didn't scare you." says Father Daniel.

"Not at all," says John, swallowing hard. "Why are you outside? I mean here?"

Father Daniel circles away slightly, his facing falling in the ring of light thrown from the porch. He smiles awkwardly.

"I didn't want to ring the bell. I was going to but I thought you'd be along. I didn't hear your voice inside, and your car wasn't here."

"Oh yes, my car ..." says John smiling, remembering.

Father Daniel takes his hands out of his coat pocket. He is freezing, John notices, but John makes no move to invite him inside. John is content to simply stand outside in the walk, in the milky black night, in the still, crisp air, still, as though no one is alive except the two of them.

Father Daniel bounces slightly from one foot to the other, making conciliatory openings which he is at a loss to fill until finally,

"I was worried. I was concerned about you. I mean that last time we met. I've been thinking about that night a lot."

"Have you? So have I, you know," says John.

"I feel I may have made a mistake as far as you were concerned. I think I acted without grace, without thought."

John pauses for effect.

"You think I did see something?"

Father Daniel shakes his head. "What I think is not important. It is what you think, what you think you saw. I just feel I could have listened better. I've taken the question up with some of my brothers. I just wanted to tell you, to let you know."

John reaches up to caress the Young Priest's arm. A strong arm, a hockey arm.

"That's O.K., Father. I forgive you," John says.

"Thank you," says Father Daniel. He draws quietly away, moving towards a rusted blue Hyundai with a blown-out passenger window.

"Merry Christmas, Father," calls John.

"And to you, Mr. Mullen," calls the Young Priest.

A movement behind him, and John is aware of Oona's eyes on him.

"John?" Oona calls from the front door. "What are you doing outside? Who was that?"

John turns on his heels with grace; so gracefully, in fact, that for a moment Oona is tricked into believing that her husband's last port of call was the Lasalle Yacht and Sport Fishing Club. But as he approaches, his face calm, un-flushed and dry, she regrets her suspicion.

John takes the stairs to the landing two at a time and grabs Oona before she can hurry back inside.

"John, it is freezing; come in now," she pleads, but John won't let her go.

He pulls her closer, deep into the folds of his worn, unbuttoned alpaca.

Snowdon Story

WOLFE AND HIS WIFE WERE survivors of the Holocaust and found their way to Montreal in the late 1940s. Originally from Rovno in the Polish province of Wölyn, it was widely rumoured that Wolfe dealt in the black market that raged immediately following the war and that in the three years that he lived in a displaced persons camp outside Munich, he had amassed a small fortune. Wolfe tried for several months to settle in England but when that didn't work out, he and his wife boarded the *Samaria* and ended up in Montreal. A tailor by profession, several eyebrows were raised when Wolfe began to invest in real estate, an expensive proposition at the time, hence the rumours of the fortune he supposedly arrived with. Wolfe was particularly taken with the Snowdon area with its commercial storefronts and residential apartments above. It reminded him of home.

Though they wanted a large family, the Wolfes had only one son, Norman. He was born soon after they arrived in Montreal, and from the earliest age he actively rejected everything his parents represented. It was the old familiar story of parents who doted and a child who was ashamed. The Wolfes, for their part, never stinted nor hesitated when it came to their only son. In their eyes, the only prophylactic against the fate that they had endured was assimilation, and to that end Norman was sent to schools that catered to the gentile elite. They could never change their *greener* ways and so, they kept their distance.

Norman grew up and learned how to sail, play tennis, how to wear the right clothes and speak with affectation. His religion was a vague after-thought, something in the dark distance, a stumbling point that his freely shared pocket money quickly smoothed over. Norman learned early how to buy friends, how to insinuate himself without standing out.

The Wolfes, for their part, were content to stoke the fires beneath their son's social success. Wolfe and his wife lived above their tailor shop in a strip of buildings he owned on Queen Mary Road. It was an ideal vantage point for Wolfe to survey his growing real estate fiefdom. And though it may have been a fiefdom, Wolfe, with his huge ring of jangling keys, was a benevolent *seigneur*. Over time, his tenants learned that their stern, unbending landlord with the broad back and hands both terribly strong but also delicate would never throw them into the street if they were late on the rent. What Wolfe wanted, more than anything else, was to be a decent human being. He wanted to be other than the so-called humans under which he and his wife had suffered. He wanted to prove that he was, after all, better than they were.

Wolfe was also no one's fool. His simple approach to business concealed a fine and calculating instinct for the deal. One would do business with him as though dealing with a naïve child until the closing time when right there, at the notary office or in front of the loan officer at the bank, he would introduce a clause, a suggestion, an idea that saved him thousands, saved the buyer or seller thousands and made everyone fairly glow in admiration.

Not Norman. Nothing Wolfe could do would ever earn Norman's respect, and the old man knew it. And since Wolfe would never get filial love from Norman, he got it wherever he could, which might be a truism of the masculine human condition.

Peter and Stavros Lykos were babies when their father immigrated to Canada in the late 1940s. Lykos was a fine antiques restorer and found work immediately with three Armenian brothers named Diryan. But Lykos was not a healthy man, and within ten years was dead from a stroke. Eventually, the two sons quit school to work for the Diryans and look after their mother, who died of heart disease a few years later.

When Peter and Stavros showed up to rent the eight hundred square foot store front on Queen Mary, a space right beside Wolfe's tailor shop, they did not have two cents to rub together. But they had knowledge. The boys had grown up amidst chipped icons, scaling picture frames and cracked porcelain. The brothers Lykos had no business plan, no line of credit, no accountant to fill out the avalanche of mind-numbing government paperwork, no insurance, no prospects, just a handful of greasy dollar bills scrounged from evening jobs as dishwashers and pizza delivery men. Wolfe figured they'd last two months but rented them the space anyway because he liked them.

Was it a coincidence, then, that every time Peter had to admit to being a little short on the rent, Wolfe would suddenly remember a chest of drawers that had to be shifted from one apartment to another or that a bed had to be delivered or that a bureau needed refinishing? Was it a twist of fate that those who owed Wolfe money also, seemingly accidentally, found their way to Athena Refinishing with cracked credenzas, wobbly side-boards and battered commodes?

And was it due to mere carelessness that Mrs. Wolfe, the great *balabuste* who knew her weekly budget down to the thinnest groschen, made too much brisket or too big a turkey and needed some extra mouths to help eat it so that it shouldn't go to waste? Norman could not be counted on, he of the raised pinkie and the watercress sandwich, to sit down to a *hiemische* meal of *chulent*, but those Greek boys could eat!

Norman lived up to the promise of his parents' ambition and entered McGill, leaving several years later a general practitioner and after several more of specialisation, a dermatologist. His Westmount offices were plush, wall-to-wall deluxe and his polished, if not to say gentile, manner generated a clientele from both sides of the cross.

It goes without saying that Wolfe paid for everything. Not for Norman, years interning in the far North to work off his education grants. No! Not Norman Wolf – yes, he dropped the "e" but then tried to pick it up again when informed that the English general who conquered Quebec used the ending vowel. It was too late, the business stationery had already been printed, the announcements of his practise had been sent. Norman spent an anguished weekend obsessively writing his surname with and without the "e" in order to determine which one looked less Jewy. It was all in vain, he never could figure it out.

It was Mrs. Wolfe who went first. Eighty years old, angina, arthritis, renal failure. Wolfe was despondent and helpless at the Jewish General Hospital. He was tempted to call his son, the doctor, but he hesitated... after all, Norman was probably busy, he didn't want to bother. Stavros was unable to stand it any longer and made the call. Norman, a little rosy-cheeked the brothers noted, showed up after hours but was unable to take his mother's hand in his. He had his official doctor's voice on and spoke of the inevitable prognosis to his father – his father! – like he was dealing with a slightly dull hick. The heartless platitudes elbowed each other aside, spilling out of his mouth. A pat on Wolfe's broad, manly, black market shoulder and Norman was off. Mrs. Wolfe didn't make it to breakfast.

At the funeral, Norman pretended that he did not know how to say the mourner's *Kaddish* along with Wolfe, confronting the rabbi with a fey, naïve smile on his face. No matter, Wolfe's friends, old *bundists* and landlords, got their licks in, shouldering Norman to the back row where he faded into the bland décor.

At the wake, Peter and Stavros brought out the ouzo and retsina and made certain that Wolfe was never alone for a moment during the seven days of shiva. They took turns sleeping in Wolfe's apartment. For a month they worried over the old man till he told them it was enough. Norman called once or twice. He never came to the shiva, never mind sat it out, a wasteful mediaeval ritual.

After his wife died, Wolfe was never the same, though he lived for several more years. His interest in business flagged; now that Norman was doing well, there just didn't seem much point. Peter and Stavros expanded their business, taking over the tailor shop, moving in to spaces on either side as it became available, opening a fine antiques business as well. Wolfe would often come down from his apartment to while away the long days of age, have a glass of wine, talk about his black market shenanigans and his time in London, a city that had left a lasting impression. The old, increasingly unkempt man might have been an embarrassment when the well-bronzed Hampstead wives showed up, their husbands' cheque books limp in their hands, but the Greek brothers drew Wolfe as "unique local colour." Wolfe even helped close the deal on occasion, and it was the brothers' delight to cut Wolfe in on the sales commission.

One morning Wolfe didn't answer Peter's morning knock on the door. Stavros wanted to break it down, but Peter was afraid. They called Norman, but the doctor was inconveniently out. The brothers waited a couple of hours and knocked again, shouting for Wolfe from the corridor. Finally, Stavros pushed his brother aside and kicked and kicked until the door gave way.

Wolfe was lying on his bed, flat on his back, fully dressed as though ready to start his day. His eyes, pale blue and milky, were wide open. Peter started and then stopped himself from making the sign of the cross as Stavros closed Wolfe's eyes.

Max Schemler, Wolfe's lawyer and executor, knew Norman and disliked him intensely. Wolfe had been one of Max's first clients. The morning he hung up his shingle Wolfe was there, a real estate transfer in one beefy fist, a civil case in the other. Through the years, Max and Wolfe became friends but Norman just grated on Max's nerves. So, was it ironic that now there they all were, Norman, Max and Peter and Stavros in Max's refined offices, negotiating the disposition of the building that Wolfe, in his generosity and blindness, had left to his son?

Peter and Stavros showed the original commercial lease, now almost twenty years old and never revised. Wolfe had increased their rent verbally, and there had always been the promise that they might buy it one day at fair market value. Norman snorted loudly, and it occurred to Max that Norman was quite drunk.

Norman's lawyer was Paul Montrose, née Rosenberg, and was more part of Max's crowd than Norman's. He also hated Norman as a smug, self-hating, arriviste, but Norman paid his legal bills without question, and Paul's firm was nowhere near as flush as Max's. Paul's sympathies were with the Greek brothers, but his duty was to fuck them over on Norman's behalf.

Max presented the brothers' fair market offer, and Paul blew shit all over it as Norman, unsteady on his feet, got up to leave. Max calmed everyone down and confabbed with Peter and Stavros. Another figure proposed and rejected. Max had had enough and addressed Norman directly, asking him to stop jerking everyone around and name his price.

The brothers blanched. It was twice the market value. Peter whispered to Max that they didn't have it. Max didn't flinch but rather wrote on his legal pad "I will guarantee it at prime, for Wolfe." Peter stared at the paper, his hand trembling. He passed it to Stavros, who stared in turn at Max.

Peter and Stavros rose from the table and looked down at Norman. Peter said a few barbed words in Greek, and the brothers left. Max turned to Paul and accepted Norman's price. Paul turned to Norman, but Wolfe's son was no longer listening. His eyes followed the Greek brothers out. There was a moment of silence and then he shouted, slurring, "What did he say? What did he say to me!?"

Wolfe's apartment had been sealed by the police, pending the results of the autopsy. The brothers had also been advised by Max Schemler that the deal would be held in escrow pending an examination of the apartment by forensic accountants that specialised in this sort of situation. The brothers did not understand until Max explained that elderly European-born Jews were notorious for secreting valuables in hiding places and for keeping money in forgotten bank accounts. With Wolfe, whose dealings were so frequently on a cash basis, this was a necessary step to satisfy Norman. Max assured the brothers that once the forensic accountants finished their work, the property would be theirs.

On the day of the examination, Peter and Stavros sat in their shop listening to the sounds from the floor above while drawing plans for the building. The apartment was going to become the new atelier for restorations, freeing up room on the ground floor for more stock. The extra financial burden of buying the building at twice its value meant that the brothers would have to do the renovation work themselves, but they didn't mind.

When the brothers Lykos arrived the next morning, they found the door to Wolfe's apartment sealed. An official from the forensic accounting firm had Stavros and Peter sign a release for any damages, and then cut the seal. The brothers stopped at the threshold. The place had been examined with thorough destructive efficiency. All documents had been exhumed, evaluated and then either taken or tossed onto the floor. Every drawer, every closet had been opened, the carpets had been pulled up, some of the hardwood floor had been split and lifted, and most of the walls had been attacked with a reciprocating saw. In the kitchen it was the same.

Christina, Stavros' wife, who had looked after Wolfe before he died, had come to help them. For the better part of the morning they simply cleared rooms of debris, created some working space, but their progress would come grinding to a halt each time they found a photo album, a book, a ledger. At one point, Christina disappeared for a long time until they heard her crying from the bedroom. They found her sitting on the floor, weeping amidst Mrs. Wolfe's undergarments, her nightgowns and lingerie, all her personal possessions, silly things, costume jewellery and old perfume in time-stained bottles.

Despite repeated calls to Norman, he refused to come over. Peter, who prided himself on his better English, his more even temperament, pleaded and then begged. He told Norman that there was tons of his stuff, his childhood things, surely he would like them? There were papers too, banking documents. Reluctantly, and fearing that Paul Montrose's so-called experts had screwed up, Norman agreed to drop by. At this news, Christina got a little hysterical and tried to put everything back in its place, and the brothers didn't dare try and stop her.

Norman arrived drunk, the brothers could smell the single malt on his breath. He was uncharacteristically, almost aggressively, friendly, putting his arm around Stavros' shoulder, calling the brothers by their first names, even showing some pleasure at seeing Christina. He acted as though the brothers were lucky to have bought the building at any price. He pretended that they had driven a hard bargain and that giving up his father's property had been personally difficult for him but that, ah well, life must go on.

Norman strode through the apartment like a conquering general, stopping only to flick at things on the floor with the toe of his shoe, to snicker at the few mawkish paintings on the wall, his father's books, his mother's cheap porcelain animal figurines. He gloated, informing the brothers that the accountants had discovered over twenty bank accounts used by Wolfe, some untouched for decades, containing substantial deposits. When he went into Wolfe's bedroom, Christina opened the dresser drawers revealing the now carefully folded underwear and lingerie. Norman would not even glance at it but rather smiled at Christina unsteadily till the woman had to turn her face away.

Peter showed him a family album of photos, some dating from before the war, amassed and mounted with care by Mrs. Wolfe. Norman glanced at it but would not touch it. Montrose's people had done a thorough job. There was nothing here of value. Still smiling, Norman reached out and gently tapped Peter's cheek. He made his way to the door, stopping only to stare, horrified, at a pair of his father's leather slippers, wrinkled, dusty and deformed with age and wear. He turned to face Peter and Stavros, throwing out his arms to encompass the whole apartment, swaying on his feet. "It's all yours!"

It took two full-size dumpsters to empty the apartment. The brothers tried to give some of the stuff away but found few takers. They contacted the Montreal Holocaust Centre, which agreed to take the photo albums and some memorabilia. The rest was placed into bags and dropped out the back window into the container waiting there.

When the apartment was empty, even though they never discussed it, the brothers simply let it sit empty for six months. Six months to help move the timeline along. Six months to help fade Norman's sneering, contemptuous face from their memories. And one day, in spring, by common accord and without any planning, Peter decided to move a wall.

So, with gusto and energy, they attacked the renovation. They put up a couple of saw horses and used a piece of the old Formica kitchen counter as a work table. The plans were rolled out, and the tape measures snapped and recoiled as the new layout was paced off and marked. Then the swing of the hammers and pry bars and pieces of ancient lathe and horse-hair plaster went sailing through the air into the rear container.

Peter brought up an old radio tuned to CFMB, Montreal's ethnic radio station. Greek pop hits filled the dusty apartment, the polyrhythms spurred on the pace of destruction and renewal. By unspoken arrangement, each brother assigned himself rooms where the nostalgia for the Wolfes would be less crippling. Peter could not bear the thought of entering the bedroom, so it was left to Stavros, who himself had fond memories of the kitchen. By the end of the first day, they had pulled down four walls, exposed most of the ceiling and pulled up many layers of linoleum.

The second day was equally productive and by the afternoon, Stavros was facing the last wall, the one between the bedroom and the bathroom. The radio sang out a popular flashback hit from his youth in Thessaloniki, a basic four/four bouzouki beat. His blows shattered the plaster and the two-by-fours behind. In the kitchen, Peter was carefully pulling down the last of the original, old pine cabinets. These, they had decided, would be spared the dumpster, would be dipped and stripped and oiled back to usefulness. As one end of the cabinet left the wall, the other was suspended precariously, too awkward for one man. Peter called for his brother.

The rhythmic hammer blows had stopped, but there was no answer from Stavros. Peter called again, starting to laugh at his precarious balancing act. He called again and still no response. Finally he let his end drop, leaving the cabinet pinned to the wall on one end and resting on the floor at the other. Peter called again as he walked through the apartment to where he found his brother kneeling on the floor in front of a wide gap that had been smashed through the wall. Stavros was not moving, and for a tiny moment Peter's heart skipped, thinking his brother had hurt himself, cut himself on a nail, suffered a heart attack.

Peter called again, quietly, to his brother, and again Stavros did not react but sat facing the gap in the wall as though meditating before a hidden deity. As Peter approached, he could better see what was fascinating his brother. A tiny bead of light, a golden reflection becoming wider, more golden, more and more.

Stavros turned to Peter, his face slick with sweat and dirt and tears and, as he turned, he allowed Peter a more direct look into the gap in the wall. In between the two-by-fours, piled one on top of another were three canvas bags, trimmed with leather. Clearly one of Stavros's hammer blows had split the top bag. Small gold ingots were spilling out.

Max Schemler contemplated the stacks of gold ingots arranged on the coffee table in his office and the two Greek Brothers sitting side by side, their faces worried, glowing, red with excitement, creased by concern. Max had done a little calculation and scribbled a number on a piece of paper which he held up to the brothers. They looked at each other, confirming their own assumptions.

Peter handed Max some faded, yellowing papers which Max looked at carefully, flattening down the folds. They were official Bank of England bills of sale for the gold. All the registration numbers matched. Obviously, Wolfe had not been idle during the few months he spent in London waiting for his ship to Montreal. Max looked at the papers with care and interest, allowing himself a rueful smile. He looked up to find the brothers staring at him. His secretary buzzed, announcing the arrival of the Man from Revenue Canada.

As the Man from Revenue Canada entered, his eyes moved irresistibly towards the gold ingots. Working in his little cubicle at the Complexe Guy-Favreau, he did not often have the chance to get close to a case like this. Illegal, undeclared gold was highly taxable, but what was being proposed intrigued him. The responsibility was intimidating. This meeting, these offices and then this lawyer, Max Schemler, whose reputation was sterling itself, was intimidating. The Man from Revenue Canada was looking for a resolution, a way off the hook of this intimidating case.

Max stated that he represented the brothers Peter and Stavros Lykos and that the gold they found in their father's home was legally purchased and duly reported and is the rightful inheritance of the brothers. Max had already performed the due diligence. He had official copies of the bill of sale from England, he had the brothers' official immigration documents, as well as their father's death certificate. And he had the original bills of sale found with the ingots. It was all wrapped up with a black-edged bow needing only Revenue Canada's approbation.

Though intimidated, the Man from Revenue Canada would not be rushed. He had received copies of all these documents with the submission for tax exemption filed by the brothers Lykos. He had himself contacted the Bank of England and had confronted the glaring anomaly that still stared them all in the face. All the documents were made out to "N. Wolfe" and yet the brothers' family name is "Lykos." Would Maitre Schemler care to explain?

Peter spoke up, haltingly but well rehearsed. At the time of the purchase, in the late 1940s, the Bank of England didn't like foreign names, didn't like foreign people. Their father was the victim of a bigoted prank. Squirming intimidation crept anew into The Man from Revenue Canada. Please, not a racial element, please! He was listened but was not following the argument, and he flashed Max a smiling, desperate look. Max handed him an English/Greek dictionary and asked him to look up the word "wolf." Stavros explained that their father was ashamed to be the victim of such a prejudiced act and afraid that the gold would be taken away from him, so he never tried to correct the mistake.

The Man from Revenue Canada's lips moved as his finger trailed down the page. Wolf...wolf...lykos! Lykos!

Max suggested that the brothers should not be penalised for a racist prank played on their father by a bigoted employee of the Bank of England, should they? Duty on the ingots at the 1948 rate had been paid. And, as there is no inheritance tax, there would be no penalty, surely? The Man from Revenue Canada examined the dictionary entry carefully, smiling and relieved.

The *Bundist* burial society Wolfe belonged to had long ago been absorbed by a larger one, and the plots he had reserved for himself and his wife had been shifted from the De la Savane cemetery to one in the suburb of Dollard des Ormeaux. Because the ground at the Dollard cemetery was once part of a flood plain and therefore subject to infiltration by water, over time Wolfe's headstone began to gently lean toward that of his wife's.

And it was a long drive from Snowdon. Peter and Stavros waited till the season or the weather or the changing light of day told them it was time for a visit. They would pick a Sunday and drive out, Peter carrying flowers for Mrs. Wolfe, Stavros a bottle of Wolfe's favourite restina. The other headstones in the Jewish cemetery carried the little stones that were the tell-tale sign of recent visitors paying their respects. Despite Wolfe's various affiliations, there were few stones on his. Most of the people who knew him were dead too. But the small pile of brass and silver door keys was irrefutable evidence that a profound filial love endured.

For Bill.

Elegy for a Hit and Run

Location hunting for films and television shows is the best job in the world. First of all, it's clean work. You have to look your best at all times because you are dealing with the public. You are constantly trying to make a good impression, and since most people size you up in the first few seconds of meeting you, looks and grooming and comportment are essential to success.

So you have to be well dressed and well groomed, which means you have an official excuse. You need not feel guilty about buying that shirt and getting that facial. It's for your work. Then there are the perks which really aren't perks so much as they are the tools of your trade. You need a car. If you own a car, the job is justification for having a nice one, as you cannot be expected to chauffeur directors and producers around in a cheesy sub-compact. If all you can afford is a cheesy sub-compact (and trust me, if you are good at your job this will not be a problem for long), then the production will round up a suitable rental for you. And since your work hours are often outside the norm, that car will be, essentially, yours for the duration with no questions asked about mileage or gas consumption.

Then there is the float, the money advanced to you for photo imaging, lunches, and other expenses you may encounter while in the performance of your duties. These might include taking a potential location owner out for a nice lunch. Or supper. Maybe you get them a chic gift to clinch the deal. Gift baskets for the neighbours are a nice touch, just so that they won't feel left out. You might need a little grease money to lubricate the skids under a sticky situation. You might want to make a little contribution to a city official's favourite cause. Or to the city official himself. It's all discretionary, and it is all acceptable.

Location hunting is also very autonomous work. One tends to make one's own schedule. Yes, sometimes you need to work evenings and weekends but then, generally, there is no reason for you to be up at five or six in the morning.

I was drifting in the late 1980s, going from one freelance contract to the next, doing whatever was required. Location hunting jobs, however, were my rice bowl. Film and television work in Montreal was very cyclical on several fronts. First, it was either boom or bust, depending on the current government and how much of a tax break or incentives they felt like handing out to producers. And second, because of consecutive separatist and non-separatist provincial governments, the work that flowed into Montreal depended to a great extent on how the atmosphere was perceived. There are people who will deny this, but I have had a great many conversations with American producers who had hesitated coming to Montreal with their millions in production money because they were afraid that no one would speak English to them. But I digress.

I had been at loose ends for a couple of months when I got a call from Pierre, a production manager on a big, very successful Quebecois television series. I had helped him out of several tight spots in the past, and so I was expecting the worse. He didn't disappoint.

"We're stuck again," he muttered between sips of coffee. "Can you go on the road and find us a house?"

"What do you need?" I asked, taking a few notes.

"Very middle class, very new. Upper middle class... the character is a Jewish guy."

"You're kidding," I blurted out, dropping my pen.

"No," laughed Pierre. "He's supposed to be the owner of an agency. In fact, he's a hockey agent but not a very big one, so we're not looking at a Westmount type of house. He's got some money, but he's not rich."

"When is this scheduled?"

"I need it in about a week. Can you get on this right away?"

At that point in my career I had it down to a science. One tactic was to peruse the real estate ads in *The Gazette* targeting ones that featured "model homes" or "model apartments." There was a development that I had passed several times in Ville St. Laurent that I had been meaning to look at. It was a dead end street, just off Cavendish Boulevard, south of Cote Vertu.

It was a late September afternoon, mild after a seasonally warm day. One could not yet smell autumn in the air, but the sky was quite blue and clear, and the setting sun raked low with a burst of colour that was intense and saturated. It had rained the night before, and the air was uncommonly clean. On occasions like this, when the sun came in low but still hot, the city became dimensional and everything one looked at stood out sharp and clean. It was as though someone had taken a razor knife and cut out every edge and shape and pushed them into relief.

The housing development was set out in an otherwise empty sub-division. Nothing had stood there before, just empty fields. The developer had put up two fully furnished model homes, and the foundation for a dozen more could be seen from the road. "Les Beaux Domaines" was the name on the billboard at the entrance to the drive. I looked around and spotted the trailer that was typically the sales office at a development such as this. There was only one car parked along the trailer, a big blue four-door Mercedes 300 sedan.

I got out of my car, putting on my "I'm-a-wonderful-charming-fellow-with-a-crazy-but wonderful-idea" face and made my way over to the trailer. I knocked at the door, but there was no answer. Peering through the window, I could see that there was no one inside. Uncanny, as I turned around, I could feel him before I could see him

There, on the balcony terrace that ran around half of the model home he stood. He was silhouetted against the setting sun so that he appeared, at first glance, almost incorporeal. Not there, but really there, his arm bent at the elbow as he brought his cigarette to his mouth. Had he even seen me? I didn't think so. Had he heard my call? He didn't appear to, as he made no move whatsoever. He just stood there in the mild air rimmed by the harsh, raking sunlight.

"Hey there!" I said in a voice that was shaped to cut through whatever was transporting this man so completely.

He didn't start, but now it was clear that he heard me. Drawing again on his cigarette, he turned his head to look at me and broke into a smooth welcoming smile.

"Didn't see you there," he said, tossing the butt over the edge of the deck. "Lost in thought."

I made my way towards the steps leading up to the deck and noticed that it had got suddenly very quiet, as though a muffle had been tossed lightly over everything.

"I love to see the city like this, at the end of the day. When the air is like this, you can see the Oratory," he said, pointing.

I followed his gaze, and indeed from where we were standing, Montreal presented a low, squatting fresco: the grey concrete tangle of the Decarie Interchange, the purple-green tree tops of the lush veldt that was the Town of Mount Royal, the mottled north escarpment of Mont Royal, the plateau formed by Queen Mary, culminating in that Catholic Taj, the blood-stained steps of St. Joseph's Oratory.

"You can rarely see it just like this," he said, exhaling deeply. "Someone might take a picture."

His accent was pure, native Montrealer. First generation, Cote St. Luc by way of the Main, the blunt consonants, the "de" for "the" and the rolling iambic rhythm. He was well over seventy, hair thin and still brown, face once handsome, now lined and filled with a salesman's squinting charm. He was dressed atypically for someone selling real estate. The short-sleeved plaid shirt revealed tanned forearms, well muscled, trim, not an ounce of fat. The shoulders were round but compact and still strong, tapered waist, short, stout legs, wide feet in expensive sporty loafers. The contractor? Yes. The architect in a pinch and by a slight stretch, but he wasn't selling anyone these houses dressed like that.

"It's a trick of the light and air," I said as took in the vista.

"Huh?" he said, turning to me so that I could see his milky blue eyes, the hairy salt-and-pepper brows.

"It's the ozone in the air. The rain and lighting last night and this morning. Pulls all the dust out of the air. It works likes a magnifying glass."

He was eying the camera around my neck and bent forward to get a better look.

"That's some camera. Whattya got there, a Nikon?"

I slipped it off my neck and handed it to him. It is another ploy to slip in under the radar. A potlatch manoeuvre; I give you something shiny to look at and hold, you let me come in here with a crew of sixty slobbering film technicians and let me shoot.

He handled the Nikon like it was the Hope Diamond. His hands followed the form of his body: the fingers were medium length, thick, blunt and well formed. The knuckles were hairy, the nails thick and well manicured. The hands of a carpenter? No, draftsman. He drew the plans! He did up the plans for the individual units. Custom design?

"You heard of Voigtlander?"

He caught me by surprise. Rare camera, of course, but his pronunciation. This wasn't ghetto Yiddish.

"Voigtlander, sure. Great camera. Great lenses."

"Have one," he said smiling, handing back the Nikon. "Belonged to my father. These new cameras look so fast, eh? Like a sports car."

Now I was stuck. My first ploy – the coincidental pass-by that results in a sudden inspiration – had faltered with finding him looking out at the city, oblivious to my arrival. My second attempt – the potlatch gimmick – had resulted in no further progress. Should I simply state my business? I was reaching for my card when he turned his back to me, his gaze resting once again on the city now ripening under the effects of the setting sun.

"I used to drive up past here on my way to Cote Vertu." He squinted into the distance as though to orient himself correctly. "The Cavendish extension was supposed to reach through Cote St. Luc right up to Ville St. Laurent. Did you know that?"

"Actually, I did."

"It'll never happen, but."

"It should. You know how much time that would take off getting to Dorval?"

"They have to go under so many tracks. You know the train tracks south of Blue Bonnets?" He motioned with one arm, describing in elegant arcs how the road extension would have to curve and bury itself to emerge near where we stood. "There's a whole yard there. That'd be some tunnel."

"Is that why you picked this piece of land?"

Again, it was as though he suddenly did not hear me. He was following his eyes, his feet following, stepping to the far end of the deck, down the steps toward the sales office trailer. I felt for a moment that I should just go. It was the end of the day. The sun was setting. There was no one there but us two.

I sneaked a look into the window of the model home. It was furnished in a rather simple but homey manner. It was pretty perfect for our needs. Do your utmost, right? I followed him, catching up.

"You know Liberty Mews?" I wasn't sure he was speaking to me. His arm was stretched out again, and then the words fell into place.

"That's on Simpson, right? Below Doctor Penfield? The 60s." I held my breath.

"That was one of ours. Sold out before we posted the plans."

Now he indicated somewhere in the direction of Outremont.

"Les Terraces?"

"Phase One or Two?" I teased.

"We did those," he chuckled. "Circle Heights. The Balmoral. Le Chateau des Hauters. Le Monaco."

"That's some resume," I said with genuine admiration. At the same time, I was doing the math and it didn't add up. What exactly did he do?

"You developed all those?" I asked, approaching him.

Now he turned toward me, opening the door to the sales office and motioning me inside. I was thinking, oh shit, it's the big sales job.

"All those and more. So much more," he said, smiling as he followed me inside, holding out his hand. "Placek, Mendel Placek."

I handed him my business card and pretended to look around, pretended to be taking it all in like, what? Like someone's betrothed? Someone's husband? The good son?

He squinted at the card, a shadow of suspicion darkening his face. "You looking to buy?"

"Was thinking about it, but--"

He cut me off.

"Good time to buy, the rates," he pursed his lips and blew away any notion that interest rates would ever be better.

"I was thinking the same thing, but looking at the place I had another idea."

He was finally looking at me, taking me in full measure, hands on hips, rocking back slightly on his heels. Scrutinizing, hell, he had me wrapped and bagged.

"I do a little work in the film business," I began. He stopped me short again.

"Oh yeah?" he drawled, smiling. "You know Herschel Blumenthal?"

"Who doesn't know Herschel?" I smiled back. "You know him?"

"Went to school with him. Baron Byng. What's he doing in the business?"

"Oh, he's a big shot," I started, only to be drawn up short.

"I know! I know he's a big shot, but what does he actually do?" he asked, settling himself down in a chair. "I read about him all the time in *The Gazette, The Jewish News*. But what does he actually do? I can never understand it."

"He owns half the film business in town," I replied, with a pretence of spilling a confidence. He sat forward, listening. "He owns the biggest rental company, the biggest studios…"

"Studios," he whistled. "How does he come to own studios?"

"He was smart. He had vision. He took some defunct government buildings, huge machine shops left over from who knows when. They were sitting there, land all around. He came in with a bid of one dollar but with an idea to build studios."

Placek had one hand pressed against the side of his face, his face crinkled, smiling.

"Imagine that. That pisher!"

"Then he got the government to advance him low-interest business loans, millions. He created the most modern, most beautiful studios anyone had ever seen outside Hollywood."

"Imagine that... imagine that," he took a breath, nodding, impressed.

"Now everyone says it was obvious, but back then he was the only one willing to take the chance. Risk."

"He had a vision, little Hershey," Placek said, shaking his head slowly, smiling inwardly. "Imagine that little pisher. He's a big shot now, eh?"

"The biggest. I do a lot of work in his studios," I said, warming up to a segue. "In fact, I'm working on something now, and I think I have a suggestion you might find interesting.

But he was no longer there. I mean, he was there but not there. He had slipped away, somewhere else in time, over there by the big picture window, watching as the low-raking sun blasted like a ray gun across the city, catching itself on the facets the face of the city presented.

I sat quietly, waiting. Did he hear me? Finally he turned and regarded me as though picking up the threads of a conversation that had started long, long ago.

"Do you know the story of Alexis Sklaris?"

I shook my head, drawing out my cigarettes from my inside pocket. I felt his eyes flick to my hands and roam longingly across something with which he had more than a passing familiarity. When he spoke, he could have been reciting a parsha of long, lost love.

"Rothman's," he sighed. "Rothman's of Pall Mall. Are they English?"

His pale blue eyes were shining, his lower lip was suddenly wet. I opened the crisply cut and folded clip top revealing a gleaming row of filtered cigarettes like the grim smile of a City banker telling you some devastatingly good news. I extended my hand, and he met me more than half way, his slim, freckled fingers expertly plucking a single soldier from the ranks.

I flicked my lighter and listened to that giddily engaging melody of divine incineration. In those days, there are no preservatives in English Rothman cigarettes, nothing between the communion of man and nature, and Mr. Placek was the kind of person who raised the ritual to a truly high plane of observance.

"That is...," he began, drawing deeply and luxuriating in the effect. "That is just lovely."

"Alexis Sklaris?" I prompted. "The real estate guy?"

The old man waved his hand.

"Real estate," he snorted, his beautiful face breaking, smiling, sceptical. "Real estate, like Haifetz is a fiddle player. Eh? Like Sinatra is a wedding singer."

He drew again on the Rothman's and turned to gaze at the world outside, the setting sun.

"We were in it for the fast money. Hit and run artists. Opportunists," he said, leaning back and squinting through the smoke. "Oh sure, there were people with a plan. No me. Not my circle. There were, I dunno, the Belzbergs, the Steinbergs, you know, Ivanhoe. Not us. We were in it for the quick cash. Hit and run. Buy the land, build the houses and sell before the bank calls in the notes."

I was loving this glimpse behind the curtain.

"By the seat of your pants."

Mr. Placek laughed, coughing, then catching his breath.

"Sometimes I'd be on my knees in front of those WASP assholes, pleading, begging until my brother-in-law would call up, 'Mendel, we broke even! Mendel! They signed the deed! Get up off the floor!'"

His laughter took him solidly by the throat, picking up his chest and shaking it. His eyes squeezed shut against the tears seeping through. Laughing, coughing, laughing.

"But not Alexis. Not him. He was different. He was … ," he stopped, looking, grasping for it. "He was singular, he was alone, by himself out there where there was no one."

"He was different," I said, confirming.

Mr. Placek drew at the last inch of his cigarette, leaning in towards me, drawing me closer.

"And you know why? Because he had vision. What we never had. He had a vision."

Mr. Placek leaned back in his chair, once more looking out the window at the blue and gold sunset as though seeking support from that light. I was caught up by what he had said and was eager to learn more and concerned that if I spoke, I would break the spell. So I settled back in my chair, feeling my left leg grow annoyingly numb, but I could not move.

Mr. Placek sat for a long time, letting the cigarette smoulder, then snuff out in his fingers. He hummed a bit. Crossed and then re-crossed his legs. Hummed, then sighed again. A refrigerator cycled on, and it seemed to remind Placek of his hunger.

"You eat today?"

I didn't notice the little refrigerator beside the filing cabinet. He walked over to it and took out a small jar of herring, an onion wrapped in plastic, two red ripe tomatoes, a half rye bread sliced, a tub of margarine, a mickey of Smirnoff vodka, a tub of sour cream.

"Sklaris came from an island off the Greek coast, a small island and I don't know for sure," he said, turning to me. "I mean, it was told to me, second hand. I didn't hear it from the man himself, but. It was an island off the Greek coast that was very small and where all the land was taken. All the land. So for a young man growing up, there were two possibilities. One, be the first-born son and inherit the land from your father. Two, go to sea. They could also become priests, that was also a possibility, but not for Alexis. He went to sea.

"This was in the period between the wars, you see? Alexis went to sea and was happy with his life. He was young, he was tall for a Greek, and he was good-looking. You know what they say about a woman in every port? It wasn't just words where Alexis is concerned."

Mr. Placek turned to me fully to see what I was doing, and in perfect concert I lifted my eyes to his. I was in him, inside his mind, and he thought it just fine.

"You understand, it was told to me. Second hand, mind you, but I never heard it directly from him."

The word "him" had mysteriously taken on a weight, a dimension that I hadn't heard before. I didn't breathe, waiting for him to continue.

"By the sea, Alexis saw the world. South America, the Orient. He was known everywhere he touched ground. He was a friend to hundreds, he learned languages, strange languages and customs. He absorbed everything, you see?"

I nodded.

"He progressed in the shipping company he worked for. After ten years seeing the world, he was first mate on a freighter. And the funny thing was that in all the years he travelled, he had never visited Montreal. Never. It was odd because the company he worked for had a regular service to and from, but his boat had never made that trip until sometime in the late 1930s. Then finally, he arrived here, with a load of Smyrna figs, olive oil and ceramics. But when they got here, there was a longshoreman strike on and they couldn't unload the ship. So Alexis tells his captain he would like to see the city, and off he goes."

I offered him another Rothman's and though he hesitated he took it, this time lighting it himself with a thumb-worn tiny gold briquette.

"You don't know this. You couldn't know Montreal then. I mean, I could sit here and talk till Tisha Ba'av and I wouldn't be able to tell you everything. Everything. How special this city was. How free. Danzig. Trieste. Shanghai. And this was the city, that was the time that Alexis Sklaris was let loose on the world."

Placek broke bread in the old-fashioned manner, piling my plate generously, filling my glass with the cold vodka, putting a kettle on the boil.

He raised his glass, "L'chaim!"

I returned the salute and stabbed at a piece of herring, waiting for Placek to down his tumbler in one go, shaking off the effects with a shiver of delight.

"I think it was at White's Paradise. A jazz club, it no longer exists, but it was there at the head of Decarie. It was a road house first, then a jazz club, but upstairs, especially on the weekends, it was a casino. How Alexis found it, who took him there I don't know. But there he was on a Saturday night, maybe it was the small hours of Sunday, and on the table was, for him, everything. A year and a half from home, the wages of a first mate, a few trinkets, maybe some pebble gold, maybe some uncut stones from Antwerp."

He paused, piling a slice of rye with a smear of sour cream, a piece of herring, some onion, some tomato.

"Who else was there? Arnie Rosen, Mikie Goldmann, Frenchie Richard, Goldie Washington and his brother Liberty - I heard about it from Morty Garellek - Morty held the bank, and Alexis was to throw down."

Placek was getting wound up and emotional, but I couldn't see why.

"Everything was on the table, but you don't understand what that means when I say everything 'cause in your mind, what do you see?"

I took a short, quick shot of the icy vodka and shook my head.

"A pile of money? A big pile maybe? American money, Canadian? Some trinkets, but that is not what Alexis saw. He was looking at possible futures, huh? That pile in which his little contribution was all but lost represented a sister's marriage, a younger brother who wanted to go to university in Thessalonica, his father's hernia operation, an extension on the family house, maybe plumbing, maybe a new he-goat - the small herd was prone to certain inbred problems... do you see?"

Mr. Placek's voice got a little hard and challenging, his lower lip was jutting out at me and trembled as his eyes narrowed.

"'Cause you and your generation don't know what that could mean. For you, that's just some money. Eh? What is that? Eh? Something to spend? But we didn't spend!" he shouted, his face reddening, his breathing short, harsh.

"For us, just like him, that dollar was a fist! It was a blow against them! Against it!"

"What?" I risked.

Placek pointed out the window, at the gloaming sky now suddenly laced in dark clouds.

"That which we didn't know. That which was always on us, always after us, biting, ripping, killing us in every way."

Placek took a moment, his eyes falling on and then fixing onto the five by seven photo on his desk. It was Placek and the family taken at a son's bar mitzvah, his wife's hair lacquered, the daughter with her '60s, bad-girl bangs and the son, dwarfed by the Torah held between him and his father, the younger Placek.

"I tried to raise my kids in the same way, but in the end I failed. We all failed. Your father too, maybe?"

His brow was raised, teasing me with the question. I took a piece of raw onion and bit into it. Placek shook his head.

"It wasn't just a pile of money for Alexis. It was that which we used to keep that thing, that hungry thing away from us and those whom we loved."

I poured Mr. Placek and myself another shot and raised my glass,

"You are a poet, Mr. Placek," I said.

Placek drank his down in one go and held me steady with his eyes.

"*He* was a poet," he said, eyeing me carefully as though deciding whether or not to go on. Finally he began again.

"It was his throw down, and they all waited. He came up with four 10's, not a high hand, but it was enough. And as he raked in the loot there, at the bottom, was a piece of official-looking paper. Frenchie Richard had put it down just before he folded. It was the deed to Frenchie's father's farm. Frenchie's father had died a few months before, and Frenchie had been cut out of the will because he consorted with Jews, the English and coloureds. While the family was planting poor dead Aimé Richard in the ground, Frenchie crept into his father's house and stole the deed. He never told anyone, and for a few weeks he waved it under everyone's nose waiting for a nibble, but no one wanted a shit farm with a dead apple orchard out in the Cote-de-Liesse parish. No one. Besides, no one believed Frenchie really owned it because everyone knew his father had thrown him out of the house years ago."

Placek got up to take some sliced smoked meat out of the fridge.

"But there it was, a legal document that Frenchie signed over to Alexis Sklaris that said the young Greek boy owned it. Garellek was a notary public, and he fixed his stamp to make it all official."

Placek was looking down, an odd smile of his face, his head shaking back and forth.

"They had to explain to Alexis what it was," he laughed, suddenly remembering. His face reddened with mirth. "He had never seen a deed of land. He seemed to have trouble grasping the concept. In the end, Morty drove him out over that shit dirt road that was once the Cote-de-Liesse to show the Greek what he had won."

"Must have been a shock to Frenchie's family?"

"To say the least," shouted Placek, doubling over with mirth. He caught his breath.

"Can you imagine? But the genius of it," he began, his voice clearing to a fine, present baritone as he edged himself closer to me, his chin lowering, the brows coming together gleaming the darks of his eyes. "The genius of it was that in a moment, in that tiny moment when he stepped out of Morty's car, this young man from half a world away understood something that to this day I can only gaze at from a distance. Looking out over that tract of land, a farm that hadn't produced for years, practically a ruin... what he saw was land. *Land that he could own!* He could have this land. It could be his own land, and in that there was a vision."

"What about the family? It wasn't legal, the deed I mean."

"Not legal!" he cried, reeling back in his chair. "Not legal but still, there it was. A deed signed over to him."

Placek picked up his shot glass and, as he downed it, seemed to gather strength and youth.

"Frenchie Richard's family were worried. What did they know - was it legal, was it not legal? But Alexis didn't even touch that. He didn't even go into that. This is what I'm trying to tell you. This was the vision he had."

Placek helped himself to another one of my Rothman's, standing and idly tapping the butt end on the pack before placing it carefully between his lips. He sat back down and faced me, drawing me into his circle. The gesture was male, positively beautiful, and suddenly Placek himself was beautiful.

"Alexis sat down with the family. He talked to them in his seaman's French. He opened a map, showing them the places in the world he had been and where he came from. He took out his family pictures and showed them his father and mother, his brothers, their children. They had never seen anyone like him before. When they saw the picture of his younger brother, the Greek Orthodox priest, Aimé's widow crossed herself. He made a deal. He gave them $100...," he whispered, getting up again to pace in front of the picture window before turning back to me.

"$100 dollars, cash!" said Placek, rubbing his hands together as though conjuring the same magic. "And then he made them sign the deed under Frenchie's signature, but he made them this deal - they would always have their house and one acre around it. But the document they signed allowed him to act legally and with complete authority as though he owned the whole farm."

"An option."

"If you want," Placek conceded. "But he then told them that they had to introduce him to other farmers in the area. And for each farm they helped him buy, he would give them a commission of ten bucks."

Placek let this sink in, watching me to see if I understood, nodding his head as this enormous truth filled the room.

"You see what he did? Do you see?" he whispered as he sat down close to me, the vodka and herring and onion filling my nostrils. "He turned fear into friendship. He turned a muddle into a plan."

"Amazing," I said, shaking my head.

"OK, the widows were old, their farms were a mess. They were all just hanging on, but they had land. The one thing Alexis understood. Do you see?"

Mr. Placek gathered himself up, balling his emotions, his joy leaping out of his mouth like a gale of garlic, vodka and laughter. He counted off the necessary conditions.

"So it was luck and timing. And vision!"

Placek jingled the change in his pocket, winding himself up. It had all crawled under his skin, but I couldn't see what was needling him. When he spoke again, it was as though he were reciting received wisdom from some long-forgotten book.

"He barely spoke their language! And without a lawyer, only a small piece of paper, his hand on the deal. And that is what he did. He went up and down the Cote, stopping at every apple orchard, every pig farm, and he spoke to the farmers and he showed them his map and the pictures of his family, and he gave them one hundred dollars and the promise of ten thousand more and that they could keep their houses and one acre around. His ship left Montreal, and he never saw the sea again."

Placek stopped, turning to me, his eyes arched, his mouth droll and expressive.

"And in a very few years, he owned most of St-Laurent and huge tracts of land all over the island."

He moved away from the window and took his seat behind his desk, taking another one of my Rothman's on the way. He sat down, perhaps a little heavy on his pins, but wiggled himself into his chair, his eyes now peering into the evening gloom. After a long moment, he began again.

"Do you know what it is, a customer peddler?" he asked, squinting through the smoke of my Rothman's.

Customer peddler. Local appellation. Native guildsman, involved in the arts of extraction.

"Like a peddler, right? But bigger items," I replied, hesitating. I knew he really wanted to tell me as he settled himself, warming up to the subject. "Well, maybe I don't know."

"You remember Brown's department store?"

"Department store? That's a joke. What a dump that place was." I was searching back in my high school memories. "A friend took me there once to pick up a dryer for his mother. On Saint Lawrence."

"Saint Lawrence, right."

Placek paused as though setting the facts in order while I thought to myself, who was this guy, this father, who had once bored his own kids to death with the daily recitation of his life and times?

"I used to work out of Brown's. We all did. All the peddlers."

"So what did you do? You were a salesman?"

He covered me with his lidded eyes, and then spoke as though waking up.

"Well, sure," he started. "Salesman, but not for Brown's. For myself. We all worked for ourselves."

"But I don't understand how you worked. How did you sell?"

"We were the bank. We acted just like a bank. Don't forget in those days, if you didn't have a good-paying job, if you didn't have a bank account, you couldn't get credit. Morgan's, Eaton's, they didn't care for these little guys, the working class."

He faced me squarely, drawing a pad and pen to him, scribbling numbers.

"If you had a regular job after the war, if you had something in the bank, no problem. Maybe you had to wait a while to get a fridge, but you could get it on payments. But what if you didn't?"

"I don't know," helping myself to another one of my cigarettes.

"The French guys coming off the farms, flooding into Montreal, they took jobs wherever," he continued, focused now on the little grid he had drawn. "They worked, they didn't work. They also didn't trust banks because they were all run by the English or by more cultured French guys whom they didn't understand or they didn't trust."

"They didn't trust French Canadian bankers?" I asked, incredulous. He was suddenly exasperated.

"Trust. Didn't trust," he whined, suddenly pulling one of my hands to him. He leaned low over the desk, fixing me again with his pale, milky eyes. "It was a question of class. Like it or not, we were of the same class. Maybe not the same, but closer. We were closer in class to them than they were to the educated, proper French. We shared the same things. We had big families, we had a connection to religion. We could work with our hands, you see?"

I nodded and he relaxed a moment, releasing my hand.

"They weren't frightened of us," he sighed, running his workman's hand through his hair. "Maybe they thought, well, if they didn't make a payment, it's not so serious. After all, we were just little Jews like they were little Frenchies. You see?"

"Right."

"Miss a payment with some big shot in a suit and tie behind a desk at some big bank, who's going to listen? Who's going to give a shit." He was warming up again and suddenly shouted, "Well, we gave a shit!"

"So how did it work?" I prompted.

"Word of mouth. Always!" he practically crowed. "One would tell the next, you see? That way, they were all the same class, the same group. Sometimes all from the same village or region. They kept an eye on each other, you see?"

"No," I said, shaking my head.

"Look here, if one of my customers recommended someone to me, and that new person bought a washer for his wife, the original guy, the one who passed on my name, made sure that the new guy paid. Why?"

"To keep his name good," I replied.

"Right! Right, that's it," he laughed, settling down again. "He wouldn't want to be known as someone who was friends with someone who didn't keep his word, didn't look after his debts, his family. So they watched each other."

He drew himself up, his chest puffing out and waggling his finger in my face.

"In twenty years!" he thundered. "Listen to me, in twenty years not one of my customers ever failed me. Ever failed to make a payment. And it was all on a handshake. Mine and theirs. You know what my business was?"

I shook my head and watched as he reached into the desk and drew out a small metal index card box.

"This was my whole business," he said, smiling with fond nostalgia. "Everything was in a box like this."

He took out a blank card.

"And on this I wrote everything," he explained, turning the card to show me. "Here, I wrote the name, address, wife's name, kids' names. Everything. Here, the item, make, model, serial number. Here, price."

He settled back again, drawing a small wad of blank cards out of the box, fanning them.

"Every Thursday evening I went out to collect," he recalled. "A lot of them got paid on Thursday, and most of them got paid in cash. So I made the rounds after supper. I'd drive out to the East End. Cold water flats. Sometimes St-Henri. They all knew me by my first name. 'Monsieur Mendel.'"

He rose and began to pace again, both his hands thrust deep into his pocket, the muscled forearms bent like brackets over his hips.

"I'd hear them from one flat to the next. 'Il arrive, Monsieur Mendel!'" he laughed. "I liked them, you see? I liked all my customers. Never had one fail me. Not one in twenty years."

He had stopped again in front of the huge picture window. There was now only the very faintest trace of daylight blue in the western sky. In the east, only lights revealed the city beyond the twist and ramps of highway.

"I'd sit down," he said quietly, as though living through it all over again. "They'd always invite me in. Somehow, they all got the idea that I liked a glass of water whenever I did business with them, so they always brought me a nice glass of water.

I was suddenly thirsty.

"In the summer they would always offer me a beer, and once in a while I'd surprise them by accepting." He turned to me, now dark against the black pane. "You should have seen their faces when I'd say, 'Oui! Merci!'"

"Probably never saw a Jew drink before," I joked, but he went on as though he hadn't heard.

"I knew them all. All of them, their kids, their mothers and brothers," he said quietly. "And they knew me. They would pay me their few dollars, I'd mark it on the card and sign it, they'd put their signature next to mine, and then adieu till the next week."

His breathing had become a little shallow, almost strained.

"If they were young, sometimes I had to go collecting on Sunday after mass. I'd go just before lunch, catching them at home before they went off to the tavern. I'd bring my kids with me..."

I thought I hadn't heard him correctly but didn't want to break his mood.

"They'd sit in the car and wait for me," he explained, turning to me. "They were my excuse, you see? If they wanted me to join them for lunch or if they wanted to give me a long story, I'd just point to the kids in the car and tell them that Daddy had promised to take them to Belmont Park. I hoped that my kids would see, would understand..."

He trailed off as though searching. Straining for a word.

"Understand what you did for a living?" I suggested.

"No," he hissed, looking back at me, annoyed.

He pointed to the city beyond the blackness of the window, thrusting his finger out.

"Understand them! The people who were putting clothes on them, feeding them, paying for Talmud Torah for them. I thought they should speak a little French like me. Know these people the way I did. Sometimes, even just seeing was something."

"And did they?"

It was not a provocation. I really wanted to know.

"Did they get to know them the way you did?"

Placek took out his handkerchief and blew his nose elaborately. He refolded it, almost waving it at me dismissively.

"They were kids, very young," he explained. "Soon after, I stopped peddling. Got into the building game, you see?" he gestured around him with elaborate drama. "My empire."

Placek rose from his comfortable chair, his legs stiffer and his gait not so spry. A huge weight had descended on his shoulders, his back was rounded by it. Whatever bravado his fate had bequeathed, failed him now. I watched it flow out of him on that meandering stream of nostalgia and bullshit.

"It took me a while, but I learned: my kids were not comfortable with a peddler father, my wife also. She was concerned that people would look down their nose... never mind that we had the same kind of house in Snowdon that our friends had."

Placek turned to me, his hands turned out, his voice plaintive.

"What did they fucking want from me? I told them, 'The work stinks, but the money smells good!' It was like a joke, but they fixed on it."

I nodded but I wondered, who was he talking to? His confessor? A stranger with common sense who would give him absolution for listening to the grating, prattling gossip of women and children? Forgive him for being led around by his nose, that wonderful man-nose that smelled good money in odorous work?

"So when my brother called me to look over a plot of land in Montreal West, I told him, 'What the fuck do I know?' He wanted ten thousand dollars from me to put up two houses..." he said, stopping to peer at me, his eyes black.

"Do you know what that meant to me, ten thousand dollars? Have you any idea?"

Placek approached, bringing up a chair to sit face to face with me and, again, taking one of my hands between his own.

"Can you imagine how many washers and dryers, how many DuMont cabinet televisions, how many fucking Hoover vacuums and how many Thursdays and Sundays of collecting that represented?"

I shook my head.

"And my younger brother, *der klieger*, is asking me for ten thousand to buy a plot of land so that he can build two duplexes."

Placek exhaled, still fixing me with his milky eyes.

"And maybe I would have got away from the idea, but my wife was speaking to his wife. After years of shaking her head over my clients, suddenly she was my partner! She wouldn't let me live!"

Placek raised his voice in a credible imitation.

"*What are you afraid of? My father would have done it. It's a sure thing. What are you afraid of?*"

Placek dropped my hand and leaned back, his fingers pressed to his eyes as though blotting out his moment of uncertainty.

"But I was afraid!" he cried. "I was afraid, I was so afraid because she didn't know, and I could not tell her because then she would be afraid, and the kids…" he trailed off, rising to his feet again, moving back into the shadows.

"I couldn't risk it. I couldn't touch it, do you see? It was a cash business, do you understand?"

"Peddlers worked for cash," I said, putting it together.

"Yes," he cried again. "It was a cash business. House painting was a cash business. Used cars was a cash business. So the money was there, but did you dare spend it? If you lived carefully, under their attention, it's a risk you can take; but investing ten thousand dollars, signing your name to papers with notaries, lawyers, building permits. Who was I?"

Placek walked slowly back to his desk, glancing at the bar mitzvah photo.

"But she would not let me live," he sighed, his mouth curling into a smile. "One evening I was going to make my rounds. She watched me dress, pick up my little box of cards, my car keys. I called to my daughter,

'Come, let's go for a ride.' There was no answer, but I could hear the television going in the basement."

Placek gave me a sick little smile.

"I didn't know, the fix was in. My wife watched me and I called again. No answer. 'What gives?' And my wife looks at me and she says, 'If you want to go, then go.'"

Placek breathed out slowly.

"And so I knew. She had drawn her line in the sand. The money would never be enough to wash away the stink."

Placek settled back at his desk, his forearms in front of him.

"That night I went to my brother and gave him an envelope with the ten grand."

"Amazing," I said quietly.

"And we never looked back. So, it really is thanks to her, you see?" He glanced again at the family photo with a mixture of devotion and love and something else.

"So, it was the right decision?"

Placek didn't hesitate.

"Of course!" He drew back, hitching up his pants. "I sold my peddler business to some greener fresh off the boat, and my brother and I became builders. But then I realised something very strange."

"What was that?"

"It was exactly the same."

"What do you mean?"

"I thought that things would be different. I had this idea about building, that we would have nice offices, with a secretary and I would wear suits. I thought my life would be different, and it was, but…"

Placek gave me a pained smile and reached again for my Rothman's.

"Last one," he winked, lighting it. "Like I said, we were hit and run artists. My brother was doing the same thing with his buildings that I had been doing with my customers. Only the scale changed. The risks were greater, the rewards richer. But there was no vision!"

"Sklaris."

"Exactly!" he replied, pointing the cigarette at me and then gesturing to the black world outside. "Look at what he built! Bellevue Gardens, the Bartholomew estates on Nun's Island, the Bancroft Apartments downtown, the Redwoods in Westmount, the Bonavista on the mountain, almost all of Ville St-Laurent! Designed, planned communities – he knew the future. He had a vision of how people would want to live. Have you seen the finishes he used, the quality of the materials, the intelligence behind it all? Maybe it's not Frank Lloyd Wright, but what homes!"

Placek paused, confronting himself.

"And what did we build? Overstuffed split-levels for people looking for places to park their two cars. Close to convenient shopping. In the suburbs."

"Don't be so hard on yourself," I said softly, chiding. "There are real people living in your homes, with real families. You've given people places to live. That's got to count for something."

Placek shook his balding head, his eyes downcast.

"They are just houses, no vision, nothing that will last. Generations from now no one will ever say, 'Mendel and Karl built the home we live in.' Nothing will matter except the numbers at the bottom of the bank statement."

The mood was too dark. Placek's shortcomings too personal, too much part of his own private war with himself. I did not feel worthy to hear him. He must have sensed my discomfort because he raised his head, his smile back on his face.

"And I'll tell you something funny. After all my fears, my terror of becoming 'official,' it's still a cash business."

"C'mon," I teased, rising to my feet as an indication that I had to go.

"Any notary will tell you. There isn't a real estate deal done in this city where some cash doesn't change hands. It isn't corruption," he smiled roguishly, "It's tradition. Now, what was it you wanted to talk about?"

By the time we stepped back onto the deck in front of the model home, it was full night and Placek had agreed to let me bring the director to have a look. More than that he could not promise, but he liked the publicity angle.

"Who knows?" I said, dangling hope. "It might bring in a customer or two."

"What are you, fishing for a commission?"

I walked up to him and took his hand and, after a beat, pulled him to me to hug him. There was no resistance.

"For a man with no vision, you've done pretty good for yourself."

Placek sighed, his hand coming up to gently slap my cheek. He gestured to the raised ground and the model home.

"Make me immortal."

Stalking the Mastodon

——◆——

Julian was reptilian in aspect and thought. That was the secret of his success. While we warm-blooded entities skidded off each other in confusion and bad temper and anxiety, Julian remained tightly coiled in his cool reptilian world of production schedules, completion guarantees, and budgets. It was an advantage for a feature film production manager to possess such sang-froid.

There were disadvantages too. Like being taken for a cold-hearted, narcissistic prick for one, and being regarded as a specimen rather than as a real human for another. I never had a problem with Julian other than fending off his constant attempts to get me to work outside the film union's collective agreement and his chronic inability to refer to me by name. To him I was always "Man."

"I want you to shine on this, Man," he muttered as he perused the latest draft of a Telefilm contract. "I want you to go out and find the locations that are missing, and I want you to find the ones we actually shoot."

"What about Ted?"

I had been hired as director Ted Kotcheff's driver and generally hung around the office waiting for things to do for him. Like pick his wife up from the airport. Or his kids. Or make dinner reservations. Or smooth the ruffled feathers of anyone offended by his brusque but usually fair temper.

Julian panned his cold, reptile eyes in my direction and held the look for far longer than was either necessary or meaningful.

"He'll be busy here all day with Mordecai," he said, his tone as unmodulated as a serpent's hiss. "If you're back in time to get them supper, you should be fine."

"Okay," I said, picking up my stills camera. "I'm gone. By the way, how much are you paying me?"

There was another Jurassic pause, followed by a number so low it couldn't even be honoured with a reply.

Joshua Then and Now was a redux experience for many of the key people involved. For Ted Kotcheff and Mordecai Richler, it was a chance to try and catch lighting in the same bottle they used for *The Apprenticeship of Duddy Kravitz*, a film that I still submit as one of the unassailable successes of the Canadian film industry.

Around those two key people was a cohort of happy and eventually not-so-happy artists, designers, administrators and handmaidens who had also cut their teeth on that earlier film. Chief among these was Don, the assistant director. Loud, large and garrulous, one sensed Don's arrival into any situation long before he actually got there. He and Ted formed an unlikely team composed of opposite strengths and weaknesses. Ted's bark was always intellectually charged, while Don's was full of explosive bombast but good-natured at heart. Both men were somehow larger than life but only a little.

Their bond was based on friendly mutual antagonism and a propensity to volcanic outbursts of physical violence. I heard from both about the epic punch-up between them on *Duddy*. Naturally, each made himself the hero and injured party of the tale. But it joined them, formed a world that they drew on and that separated them from us. To me they were beasts of a distant world, like figures drawn on the cave walls at Lascaux. I could only glimpse them through the dark as they passed. I could track them but never catch up.

Between them, Mordecai appeared as the lumpy cousin, a wit held in reserve like a potent Imperial Guard but a presence always deferred to. Through the weeks of pre-production and evening script work, they would *flanner* through the lobby of our production HQ on Guy Street, and I would observe their passing. They were exotic, star-like, and just being around them made me crazy with excitement and nostalgic for a time that I had only heard about, not lived myself.

For these were the guys who made *Duddy Kravitz*!

I would get giddy just thinking about it. I was at one and, the same time, a passionate fan and dispassionate critic. My post-graduate years at Columbia film school hadn't worn the charm off that film. Its range, its scope, the absolute riotous certainty of its depiction of that time, that place and those people, were breath-taking. And these were the guys who made it. These guys! And I am working with them!

I was also not unaware that my job was, as Julian was quick to point out, an "opportunity." He knew of my writing ambitions.

"Man," he slurred, his forked tongue testing and re-testing the air, "You're going to be with Ted every day. And you'll meet Mordecai. You're going to hear things. You're going to be running around. Don't let it slip by."

So for those five months in 1984, I became the fly on the wall, a kind of post-graduate, cultural paleoanthropologist. My thesis? "Mordecai and Ted: The Glorious Results of Misspent Youth."

Ted Kotcheff loved to talk, and I liked to listen. He also liked to play classical Name-That-Tune of which he was a master, given his precocious early success as a violinist in Toronto. We would fill the long hours spent in the car together flipping the radio dial in search of Scriabin or Dvorak while he kept me awake (and out of ditches) with ribald and hilarious tales of romantic conquests on every continent and with every type of woman.

When it came to Mordecai, however, Ted was circumspect. Apparently, Mordecai was never part of *that* scene. So in my mind, I naturally separated the two. Ted was the raucous libertine, the film director, alive and playing the role for all its worth. Mordecai was the dour scribe devoted to his work and, above all, his family. To be sure, Ted was a doting father as well, but none of his stories of lechery ever involved Mordecai except as witness to the goings-on.

My few moments in Mordecai's company only confirmed this impression. I remember several trips out to his country seat on Lake Memphremagog and the green envy I felt assessing his world and situation. I remember a couple of visits to his Chateau apartment and thinking how perfect it was in its mid-Atlantic synthesis of *Punch* and *New Yorker* aesthetics. This was the man who dared become what I was still only vaguely dreaming of.

Ted told me that when they were still reckless callow rakes living in London, they used to get comfortably buzzed and then go to fashion shows where Mordecai's future wife worked and try to make her crack up as she floated down the runway. It was a courting strategy that worked and not dissimilar to Jake's reluctant, grudging method in *St. Urbain's Horseman*. When I saw Mordecai and his wife together at their homes or on set, I was immediately aware of a bond, a kind of absolute link. They were clearly *beschert*.

And before the meeting of these two souls? Well, I knew that his wife had been married before. But Mordecai? There was a short marriage, wasn't there? And before that? One might assume a prior romantic life, but there was rather scant evidence. Certainly not in the novels. Mordecai was not Leonard Cohen, poet breaker of hearts, singer of love-laced odes to the soon to be disappointed. Mordecai's books offered very few clues to alter this view. The classic Richler hero is always faithful to the marrow but compromised, if only for dramatic purposes. Joshua in *Joshua then and Now* and Jake in *St. Urbain's Horseman* (in essence, the same book) slip up but only a little and are then redeemed by love. By family. By the only things that really matter.

The take-away from any encounter with the author was an impression of a jaded cynical man with few illusions. Unlike his less jaded, less inhibited friend, he eschewed the pleasures of the flesh that London in the moribund 1950s and swinging '60s had to offer for the life-long bonds of spousal fidelity and mutual respect.

So I had to shine, as Julian put it, if only to earn my place at their table, to consolidate my claim as a potential heir to their world which was, if I was honest with myself, what I really wanted. Find the missing locations? I would serve them up on a silver platter, no matter how much Julian was shafting me. And the locations?

As usual, there were several that persisted in eluding the location scouts. The principal problem was the character of Joshua's house. The brief from Ted and Pierre the location manager was simple but described an Escher-like conundrum: modest on the outside, very large on the inside.

My modus operandi was simple. I concentrated on the actual. If the script described a terraced house in Westmount, well, that's where I looked. Being a true Montreal Anglophone, I considered the west end of town my home turf, and I started ringing doorbells. The con is always the same. Dress neat, have your camera ready, and try to read the envelopes in the mailboxes so you could greet the occupants by name.

You ring ten doorbells, you hand out ten business cards, and you get invited into one house. Of the houses you get inside, nine out of ten are inappropriate for one reason or another. So in a day of hunting, you might end up with two possibilities, which you then show to the location manager, who will almost certainly eliminate one of your possibilities for one reason or another.

You then show the last possibility to the production designer, who will either instantly love it or hate it, depending on what he or she ate for lunch, what he or she is wearing that day or how much a certain lizard-like production manager has squeezed down on the art department budget.

And so it goes. *Joshua's* house was proving to be a tough nut to crack. I was only one of a half-dozen scouts working fourteen-hour days trying to find it.

At the end of each day, I would return to the office usually in time to see Mordecai arrive, and he rarely disappointed. The rumpled couture, the half-smoked Montecristo Petit, the quick, defiant glance and the grunt in welcome, it was all there. Like McGill's Redpath museum, the exhibits never varied. He would walk up the two flights to Ted's office where they would cloister, ostensibly working on the script but also, no doubt, reliving their progress from way back there all the way to here. After half an hour a call would come for me. Smoked meat was needed, stat! With all the trimmings, thank you. And would Schwartz's be all right?

"All right? It's *de rigueur*," snarled Mordecai as Ted peeled off a few bills to cover *le facture*.

My production Plymouth convertible could make the allez/retour in under thirty minutes. The counter Greeks at the deli got to know me to the point where the order was automatically assembled and ready for me by the time I struggled to the front of the line. It was de rigueur!

By the end of the first week, I had settled into a comfortable but efficient routine. Joshua's house had already been found. What I mean is, among the hundreds of photo files already compiled and all the houses looked at and rejected for one reason or another, was Joshua's house. Only no one knew it yet. This often happens on films; it is the forest-for-the-trees-syndrome. Too many choices, too many flavours to choose from, so no one makes a choice. Inevitably, the house that finally gets picked is usually one of the first scouted but, for some reason, originally rejected.

Secure in this knowledge and luxuriating in my paltry daily stipend, I refocused my energies on exploring every single house I had ever looked at from the outside, wondering what it was like on the inside. For that reason alone, the old Bronfman estate received several of my business cards through the mail slot, and Senator Kolber's housekeeper on Summit Circle and I became very chummy indeed.

It was on one such jaunt in the twee upper reaches of Westmount that I discovered a small street, a cul-de-sac that I never knew existed. In fact, for years after I could not find the street again, though I tried and tried. It meandered up from the Boulevard, getting narrower and more rustic as it went. The houses were small bungalows fronted by neat little lawns and flowerbeds under the front windows. Charming.

I parked, walked up to the first house and rang the bell. From inside, I heard the barking of a small dog, followed by the sound of a latch lifting and then, there she was. She was a woman of a certain age, a gentile, with blonde/grey hair, beautiful smooth clear pale skin and blue eyes the colour of a late winter sky. Her mouth was wide and friendly, and her body, from what I could see, was trim, fit even, if I can say that. It was a body used to gardening, serious amateur tennis, sail boating and informed *paso dobles..*

The dog, a tiny golden-haired Pomeranian, yipped and sneezed at her ankles, which I noted were slim and well turned. Her small feet were bare, the perfect nails shiny under a coat of modest but engaging "Naked Pink" polish. She was a crème parfait.

"Hi!" I said brightly, turning my head in the direction of the street and allowing her to look me over. I found that once people get a chance to look you over safely, they tend to trust you a little more.

"This is such a beautiful street. You know, I never knew it even existed before I drove up."

"It's a cul-de-sac, so…" she replied, her voice incongruously throaty and young.

"Right. So why would anyone… My name is Jacob," I said, thrusting out my business card.

She hesitated for only a second before taking it, focusing on it in a charming far-sighted manner.

"Joshua…" she started, then as though catching her breath, started again. "*Joshua Then and Now.*"

"Yes, we're making a movie of the book. You know, by Mordecai Richler?"

Can a woman simply melt before one's very eyes? Melt is the wrong word because then we would be talking of a simple change in the physical state rather than a physiological transubstantiation of the corpus. But can a woman's molecular essence change in an instant? Because that's what appeared to happen. Clearly, the mere mention of Mordecai's name had affected her in a manner that was profoundly moving. She kept looking at the card, then up at me, then at the card again. Finally she closed the card in her tiny hand and put it behind her back as though I might take it from her if she wasn't careful.

"And how is Mordy these days?" she asked softly, leaning into the door frame as though seeking support.

The waves of sensual vibrations emanating from her body caught me by surprise and were as palpable and potent as a whiff of pure oxygen. She was vibrating like a deep-sounding blue whale, moving the very air between us in a push-pull manner. In a few seconds, my own cheeks were burning, my forehead chilled, and my thighs started cramping.

"Mordecai?" I fumbled. "You know Mordecai?"

She didn't answer, at least I never saw her lips move. She simply pressed herself a little tighter against the door frame and did some trick with the time/space continuum, bringing me nearer.

"He's great," I stammered. "You know… working on this… this… film…"

Were my lips moving or had she achieve a direct link to my brain stem? She was looking deeply into me, kind of like a vampire mesmerising a virgin.

"You know, we're doing this film. With Ted. Ted Kotcheff. They did *Duddy Kravitz* together." I was babbling, held captive by her eyes, which had magically gone from pale blue to cobalt. Finally, mercifully, she interrupted.

"How does he look?"

Look? Describing Mordecai was hardly in my job description, but I took a stab at it.

"Oh, you know," I began.

"Yes," she nodded slowly, her smile elfin, sadistic.

"He's probably the same, you know…" I trailed off.

"Yes," she nodded again.

I somehow managed to pull myself away from the mind link she was forging and gathered what remained of my hot-wired wits.

"Do you know him? Mordecai?" I asked, wiping the drool off my chin and regaining partial control of my mouth.

She breathed and sighed lightly, pulling herself away from the door and back on her two, now unsteady legs.

"A long, long time ago," she replied, as though taking control of some wildly unpredictable thoughts and stowing them back out of sight and mind.

"Yeah, well. I'm looking for locations and I thought that...," I started but she was clearly no longer there. Her eyes were fixed on something past me, over my right shoulder, somewhere off in the far distance.

"It's so nice that he's back, isn't it?" she said, drawing back slightly. "I heard that he has a bunch of really nice kids."

"Yes In fact, his daughter..."

"You tell him 'hello' when you see him," she said coolly, closing the door with a smooth definitive gesture. She kept the card.

It was only when I got back in the car that I realised that I had no idea who she was, how to refer to her, nothing. And the next day, when I worked up the courage to ring her doorbell again if only to get her name and remember her to Mordecai, I could not, as I said, find the street.

I did mention the incident to Pierre the location manager, who, though very busy and now in negotiations for the house that would eventually become Joshua's family home, listened patiently. When he asked me to point out the street on the huge map we had of the city, I was unable to.

"Were you drunk?" he asked archly.

The next time Mordecai sauntered rumpily through the office, I took another hard look. The impression was still Neolithic: the large full-featured head and face, the thick wave of swept-back hair, the furtive yet challenging glance.

"Jake," he muttered by way of a greeting before he ambled up the stairs.

Was this the man to set hearts aflutter from the pre-historic past? I had wanted to prepare a clever salutation invoking regards from a certain woman on a certain street, but he seemed so unreachable. Untouchable. I choked.

Change the venue. I was now looking for another house, impressive on the outside, huge inside, that was to play for one of Joshua's rich friends. Having already out-rung my welcome in Westmount, I decided to try Outremont. This was dicey, as my French at that time was non-existent. A fumbling pidgin patois at best. Still, hunting for houses was better than sitting in the stifling office.

Another house, another chance to see how the moderately rich live. I was having a very good day and, to my own surprise, had wangled entry into about a dozen impressive homes. This next was a white, curvilinear manse, pretentious and unsuccessfully Deco. The front door was black, massive and, after one ring, it swung widely open to reveal the woman of the house and, judging by the looks of her, I was just in time.

She was another woman of a certain age but reflecting a more aggressively aesthetic and managed response to the problems of aging. She was dark-haired, of medium height and deliciously plump. *Zaftig*. She wore a simple white silk shirt and a black skirt. A string of large white pearls hung around her neck, and at the point of her cleavage a small white gold cross nestled comfortably. Two perfect pearls of the same colour were pinned to her earlobes. Her shoes were the kind of chic pumps that led men to think of how a woman would look dressed in them only.

About her underwear: I have no comment to make concerning what was under her skirt, but if you quizzed me I could testify to what was under her shirt because it was pretty much see-through. *Zaftig*. Her large breasts were held in a kind of loose, cupping embrace by a clever French-cut lace bra, transparent enough to reveal the colour if not the exact texture of her large, prominent nipples. As my cousin Ruthie used to say, "I shit you not!"

In one hand she held a shiny black cigarette holder, on the end of which smouldered a Nat Sherman gold leaf-tipped cigarette, while the plumply tapered, French-manicured fingers of her other hand were wrapped with comfy familiarity around a cut lead crystal tumbler filled with two fingers of a fragrant single malt Scotch.

She was a package as sweet and hot as a Szechwan pepper in honey. I don't know who she had been expecting, but I would have given anything to be him. Pierre insists till this day that, and I'm quoting here, "It didn't matter who she was expecting. You should have nailed her."

Once again I fumbled through my opening shpiel, giving her a chance to look me over, and before I knew it she was inviting me in to see her authentic period kitchen, which she swore hadn't been changed since the early 1960s.

"So, what is the movie?" she asked, refreshing her drink and adjusting the air-conditioning. Her English hinted faintly of her Francophone origins.

"It's a production of Mordecai Richler's book *Joshua Then and Now*, I said, handing her my business card.

And suddenly, once again I found myself basking under waves of excited pheromones. She had the card in her hands and was staring at it so intensely it was as though she expected Mordecai himself to appear from behind it.

"Mordecai?" It wasn't so much a question as a final judgement on a case, a situation, an equation I could not guess at.

"Yes. Mordecai. Mordecai's book...," but she was no longer listening.

Once more, the intrepid house hunter had stumbled over the spoor of the great Palaeolithic beast. The air was suddenly redolent of Cuban leaf, her scotch was suddenly his, and her breath stopped and started and stopped and started again.

I didn't know what to do. For all intents and purposes, I was no longer present. Two worlds existed simultaneously in that kitchen. I occupied one, and my presence had thrust her back into another. So we stood there, she lost in the memories that meant enough to her to require yet another two fingers of scotch, and me testing the ground, following the evidence, hoping it led to a trail that would take me back to some truth about him that had, till then, evaded public scrutiny.

It was not the way I thought of him; and when I have tried to tell this story, I find that it is not the way other people think of him, either. It's always about the old neighbourhood, his family and his wife. The young Mordecai, the lover of sweet, gentile torch-burning girls cannot be found. Oh, maybe in the sexual chutzpah of the reckless Duddy Kravitz, but that was fiction, wasn't it? The only true life evidence we have are the yellowing class photos from Fletcher's Field High that hang in basement rumpus rooms from Hampstead to Mississauga.

I was sifting through the elusive evidence of another life, an earlier life that somehow got sifted out of the life that he wrote about. I was rooting through the case box of another Mordecai; Mordecai the jungle beast from a Pleistocene past. Mordy the debaucher of certain women, of a certain type. Mordecai who leaves the invisible scars that make women stop breathing. The mastodon left traces. Why not Mordecai?

Was there a history that he didn't write about? Things that he never put down? Was the grumpy, carbonated mask a ruse to throw the hunter off the scent? Or did I, caught in the grip of an over-stimulated fugue state, imagine it all? No. I had him. My darts were now dipped with the correct potion. I could bring him down, make him mortal. All I had to do was get close.

I had my chance. One evening Ted asked me if I could give Mordecai a lift back to his apartment. As we pulled away from the office, he settled himself back and lit one of his small cigars. Up until this time we had not exchanged more than a few words. As I thought of a way to break the ice, I felt him looking at me fully for the first time.

"Ted says you write," he said, and I could tell from the tone that this was Mordecai trying hard to be nice.

"Yeah," I said, surprised that my name had come up between them at all. It threw me, but it didn't stop me. I fitted the stinging dart and raised my blow pipe, prepared to ask the smart-ass, innocent question.

Mordecai took a pull on his little cigar and gazed out at the city now glowing with the setting sun. He revealed his flank, his guard down, allowing me to take his measure. Squinting into the harsh, white-gold light, I found in a moment of recognition that his face was no longer beast-like. Not a curious exhibit, no cave painting. He was cut in relief but human in scale, after all. He sighed deeply, letting himself off the hook.

"It's a tough life," he said quietly.

The Golem of Hampstead

Max Schemler lived in the Town of Hampstead, on the island of Montreal. Hampstead was founded in 1914 and planned following the "garden city" design that was popular in Britain at the time. Initially, the town absorbed farms and orchards that had been part of the Parish of Notre Dame de Grâce, and the village founders either annexed or optioned fallow land that lay at the northern tip of Queen Mary Road as though in anticipation of the crowd that would move in, break sod, and eventually become Max Schemler's world.

The early resistance to the encroachment of Jewish families into Hampstead expressed by the original Scottish and English citizens is not important here. That these Hebraic interlopers inevitably took over the civic administration of the township, turning it into a high-end, cottage ghetto, is also not all that important. Most large cities with an established Jewish bourgeoisie have an enclave like Hampstead. In Toronto it's called Upper Forest Hill. Nashville has Bellevue, while Westchester has New Rochelle. Even Melbourne has its St. Kilda East, and São Paulo prides itself on Higienópolis. What is important, as far as Max's story is concerned, is that Hampstead is where the rich Jewish people lived.

When Max married Ellen Shatsky, he followed his young law firm partners onto Netherwood Crescent. In a few short years, all the vacant lots had been gobbled up, synagogues built for every religious taste, and tolerance and the idea of neighbourhood distilled.

Max and his neighbours were wealthy but not, at least as he liked to think of it, "shvitzy wealthy." In other words, when it came time to buy that country house in Morin Heights or write the cheque for Mindy's Harvard tuition or take the plunge on that shopping mall in Dollard des Ormeaux, there were no sweaty palms, no damp shirts. Pishers in Cote St-Luc living off *Bubby and Zaydie's* trust fund interest could hop from one foot to the other weighing the cost/benefits, but not Max's crowd. The Loire vineyard futures, the Manhattan west 1970s townhouse – the wealth was, as the French say, *profonde*.

Max's crowd were mostly professionals. If they were in business, it was big business, but on a human scale. There were no bank presidents, no Bell Canada executives. The preferred professions were lawyers, corporate accountants, brokers, the hit-and-run real estate developers that built so much of urban and suburban Montreal. They were the owners of businesses that provided those necessities that one never thought of but that were the very stuff of large economies and national capital. In boom times, these people made money, serious, legal, solid money. In recessions, there was no belt tightening, just clever accounting.

Max was a lawyer and although he was highly regarded, even envied by his peers for his position, his beautiful, sexy wife, his accomplished daughters and his stoic wisdom, he was unhappy. Ironically, his unhappiness was the real source of his power for, as much as he was admired for his command of the civil code, and his ability to cut straight to the true heart of any legal dispute, what really earned him his stripes was his detachment. For Max was detached.

Max never got excited by a legal argument, never got red in the face. Not shvitzy. The greatest financial coup, the trickiest industrial negotiation, never raised his blood pressure one degree. He was the consummate closer, the tie-breaker that all sides respected. His partners called him the "Ice Man" behind his back. They loved the fact that in the face of cataclysmic legal disasters, Max was as removed as the North Star. It was this clear-headed detachment that made Max invulnerable and held in awe by his peers. He could keep himself above the petty side bar arguments and egos because Max was detached. And for good reasons.

Max's father had been a religious tyrant and hypocrite. A rabbi by training, Avigdor Schemler could never find a place for his ass in this world. Before the war, in Prague, no synagogue would have him. Too argumentative, too inflexible, not wise enough. Avigdor Schemler did not know where the line between principle and obstinacy was, even when it was shown to him. He would, as his wife would mutter, make himself *tamavate* rather than admit to being wrong. Avigdor Schemler was never wrong.

In Prague, he had been somewhat reluctantly acknowledged as an insightful Kabbalist. Even in his late youth, his red-bound copy of the Zohar was frayed like lace from constant thumbing. Then, one day, just prior to the annexation of the Sudatenland, Avigdor Schemler raised his eyes from the text in front of him and snapped the book shut. Responding to questions, Avigdor placed his book under his arm and replied that he was beginning to see into the shadows and had no desire to behold any more truth. At least, not in this life.

What had Rebbe Avigdor Schemler seen in those yellowed, lace-like pages, we can only speculate. Whatever it was, it did not weaken his *angeshparte natur*, his self-righteousness, one iota. When his co-religionists were panicking at the Nazi approach, Avigdor Schemler insisted that there was nothing to worry about and he was never wrong.

He was not wrong when he ignored the warning signs in 1933, he was not wrong when he refused the offer of an uncle, already well established in Canada, to sponsor him and his family as immigrants. Avigdor Schemler could have got his wife and infants safely into Canada right under McKenzie King's racist nose, but no! And later, he was not wrong to hang around Prague after most of his extended family had been carted off to Thereisenstadt. He was not wrong to have survived the war when his wife and two infant sons had died. No, he was not wrong, but at least he was changed.

Yes, it might be rare, but it is possible for a man to change. Even Avigdor Schemler. In 1946, the Canadian uncle found him in a displaced persons camp in Wolfratshousen, Germany, and brought him to Montreal, installing him as the rebbe in a neighbourhood *shtiebel*, a basement prayer house, that served older Jewish men who were too feeble to make the walk to the nearest Orthodox synagogue. Avigdor Schemler was a shattered man, now a quiet man, who led the daily prayers and spent most of the day huddled in a pew, thinking about eternity and wishing it upon himself.

The Canadian uncle whispered, "Every pot has a lid" as he introduced Avigdor to Ruth Belaz, herself a Holocaust survivor and shattered remnant of a once noble Hungarian rabbinical line. Ruth was not a young woman. She had lost a husband and four children to the fascists in Budapest. She herself had escaped by posing as a gentile, assuming the identity of a girl who had once served her family as a maid. Well, we can say she escaped, but there are such things from which you never really escape.

When they were first introduced, something awoke in Avigdor. Later, he would tell people that he had stepped out of a dream and landed right in front of Ruth. For her part, Ruth just wanted all the pain of memory to stop. If sharing a bed and laundry with the scaly, wizened rebbe would at least crowd out the painful shadows, it was a leap she was willing to make. In any case, the small community surrounding Rebbe Avigdor Schemler's *shtiebel* regarded the match with nodding approval. Auspicious *yiches*.

And so they were married and, to Ruth's surprise, and to the smirking delight of everyone, in nine months she was delivered of a son. Maxwell Isidor Schemler was a fighting, screaming little *goniff* as had never been born into so faded a blood line. The fruit of two venerated, if obscure, rabbinical families, grafted, nurtured, tempered in sorrow and rage and now shouting, "Behold, world! I am born!"

Avigdor's delight practically burst his heart. To the outside world it was the father's joy at the birth of a son, the pride and the *naches*. A son, a healthy, robust son was reaffirmation after desolation. It was life after so much death. But that was not what was in Avigdor's mind. Sitting in that old, worn pew, day after day, Avigdor had the time to figure it all out. And now the way was clear.

Life was not the martyr's path, but the killer's. Not the ascetic but the warrior prince. Max would not be a pale-faced, sunken-eyed chader mouse. No! Max would be Judah the Maccabean. Max would be a Rothschild, a Montefiore. Max would be a man who could smash in the face of any bully and bind his bloody knuckles with his talis. Max would storms the gates, bring low the oppressors, be a man for all seasons and all purposes. And the greatest purpose was vengeance.

Max Schemler's youth was a cycle of increasing returns. Every goal, every task put before him, he exceeded. He skipped two primary school grades at Talmud Torah, and then proceeded to mature physically at the level of his classmates. By grade seven, he was shaving a full beard. In high school, he learned to hide his contempt for his mediocre teachers by a veil of kindness and good nature. It was only at home, sitting across from his father, their Talmuds touching, that Max Schemler unleashed the true powers of his brain and nimble tongue. By Max's seventeenth birthday, Avigdor Schemler could only sit back, exhausted, and marvel at his son's devastating mind. And what of the warrior?

Ruth Belaz wept when Max went off to make aliyah in Israel. Avigdor Schemler cheered him on. Ruth cried and tore her hair when Max was, willingly, dragooned into the Israeli infantry in late 1966. Avigdor closed the doors to the shtiebel after the Ma'ariv service and, alone in the gloaming, danced with unbridled, tendon-snapping, Hassidic fervour, imagining the fields of enemies his son – his son! – would scythe down. Vengeance!

And when pictures of Max in uniform, his rifle slung over his shoulder, davening at the Wailing Wall, appeared in *Look* and *Time* magazines, Avigdor clenched his fists and punched the heavens, shouting, "My Prince, my Prince!" over and over till Ruth had to apply a cold compress to his forehead.

When the war hero returned and expressed an interest in studying law, Avigdor Schemler insisted that Max attend the University of Sherbrooke, even as all of Max's friends were squeezing into McGill. This time, thought Avigdor, this time I'm listening. The French were too numerous, they will not toe the line for very much longer. The Prince will be as Maimonides, conversant in languages, able to meet the enemy on his own turf and make himself indispensable.

Thus Max was launched into, what Avigdor Schemler called, "the world." There was only one caveat. Avigdor made Max promise that as soon as he had made enough money, he would stop and turn his attention to Torah. What that meant, how long, how much money, was never specified. The promise, however, was reiterated again and again until, on Avigdor's deathbed, it was asked a final time. "When you have made enough in this world, promise me you will turn your attention, my Prince, to the other." Max, pressing his father's hand to his lips, promised.

Which was why Max was unhappy. You see, for the other men in his crowd, such a promise would, well, simply not have been taken very seriously. Make the old man happy, of course, but life goes on, eh Max? Life is for the living. What Max's friends couldn't understand was that this was a promise he longed to keep. He wanted to keep his word to his father and not out of some misguided filial guilt. Max was not susceptible to such psychological passive aggressive manipulations. He was too intelligent for that.

No, Max really wanted to stop this business of business and settle down and study Torah. He wanted to spend his days in his father's shtiebel, shrouded with his father's talis, bound up in his father's tefillin and shake and moan with the other true believers. Why couldn't he become a Kabbalist like his father?

He remembered once, when he was eight, that he crept into his father's bedroom and took down the red leather-bound copy of the Zohar. He had just settled down with it when he felt his father's sharp rapid slaps, like bee stings, on his cheeks. It was the only time in his entire life his father had struck him. What hurt were not the stinging blows but the wild fear in Avigdor's eyes. As he placed the book back in its place, he elicited a promise from Max to never touch it again until he was a man.

And now Max Schemler was a man, and he wanted to study, to pore over the Midrash and the Talmud and to discuss, probe, debate, parse the ineffable and plait pilpuls till his mind slipped the cranial limit and ascended the realm of the unpronounceable.

When Morty Metzger at the office heard about the deathbed promise, he said, "That's a fucking heavy load to live under, eh?" Max never saw it that way. It was what he had wanted to do. Slip off the throne of princely delight and fade into the feeble daylight of the chader and be a questioning boy once more. And it was so close, so near his reach.

Max's thirties and forties had been very good years, the halcyon days. During this time, his nut was augmented and polished, hoarded and banked like a fire, enough to burn for his life, his daughters' lives, their children. But it was not enough for Ellen Shatsky. It never would be. Which was the point.

Ellen Shatsky was born and raised to be a certain kind of Jewish wife. When they met in high school, Ellen was the queen bee of her class. She had developed early, her reputation as a full-grown woman was set and assured in grade eight. She was one of those women whose body bestowed a certain status that could not be touched by poor grades or unrealised potential. In short, she was always able to wrap any social situation around her little finger.

Ellen was calculating, even as a young girl, and when she saw Max, who was only a few years older than she was, she calculated that he was the man onto whose rising star she would hang her own.

Max had no chance and never resisted. Ellen was possessed of a shocking, paralysing beauty that was fascinating. Within their circle, Ellen was famous for being sexy. She exuded a potent sex appeal that was impossible to resist. Her skin was flawless, her chestnut hair was thick and shone with a careless healthy glow. Her eyes were a unique tone of green, forest green, deep and hypnotising. Ellen did not have to work at keeping her voluptuous body in shape. It was genetic, and whatever physical activity she indulged in was sufficient to keep her highly desirable. It was men's desire for her that fed her own sexual appetites. Ellen was, as her closest friends confided, "very sexy." The rumour was "she had to have it."

And she got it. The first few years of their lives together were golden and sustained both of them through the struggling years that followed. They lived charmed lives and were regarded as anointed. They set the pace for their crowd, the style and the fashions.

Max and Ellen had their children at around the same time as their friends. The kids attended the same private schools, the same summer camps where they learned to ride and sail. And Max and Ellen were never bored with each other. The heat was always there, at hand, never diminished, never mitigated until, finally, mitigated. By what?

"The first two years you screw all the time," exhaled Bryna one afternoon at Spa Jardin as Tran worked his deep tissue massage magic on her shoulders. "They can't keep their hands off you."

"You never hear, 'Sweetie, I'm tired. Honey, please, I have court tomorrow,'" smirked Rivka, waiting her turn. "Now that's all I hear. That and snoring."

Ellen smiled inwardly, listening to her friends complain. Bryna caught her.

"Look at her, what's that face for?" she laughed, pointing. "What?"

Ellen took a breath, her toned body moving like something carnal beneath her thin cotton robe.

"You know, we made love every single day for four years after we were married," Ellen sighed, raising the tension in the room sharply. "Every single day when he was in town, I mean, when we were together."

"Jesus," moaned Rivka, her mouth open.

"And if we had to spend a day or two apart, when he came back we used to just do it. Just not stop."

The only sound now was the damp, slick lapping of Tran's quick, narrow hands moving with rhythm over the well-larded flesh of Bryna's lower back.

"Shut up," snarled Bryna, turning her head away. "You and your husband make me sick."

Rivka was intrigued.

"But not now," Rivka suggested, her tone searching, hoping.

Ellen stood up quickly as Tran finished with Bryna, wrapping her up tightly in the thick, white Turkish towels. Ellen dropped her robe to the floor carelessly, revealing her naked body. The tension in the small room rose again as she walked over to a massage table and stretched herself out on it. She couldn't know that Tran, an ethnic Chinese immigrant from Vietnam, had stopped breathing.

"No," muttered Ellen, nestling down into the massage table, her arms cradling her head. "Not now."

Certainly not at the present time. Three daughters came quickly, and by her late twenties Ellen had become one of "those" ladies. What she had, what Max could buy her and her family, was simply what was due. She never paused to consider where the money came from or whether it had been difficult to obtain. These issues were not important to her. Simply, she lived for the day, which came when she reached thirty, when Max informed her that when she went shopping at Holt's there was no longer any reason to look at the price tags. With this news, Ellen was complete. And having achieved this level of uncaring and unconscious affluence, she was determined to keep it.

It also signalled what Ellen had titled in her mind "The Age of Not Caring." And whose fault was that? Who started it? The guilty party? Did Max care to join her at the annual Canadian Jewish Association dinner to honour Chaim Weizmann? He didn't care. Would Ellen prefer to see Nureyev on the Thursday night premiere or the Saturday? Ellen didn't care. Do we spend one week at Vail and one week in Palm Springs? Don't know, don't care. Just make a decision.

There was no creaking, no splintering, nothing broken. They just drifted, inexorably, apart. This happens all the time, Ellen thought to herself. It is that natural state of all our friends. You cannot sustain. Life wasn't meant to be like that. It stands to reason. Two people. Maintain.

Something. Something. And it still to be good after so long is, well, unreasonable. Happiness is attenuated and happiness is strained and happiness isn't all it is made out to be; there are other things to consider. The girls. Our friends. Our security.

For Max, achieving this level of financial security meant that he was steps closer to his goal of giving it all up. He had never hidden his promise from Ellen, but she always managed to laugh it off. This could not be a serious wish, she thought. She indulged it as one would a childish whim. She should not have been shocked, then, when Max, having achieved the age of forty-two, gathered his wife and daughters around him on the eve of the Sabbath and announced with warmth and humility that he was retiring from the law firm he had founded twenty years previously. He informed them that he intended to keep the promise he had made to Avigdor Schemler (of blessed memory) but that their lives should not be gravely interrupted.

However, certain things would have to change. The Sabbath, for example, which they had celebrated after a fashion, was now to be strictly observed. The girls were going to have to start dressing a bit more modestly, and dating would be forbidden. The house would have to be koshered from top to bottom – no more pizzas from Mama Mia – and his wife and daughters were expected to make use of the local mikvah.

Ellen had listened carefully to Max as he set out his plans for them. She was too smart to show emotion, preferring to let her husband dig and dig the grave that she was about to plant him in. So she waited, and when Max was finished, she stood and walked around the kitchen table so that she stood behind their three daughters. Together they formed a formidable tableau of resolute, feminine will.

Ellen stood up tall, and one peering in on the scene would have been startled by the intensity of the raw sexual power that came off her face and body. Max was awed and confused. Ellen drew in a long breath and then simply said, "No."

Max started to reiterate his position, but Ellen cut him off. Their eldest daughter stood up beside her. Ellen's hands went to the shoulders of the two daughters who remained seated, peering at their father as though he were a specimen. Ellen drew herself up, daring him to look at her, to look at his wife and imagine her going to a mikvah.

"Not for love, Max. Not even for you," she said. "How could you even ask me?"

"I'm your husband," Max whimpered. "You …"

And Max knew then what he had only feared before. He had left it too long. He suddenly saw himself as Ellen and his daughters must have seen him and realised what a pathetic, ridiculous figure he struck. In their eyes, he had ceased to become a reasonable, likeable person with whom one might have an empathetic relationship. No, in their eyes, Max had become a thing. A funny, curious thing that made money. A thing that had odd ideas, puzzling notions, but a thing nonetheless. And one didn't have to listen to a thing. A thing was not to be obeyed.

Of course the answer was no. He merely had to think about it, all of it. Their house, the Manhattan brownstone, the Safdie-designed villa in Jerusalem they shared with Metzger and Dougie Lewittes, the manor in the Midi Pyrennes. All of it, everything. Was this the vengeance that Avigdor had blessed? Max then looked at his wife, her face shiny with anger and vindication, her body bursting with sexual energy. No. The answer was no.

That night, Ellen tried to make it up to Max by initiating a kind of sexual contact that, previously, Max had been unable to resist. His body, however, refused to respond. Affronted, Ellen tried again, and then again, but Max's body remained inert and unresponsive. He even had the nerve to apologise.

That was eight years ago. For eight years Max and Ellen continued to share a bed but did not have sex. After failing to keep his promise to Avigdor, the idea of sexual contact with his wife seemed to Max repellent. She disgusted him physically, and desire ceased to course within him. Ellen passed right through her sexual prime without a lover. Max passed into his fifties with only a vague memory of what a physical relationship was.

It was a scandal that provoked pity among the friends and a bizarre sense of tragic awe among the women. Such a handsome, striking man, such a lusty, hot-blooded woman as Ellen, and no sex. Ellen wore this as her cross, sublimating all her energy and urges into her social life, spending money and raising her daughters. The girls, of course, were not unaware of the impasse between their parents. Once, late on a Friday night in mid-winter, the middle daughter dared to broach the subject with Max.

"Why don't you sleep with Mom?" she asked, expecting the worst but thinking it worth the risk.

"We do sleep together, honey," Max replied, trying to continue reading his selection from Maimonides' *Guide for the Perplexed*.

"You know what I mean," she insisted. "Why?"

Max looked up and stared at his daughter with a blank, slightly bemused expression. She stared back with a contempt that was far more sincere and powerful. Max then smiled, trying to brush aside her challenge with a display of well-rehearsed, but ultimately false, warmth. His daughter stared into the emptiness of his face, his thing face, and stalking away from the table muttered, "You're such an asshole."

Max could not manage to make himself angry.

So Max Schemler was unhappy, but, as we can imagine, deeply, completely unhappy. His unhappiness made him more removed, more detached, and the impression he made at work was therefore more awe-inspiring. What was behind his silent, grave, thing-like face? Metzger didn't really know. Lewittes could only guess. Jacques Vaillancourt, Max's roommate from Sherbrooke, only thought he had the answer, but all this served a greater good. They left Max alone.

His business, at this point in his career, basically ran itself. The junior staff took care of the quotidian un-pleasantries of the firm, leaving the senior partners only those cases and issues that required the human touch. And in that upper echelon of legal practise, Max was placed at the pinnacle. Even his peers reserved Max as a kind of Imperial Guard, brought out only when the cavalry and field howitzers had already softened up the issue.

He could have carried on in this manner for years, but each time the sun set and Max found himself not davening with the elders of the shtiebel but rather at the opera, at a museum opening, a fund raiser or other social event, his soul was further desiccated.

Impossible to live with a desire burning so strongly, feeding so completely on hope. The last thing we can say about Max is this: If he had been wrong, well then, Max would have been able to accept the circumstances and would have simply carried on as best he could. But every time he found himself in a synagogue or at a Jewish society event or whenever the Lubavitchers would descend on the office for their biannual shmear, Max was taken, like a blushing, red-cheeked bride, with the overwhelming notion that he was living in sin. This desire to withdraw from the material world and enter the spiritual was right. Max was right and right was right. Why couldn't Ellen see this?

There was a final straw. It didn't result in any immediate change to the familial status quo, but it dimmed the lights and primed the curtains for the next act. Max turned fifty, and Ellen decided to have a few people over to the house on Netherwood Crescent for cocktails, laughs, a little cheer to wish Max well. It was a typical evening, catered to the hilt, only the best and rarest, the men gleaming as though carved from iron wood, the women ripe, tawny with lust bubbling under every pot of flesh.

Max remained, as always, considerate, charming in a back-handed, detached manner, but inside, dying by inches. It was all he could do to remain civil. Metzger presented him with a tentative plan for the summer, a small tour of Southeast Asia.

"Haven't we done that?" Max asked dryly.

"Yes, but this time, as per your preference, we're shipping out on the H.M.S. Glatt Kosher," giggled Metzger. "The ship sails on *schmaltz* and *greiven.*"

"Stop it," Max dead-panned to Metzger's delight. "Stop it, you're killing me."

And as the evening dripped on, with all the Hampstead glitterati getting suitably juiced, Max had an odd, reverse epiphany. Looking around him at all the friendly, amiable faces, the familiar faces of those who allegedly loved and respected him, Max thought, was this so very bad? To be condemned to this level of comfort in a world of so much pain? Lewittes once studied at a Borough Park yeshiva, he kept a semi-kosher home, had a seat at the Bailey Road shul. He appeared happy. So what if his kids brought home *treif* once in a while? Was this such a bad thing, to have a life where everyone was happy?

These thoughts disturbed him deeply, as they were the first indication that maybe he was wrong. He then spotted Ellen across the den, sparkling and scintillating with Brian Wise, the tall blonde junior partner and litigation expert. He could tell Ellen's hormones were on high alert, as the sex was coming off her in waves. Young Brian, himself possessed of a fine Ellen-in-training wife, was not oblivious. They were sucking each other's breath as though it were the life force itself.

OK, thought Max. All right.

Preparing for bed, Ellen knew, through her extraordinary feminine sense, that something, in this case, Max, was up. So she took time in her bathroom to make herself interesting. She left on her make-up but removed her lipstick. She refreshed herself, spraying her body strategically with perfume. Removing her clothes, she slipped into a diaphanous nightgown that was, for all intents and purposes, transparent. It was in a shade of dark green, and her lush body was clearly visible as though through a screen of smoke.

She was definitely on her game, and things would have gone her way if only ... if only she had paused to consider that there might have been a reason Max had not taken her, as a husband takes his wife, for almost ten years. If only she had stopped to consider her plan of attack. If only she had merely allowed Max to finish cleaning his gums with his rubber-tipped dental pick. But she did none of this.

Impatient and emboldened, she entered his bathroom as he stood, half-naked, in front of his mirror, his face twisted into a grimace as he performed his oral hygiene. If she had emerged out of herself even for a moment, maybe she would have caught the first signs of annoyance in Max's face. She didn't. Instead, she rested her ass against the commode. She leaned back on her hands, her shoulders rising, her heavy breasts rolling from side to side, her fragrant hair spilling across her neck. She fixed Max with smoky, glistening eyes and spoke in a husky, throaty growl.

"I'm ovulating."

In their almost twenty-five years of marriage, Ellen had often shared the news of her various bodily functions with Max. She assumed, very wrongly as it turns out, that such information was somehow sexually stimulating to him. The fact was that every time, in their more than twenty-five years of marriage, Ellen informed Max that she was "ovulating," he was swept up with an insane, almost irresistible urge, to laugh in her face.

This time, Max merely stopped torturing his gum line for a long beat, and then shot his wife a look of such naked loathing that even she, through her narcissistic stupor, realised that if ever there had been a chance for a sexual reconciliation, she had, by her own reckless mouth, blown it.

More than that, she had fixed in Max's mind, even as he lay beside her still-smouldering body, the idea that something had to change. And soon. Or he would go out of his mind.

Sam and Sonny Singh had been doing business in Central Eastern Europe since 1989, and it was a good business indeed. From their base of operations in the Pointe St. Charles area of Montreal, they shipped container loads of consumer goods into Hungary, Bulgaria and the Czech Republic and imported leather goods, jams and other speciality food items to the West.

The Czech Republic had been a particularly hard nut to crack. The market was already inundated with goods from Germany, Spain and France. Finding a foothold had been difficult, and finding Czech managers who would take care of business without constant supervision was a trial. Lately, however, things had been turning around. Sonny had a tentative agreement to supply Julius Meinl, the grocery chain, with speciality food items from Canada. The contracts had been negotiated by Metzger, but finessing the final details and the signing were to occur in Prague, and Max Schemler was to preside. The partners felt that Max's Czech background and his familiar, though imperfect, knowledge of the language might be an advantage.

Initially Ellen was to have accompanied Max on the trip, stopping in Paris to shop and waiting for Max to join her there for a few days before flying back to Montreal. At the last minute, however, Ellen came down with the flu, so Max went alone, eschewing the offered company of young Brian Wise. Max looked forward to the anonymous solitude that business trips like this afforded.

The last details and contract signing went relatively smoothly at the offices of the firm's Czech partners. The Singh brothers were a bundle of nerves, but Max's presence calmed them. This was a big step for them and a large commitment from Julius Meinl, representing several million dollars. Max's imperturbable detachment allowed him to join the fluttering mitigations into a deal that was fair and that would last.

Sonny and Sam begged off a celebratory glass of Becharovka and, after hearty congratulations, the principals left, leaving Max Schemler alone with Frank Daniel, a Canadian lawyer of Czech extraction.

"What a relief," sighed the younger lawyer. "I can't thank you enough for closing this for us. Have you seen the fax file?"

He indicated several bankers' boxes plump with over-stuffed files and draft agreements.

"It just seemed they would never close. You will thank Metzger for me when you get back?"

"Of course I will," replied Max, gazing over the city towards the castle mount.

"Look, I hope you don't think this is presumptuous, but my wife and I managed to get these excellent opera tickets. It's *Rigoletto* at the State Opera, and we'd be so happy if you'd attend with us."

Max was genuinely flattered by the offer but quietly declined.

"Well, then, how about a quiet dinner, just the two of us? My wife and I can always exchange the tickets…" suggested Frantisek.

"Actually," said Max slowly, "I've changed my flight for the first thing tomorrow morning. I think what I'd really like to do is just spend the rest of the day walking around the old town square."

"Really? Well, then, I'll arrange a driver for you."

Max put on his overcoat and handed his briefcase to Frank.

"No, thank you," said Max politely. "Can you have this brought over to the hotel? Does the Coloniale Café still exist?"

Max Schemler spent some time in the Pinchus synagogue searching the walls for Avigdor Schemler's family. The names of the Czech victims of the Holocaust were written so tightly and covered every square inch of wall space, that after only a few moments Max's eyes began to lose focus. He had to turn away every so often in order to calm down. These were the dead. The holy and blessed martyrs. And the Schemlers? There they were. Avigdor's brothers and sisters. There were a few cousins and one or two uncles.

Max removed the small moleskin diary from his jacket pocket and wrote down some names, wrote down most of them and then, drowned by the futility, he stopped writing. Something had to change. Something. Right now, Max needed air.

It rains a great deal during the fall season in Prague and as the afternoon sky darkened, the drizzle turned into a grey, steady downpour. The busloads of tourists vanished off the streets, disappearing into the Pinchus and Maisel and the Klausen synagogues. Or they found shelter in the shops and boutiques of the Old Quarter. Max zipped up his Barbour and headed for the old Jewish cemetery.

The rain had driven away all the visitors, and even the Czech guardians had found themselves some place nice and warm and safe. Max Schemler was the only person to be found that afternoon picking his way through the collapsed and leaning tombstones. Max followed a visitor's path laid out by cordons of rope and a pamphlet he had picked up at the ticket booth.

The air had been refreshed by the chill rain, and Max found himself breathing the cool air deep into his lungs. He began to focus more intently on the cemetery and to marvel at the number and state of the thousands of headstones. Avigdor Schemler (may G-d rest his soul) had never returned to Prague after the war. Max himself had no delusions regarding the spiritually renewing powers of "roots" trips. However, he had to admit that, as he stood there all alone, in the six-hundred-year-old necropolis, that he was beginning to feel better. His soul, cramped after travelling around for the last decade in the small box of his disappointment and fear, was beginning to unravel and stretch. It was like taking off too-tight shoes after a long hike. The relief was deep and made Max giddy with energy.

He found the tomb of Rabbi Liwa ben Bezalel, known more commonly as Rabbi Löw, and noticed an image of the Rabbi's Golem in the pamphlet he had picked up at the ticket booth. He remembered, with cloying nostalgia how Avigdor Schemler used to entertain him when he was a boy with tales of brave Rabbi Löw and his son-in-law Rabbi Katz. How they created Yossele, their Golem, an artificial man, out of clay, to serve them and protect them from evil, and how it confounded every good intention by an act of clumsiness and stupidity. He remembered how his mother Ruth would gently cuff and curse him when he tripped over his own feet or knocked something to the floor, "What is with you, you little *goylem*? Out from the kitchen!"

As he tried to remember specific references to Golems he had found in the Talmud, something stung the side of Max's face. He raised his hand quickly, expecting to feel the brittle, fuzzy body of a bee or a wasp stuck to his face, but there was nothing there. And yet the echo of the pain lingered. Another stinging pain, this time on his forehead, and again there was nothing. Nothing.

It's the rain, thought Max. This stinging cold rain. He looked again at the tomb of Rabbi Löw and noticed that the rope cordons allowed the visitor to walk completely around it. Crammed into every cranny Max noticed notes addressed to the rabbi similar to those that Jewish people cram into the crevices at the Wailing Wall. Now this was curious, thought Max, this gentile-like appeal for intervention. He wondered what people were asking for these days. Looking about, Max noted that he was still quite alone. He picked up a sodden note and unfolded it carefully. It was written in Czech, and he could not make it out. He replaced it and tried another. It was in English and though the ink had run, Max was able to make out

"...tell my father to let me go... as it is killing me..."

Shocked, Max hastily folded the paper and thrust it back into its nook. He felt foolish, but he took out his moleskin and was about to write his own wish when he noticed the pages of names he had written back in the Pinchus shul. It seemed to make some sort of sense, so Max tore out the sheet of names, the names of the dead, his dead and martyred family, folded them up and searched Rabbi Löw's tomb for a safe place to put them.

All the obvious places overflowed with notes. Max kneeled down and searched the base, and close to where the side of the tomb entered the sacred earth he found a hole and into this hole Max placed his notes. And then, for no particular reason, he clawed up a small, walnut-sized mound of earth and folded it up in another sheet of paper torn from his moleskin.

On his way out of the cemetery, Max passed a line of stalls selling tchotchkes and engravings and postcards from the old Jewish Quarter. One stall sold nothing but Golem figures in every size and for every pocket. Max thought of his daughters; perhaps the youngest would like one of these tiny statues? Max noticed that all the Golem figures were exactly alike. He marvelled, in an appreciation of pure market forces and commercial design, how standardised the figure had become with its atypical head, its squat barrel-like torso and unarticulated limbs. Each figure had a small crack in its side where Rabbi Löw was supposed to have inserted *shem*, the life force that powered his creation. Looking up, Max noticed a display of books, all with the same cover art, but in perhaps twelve languages, on the subject of the Golem myth.

As he walked away from the Jewish Quarter, his Barbour zipped up tight against the chill, he let the falling rain wash away the dirt that clung to his fingers and stuck under his fingernails. Max thought that he would take his little lump of earth back and carry it to Avigdor Schemler's grave. In the spring, on the old man's yahrzeit he would sprinkle it on the grave so that, somehow, the old and the forgotten would be rejoined. At least, that was the plan.

But what force led to the Old Town Square, may we ask? And what made Max Schemler stop to look again at the famous clock tower, the Hapsburg-yellow buildings, the plump, pretty little Bulgarian prostitutes trotting about on needle-sharp, stiletto heels?

"Hi, would you like to go have a drink?"

She was probably eighteen years old, but the monster of sexual awareness was upon her and Max observed, that like all true professionals, she led from the hips.

"Come, let's go have a drink. Where are you from?" she sang by rote in a powerfully accented, phonetic English.

It was like looking into a fun house mirror, a distorted reverse universe where his wife, the former Ellen Shatsky, a woman known for being sexy, had been distorted and shrunken down to this potent, caricature lust bomb, with none of the finesse and all of the juice. I am going out of my mind, thought Max, noticing, that for the first time in years, he had an erection that was not related to the morning need to micturate.

That night in his hotel bed, Max had a very odd and powerful dream. It disturbed him greatly, causing him to turn and roll, but it did not wake him. In the morning, when he rose at six to prepare himself for the flight home, he felt himself vibrating. He could not remember even the slightest

The Golem of Hampstead

detail of his dream, no matter how hard he tried to concentrate. It was all shadows, there was no form. But he had been left with an answer to his problem. A solution to his unhappiness. Something was going to change.

There was a time when Ellen would meet him at Dorval Airport after a business trip. When they were younger they would often never even make it into the city but would take a room at the Dorval Hilton and simply disappear for a few hours. Sometimes longer.

When Max made his way through customs, he found young Brian Wise waiting for him. Max was affronted.

"Did Metzger ask you to pick me up?"

The young man took Max's grip and led him towards the waiting limo.

Max didn't even know why he was angry. Brian was simply following a request. Clearly, the office didn't want him landing without a friendly face there to greet him. What was the problem? They rode in silence, Max going through *The Gazette* with his usual angry rustling. Brian Wise sat watching the city slip by until the expressways were replaced by the duplexes of Note-Dame-de-Grâce, and then the split-level bungalows of eastern Cote S. Luc and, finally the disparate and, at times, architecturally unique homes of northern Hampstead.

As he walked up the front steps, Max felt the little Golem statue in the pocket of his Barbour and, on impulse, handed it to Brian Wise. The younger man was caught off guard. Amused, Max observed his awkwardness.

"Don't let it go to your head. I picked up a gross."

Of course, in his absence, nothing had changed. Nothing, that is, except Max. The daughters didn't notice. Ellen didn't notice. Nobody noticed. It was Max's impenetrable detachment. Nothing got out, nothing got in, but this strange new idea.

Max exchanged minor pleasantries with Ellen, who had recovered from her flu and, as usual for this weeknight, was joining some friends at the symphony. Max waited till she left and assured himself that he was quite alone before descending to the basement.

Inchan, the Filipino girl who lived in the basement maid's room, was off that night. Max only had to watch the clock for when the daughters came home. He went towards the back of the basement to the sub-basement that housed the wine cellar, his workshop and the entrance to the garage. These were generally conceded by the entire household as his places. No one, not even Inchan, ever came here. There was another door to the garage from the side of the house and another from the basement rec room that his daughters and wife used. The steps leading down to the workshop door were too dark and scary for any of them.

Max entered his workshop for the first time in months. There was a time when he was a regular visitor. He had prided himself on being good with his hands and handy around the house. He loved to make things and had an admiration for good, precise tools and machines. He had quite a collection, but after a while there didn't seem to be much point. None of the furniture he made went well with Ellen's taste. If something needed repair, Ellen preferred to entertain a parade of fix-it types and servicemen than bother him. In fact, beyond changing light bulbs, Max could not remember the last time he had actually had to do anything in his own home.

In the centre of the workshop was a massive four-by-eight foot work table which Max now cleared. Although he really didn't know what he was doing, anyone spying on him would have thought that he was following an intricate and well-known ritual. Max went up to the garage. Along the back wall, beside the cord and a half of stacked fire wood, he found what he was looking for. Two large yellow plastic bags of black earth. His middle daughter had caught the gardening bug a couple of years back and though the bite didn't last longer than one season, these bags of earth remained. Max humped first one, and then the other down into his workshop and closed the door.

Max was not artistic by any means, but within a couple of hours he had managed to fashion the mounds of black earth piled onto his work table into the shape of a man. He worked from memory of a summer on

Bradley Beach, New Jersey, when he and a friend had sculpted a figure out of wet sand on the beach. That time the figure had been a woman. Max had watched as his talented friend had shaped and defined the limbs and the torso, striving for proportion and symmetry. Now Max did the same. He moistened the earth with a watering can and moulded it, using his own arms and legs as guides. Slowly, the figure of a man stood in relief from the earth on the table.

Max glanced at his watch and was alarmed to see how late it was. He wiped off his hands and stepped quickly into the house, heading for his study. Even in the dark, Max's hand fell exactly on the right text. He placed the red leather-bound book under his arm and went into the vestibule closet to find his Barbour raincoat.

As he descended toward his workshop, he heard the front door open and his two youngest daughters enter the house, followed quickly by Inchan, who caught up with them inside. Their giggling laughter faded as he stepped down deeper under the house. When he re-entered his workshop, he was caught up short by the figure on the table. He had done a far better job than he thought possible. He opened the book, propping it up beside where the figure lay. Using two fingers, Max carved out a hole in the earth man's side and, unwrapping the folded paper, placed the earth from Rabbi Löw's tomb inside. Smoothing it over with his moistened hand, Max covered his head, turned to the text and began to recite. He spoke softly, allowing the rhythm of his laboured breath to dictate the cadence of his invocations.

Nothing happened. Max kept it up for over an hour, following his instincts, praying for deliverance and hoping for relief, and still nothing. His sensitive ears picked up the sound of Ellen's Mercedes pulling into her garage space and the door coming down. He looked at the earth man stretched out like some beachside novelty attraction and, for the first time, a feeling of embarrassed foolishness crept into his mind.

He collapsed onto the floor, his back against a half-opened sack of fragrant black earth. He buried his face in his hands. I have to see someone, thought Max. This is not normal. I am not normal.

He rose, straightening himself up, and reached out to close the red-bound book when his eyes caught his hands. They were caked with dirt, mottled by the stain of the earth. If I am nothing but dust, he thought, then he and I are brothers. Impulsively, Max leaned down low over the earth figure, leaned down so that his mouth was directly above where the figure's mouth would be if Max had possessed the skill to have formed one. He uttered a brief prayer to G-d, creator of man, and then, carefully fastening his mouth onto the form, breathed into it.

Instantly Max's mouth was on flesh. Cold, wet flesh. Max recoiled in blind panic as he beheld what he had created. A Golem, in his own image. He slammed his hand over his own mouth to stifle the cries of shock and exaltation rising in his throat. Golem was a perfect replica of himself. Precisely, hair for hair, each pore and beauty mark a clone of the original item. What caught Max up and entranced him was that this was not a mirror image reversed by the physics of optics. This was him! It was Max Schemler presented in a manner that perhaps only twins can delight in.

Max observed, with a skip in his chest, that Golem didn't seem to be breathing. It lay still, inert. Dust. A cadaver. *What have I done?* thought Max, his detachment ripped and tattered like a storm flag in a hurricane. Above, Max could hear the strident, crisp click of his wife's heels on the rosewood parquetry. He knew he would start to be missed and, wiping himself down, Max prepared to make his appearance. Leaving the workshop, he cast a last, lingering look at Golem, still unmoving, laid out on the work table. It was a luminescent figure, pale and so vulnerable under the hanging fluorescent fixture. Max felt an odd sensation in his chest. What was that? Empathy?

Did he help design this house for some future subterfuge as yet undreamed of at the time? Max was able to slip from the workshop into the garage, up the rear stairs that only Inchan used, to the second floor corridor, through the linen closet, into his study and through to his bathroom without anyone noticing. Pausing for a moment to refresh himself, he examined his face in the mirror and saw that he really was completely decomposed. His detachment had fled, he looked screamingly engaged, and he resolved to quash this emotion immediately.

When Max joined his wife and two of his daughters in the kitchen, where they were muttering sharply over instant coffee, he had reassumed his regular, bland demeanour. Nothing was up. Certainly not Max Schemler.

He needn't have worried. He could have shown up with Inchan's severed head poking out of his pants and no one would have noticed. There were no welcoming noises, no display of teeth through smiling lips. They barely stopped their bitching. Ellen did eye him for a moment as he approached the refrigerator, but she returned to sniping at her eldest daughter when he retreated. Max backed out of the kitchen, holding the scene in one eye as he carefully closed the other.

Later, Ellen never noticed him slip out of bed. She had dropped a couple of Ativans and had her ears stopped up with wax plugs. The girls' rooms were far along the corridor, and Inchan was a heavy, snoring sleeper. Max opened the door to the workshop slowly, his heart racing with adrenalin-fueled anxiety. All was as he had left it. It wasn't till he was within a couple of feet of the work table that he noticed that Golem's eyes were open. Max felt his entire body swell with, with what? Was this pride?

Golem breathed in irregular, shallow gasps, and Max feared that perhaps something was lodged in its throat. Golem rolled its eyes down and, for the first time, saw Max Schemler, and quickly its breathing became deeper, more regular, and eventually Max realised that he and Golem were breathing exactly the same.

"Who am I?" Golem asked, its voice Max's, if somewhat drier.

Max stepped back, seeking with his hands the support of the work bench. A man could explode, he thought. He gathered himself and approached the figure on the work table.

"You are Golem," he said, growing in confidence as his creation followed him with its eyes. "You are Golem, and I made you."

Golem slowly stretched out his hand and Max, confident now, took it, pleased at its familiar dimensionality and texture. Pulling on Max,

Golem lifted its upper body into the vertical and allowed Max to swing its legs over the side of the table. Golem's eyes fixed on its feet. It seemed intensely interested in every part of itself. Finally, Golem raised its head to fix Max with its eyes.

"Why?"

Max drew Golem to its unsteady, but strengthening legs and, holding him at arm's length, said evenly, with perfect detachment.

"To help me."

Holding Golem's hand, Max led him up into the garage.

"Remember this path up from the workshop. If you ever need to speak with me, that is where I'll be."

Golem nodded, taking in the house as they ascended.

"It's as though I have been here before. Have I?"

"In a way, I suppose you have. We will have to find out how much you know of me. How much of what I know, is in you."

Once on the second floor landing, they moved swiftly into Max's study.

"If, for any reason, you need some peace and quiet, if you simply want to disappear, this is the room. They never come in here."

"Never in here," repeated Golem.

Max led him into his walk-in closet and showed him the shirts and suits, the underwear drawers and the shoe cubby holes.

"Every day you take a fresh shirt and choose a different suit. It doesn't matter which you pick, it will all look fine. If it doesn't, she'll let you know."

"She?" said Golem, putting on a pair of Max's pyjamas with movements so deliberate and familiar that once again, Max's heart swelled.

Max motioned Golem to follow him into the bedroom. Ellen was deep into some beautiful, drug-laced, dream. She was at Holt's, and a gorgeous young saleswoman was helping her into a pair of Manolo Blahniks, telling her to "...take them, just take them, they are only good for you..." Golem observed her, surprising Max by sitting down on the bed in the curve formed by her bent legs and waist.

"All you have to do is say 'Yes,'" Max whispered. "Whatever she says, you just say yes. You agree with her. If she asks you a direct question, simply raise your head and look into her eyes. In a few moments she will tell you the answer. And then you say 'yes.'"

"Yes," replied Golem, its eyes fixed on Ellen.

"Same with the girls."

"The girls. I say yes."

"Yes. And smile. Not often. Just every so often, smile at the girls. It makes Ellen feel good."

"Smile," repeated Golem, trying one on for size.

Max was startled by the effect. For the first time, he didn't recognise his own face. Who was this charming man? From where came this warmth, this comforting, crinkle-eyed fellow? Had it been that long since he had been happy?

They finished the tour of the house, with Max pointing out the important points; the house alarm system, which Abloy key went where. At first Golem tried to take his hand as they went from room to room, but after a while Max would not let him. From then on, they moved like substance and shadow, synchronised like schooling fish. They ended up sitting in Max's Jaguar in the garage.

"Are you getting all of this?" asked Max as Golem clicked through all of Max's pre-programmed stereo stations.

"Yes. As soon as you talk of something, it's there," replied Golem, pointing to its head. "It's here."

"Tonight, you will stay in the workshop. In the morning, I'll bring clothes for you, and we will leave together. I'll show you the route to the office and to the shtiebel where I will be most of the day."

"Shtiebel," replied Golem.

"Yes. The shtiebel is where I will be, studying, praying. I can see that this is going to work out perfectly."

"But what am I to do?" asked Golem as Max led it down to the workshop.

Max opened up a summer chaise lounge and laid Golem down in it. He kneeled down beside his creation, looking into its eyes, marvelling yet again at what he had done.

"I told you. You are going to help me."

"Help you?" repeated Golem, apprehensively.

"Yes. I made you," said Max, reaching out for some of the dirt on the work table. "And I made you to help me."

Max opened his hand and allowed Golem to look at the earth. Golem's apprehension seemed to fade. He sighed and lay back, his eyes returning to Max's.

"To help you," said Golem with a sense of detachment and finality that was Max's hallmark.

The next morning, Max Schemler was so giddy with excitement, that he almost blew it. He practically sprang out of bed like a newly shorn lamb. Ellen eyed him with a flicker of suspicion, but as soon as he felt her scrutiny, Max calmed himself, masking himself behind his usual indifference. He needn't have worried about his daughters; he barely registered on their radar during the best of times. Max did wonder, however, about Inchan. Generally, she took her cues from the women in the household, but he speculated that she was more sensitive than they were when it came to him. Still, no, she did not give the slightest indication that anything was amiss. Perfect, thought Max.

After dressing, he carried a suit and other clothing down to the basement as though preparing it for the laundry. He needn't have bothered. No one noticed, no one cared what he was up to. He found Golem as he had left it, lying on the chaise lounge, eyes open, not anticipating, not wondering, not anything. Max thought wryly to himself that Golem's natural state was so much like the one he had assumed over the years. Detached, adrift, one to himself with no port, no safe harbour and no real need for one.

He helped Golem dress and noticed how swiftly it picked up cues and routines. He watched as it buttoned the clean white shirt he had brought down, watched as the hairy knuckles curled as each mother-of-pearl button slipped through each hand-stitched oval. Uncanny. When it was dressed, Max stepped back to admire his work. It unnerved him, juiced him with giddy, bubbling emotion to see Golem assume a pose, one hand in a pants pocket, the other brushing back its hair.

Max led Golem up to the garage to the Jaguar, letting it into the front passenger side and instructing it to crouch on the floor and to keep its head down. He activated the garage door and noticed his youngest daughter had left her bike, again, directly in front of his car's path. She never left it in front of Ellen's car. Always his. Now, some dime store therapist, such as Ellen had once dragged him to a few years into their celibacy, might have read this as a daughter's cry for her father's attention. Indeed, it was such an obvious notion that Max thought he should pay attention. He took the time to seek out his youngest, to engage her in conversation, to be in the same space as she. It didn't work.

"I don't need you, Daddy," she said finally, after he had tried once again to attract her confidence. "Just leave me alone, please."

At least she had been civil. Max moved the bike to the side – maybe she just did this to piss him off? – and took the driver's seat. Golem craned its head up to watch.

"Keep your head down till we get moving."

"I can drive, you know," replied Golem evenly.

The Jaguar slipped slickly through misty, early morning Hampstead, encountering only a few joggers, Italian gardeners and other servicemen. There were a few Filipino women walking family dogs that had been marginalised soon after losing their puppy cuteness. What a shit hole, thought Max.

With Golem paying close attention, Max showed it the route to the shtiebel, and then the route to the office. Golem reacted to everything as though experiencing a long spell of déjà vu. Nothing surprised it. Several times it opened its mouth as if to say something or raised its hand as though to point at something familiar. Otherwise it sat, taking on the aspect of a creature drinking after a long-suffered thirst.

At the office, Max drove into the underground garage and parked in his spot. The firm had its own set of elevators, so Max told Golem to wait while he went up. As soon as the information came to it, Golem was to follow. It worked perfectly. It seemed, whatever Max thought of or experienced found its way to Golem and became part of the creature's knowledge. Golem pressed the correct button, got out at the right floor, made its way through the executive lobby down the corridors to Max's office.

Max was waiting for it and when Golem was safely inside, he closed the door, locking it.

"Sarah will come in here at 9:00. She'll leave anything for your immediate attention in this box here. Messages will appear on your computer screen here."

Golem seemed fascinated by the large dark office forty stories above the city. In the near distance, downtown Montreal was laid out like a grid, the morning traffic proceeding sluggishly down René Levesque. Further north, the streets rose up the side of Mount Royal, and Golem's eyes were drawn north to the mountain itself, now mottled with fall colours.

"It's so quiet," it said after a moment. It turned to face Max, who was busy clearing his desk. "What will I do?"

Max smiled and led Golem around to the conference area, which consisted of three couches arranged around a low coffee table. They sat facing each other.

"That's the great part. Nothing. You do nothing," said Max, getting giddy again.

"You work here," replied Golem.

"And you will too. Look, I'll show you," he said, getting up. "Let's pretend someone knocks on the door and enters and asks you about a divorce case."

"Divorce."

"You simply look up from the desk, pause a minute, then say 'Metzger.' Then you return to reading something."

"Metzger," said Golem, rolling its tongue over the name.

"Suppose someone comes in with a question involving taxes. You do the same thing. Look up, pause – you can even look out the window for a moment – and then you say, 'See Lewittes.'"

"Window," said Golem. "Lewittes."

Golem rose and walked slowly over to the window, seemingly charmed by the view. Max sat down on a couch, watching. Golem stood at the window, turned its head towards the door, waited a beat, and said, "Lewittes."

Max clapped his hands, delighted.

"Perfect! And if someone comes in with a question you don't understand, simply look them in the eye for as long as you care to, and eventually, they will leave. I'm famous for that," said Max, stretching himself, almost laughing out loud.

Golem turned from the window and took his seat at the huge, cherry wood desk. Max was sitting with his back to the door when Sarah opened it with her key. She stopped in her tracks, startled to find the room occupied.

"Oh! I'm so sorry, Mr. Schemler," she cried, addressing Golem. "I didn't know you were in a meeting."

Max did not turn his head but stared straight ahead, daring not even to breathe. His eyes darted over to Golem. It was in the act of raising its eyes to look directly at Sarah.

"Shall I bring in coffee for you and your guest?"

Max watched as Golem held Sarah's eyes with his own. There was no expression on its face, just a steady stare. After only five seconds, Sarah backed out, bowing and scraping with apologies and excuses. As she closed the door, Max sprang to his feet.

"How does it feel?" said Max, clapping Golem on the shoulder.

"Feel?" asked Golem.

Max Schemler paused at the door to the shtiebel, paused a moment before plunging into his new life. It wasn't that he was nervous, but that giddy feeling was welling up inside him and he didn't want it to show on his face. Calming himself, he entered, placing his kippa on his head, touching the mezuzah on the door frame and taking a quick survey of the room. It was after the morning services and most of the elderly regulars had already shuffled off for their tea and challah toast.

Max's eyes were drawn immediately to Avigdor's old place of honour, a pew on the north side of the room, two back from the altar. There was no one sitting there, so Max slipped into the pew and unzipped his tallis bag. With every gesture and ritual movement, Max felt himself rising, rising higher and higher to a better, a finer expression of his true nature. Everything fit. The sickly colour of the jaded fluorescent light, the smell of mildew and indigestion, the pious bleary eyes. It was all he could have hoped for, and yet so much more.

His arrival had aroused only a tiny stir of curiosity, but now that he had settled into Rebbe Avigdor Schemler's place, the cutting glances and the arched brows fell on him like question marks. Eventually, the shamus, a rambling, fat, balding man, ambled over with the pretext of gathering siddurs. Max had cloaked himself in his tallis, tied on his phylacteries, and was rapidly, but with crisp articulation, reciting the morning prayers, rocking with a practised, controlled rhythm. The shamus nudged him with an inquiring prompt and Max, stirred out his meditative trance, looked the man right in the eye. In an instant, the shamus had him pegged. A smile broke out on his pudgy face.

"Schemler? Schemler!" he cried out, his hand searching for Max's.

Max allowed himself to be welcomed and then, abruptly, went back to the ritual prayer, letting the shamus leave and spread the word: the Rebbe's prodigal son is among us. The warrior prince of Hampstead is here. Now we'll see some davening!

As the news spread, the shtiebel, normally a place for quiet study and meditation during the day, began to buzz and pulsate with a fresh, invigorating hum. By midday, some of the older members had been drawn back, and towards the late afternoon, aggressive young Lubavitchers, some with students, arrived in a noisy, chattering group. All expressed curiosity at the presence of the new man, and all questions were answered by the shamus or by those old adherents of the Rebbe.

Finally, one of the braver Lubavitchers slid into the pew beside Max Schemler and, after a few moments, tried to engage him in a discussion. Pleasantries were exchanged, followed by questions which led to more questions, which led to tiny disagreements, leading to larger disputations and, then they were off!

Golem spent most of the morning gazing quietly out of the huge windows of Max's office. Montreal can be quite beautiful at certain times of year, and Golem had the unique pleasure of looking at the scene with eyes both familiar and fresh. True to Max's word, nothing much was demanded of Golem. Once or twice some young lawyer would knock, then enter, holding a file or two. Golem would respond following Max's suggestions, and the young lawyer would leave.

At around one o'clock, Lewittes entered.

"Going down for sushi," he stated.

Golem thought for a minute, gazing into Lewittes's eyes, but it seemed that an actual response was needed.

"Metzger?" replied Golem.

"He'll meet us downstairs. Come on," answered Lewittes, still holding the door open.

Golem followed Lewittes's lead and in a few moments found itself at a table in the sushi restaurant that was on the ground floor of the office building. Metzger showed up a few minutes later. When the waitress arrived to take their order, Golem was momentarily unsure how to respond.

"Lemme order, it'll be faster that way," said Metzger, taking the menu from Golem's hand.

Metzger rattled off his choices and when the waitress left, he turned to Golem, smiling wryly.

"If we leave it to Barney, we'll be here all day. He's always looking for the smoked sable. Eh, Barney?"

The two men laughed, and their cutting banter continued right through the meal. In this way, Golem learned that it actually never had to do anything or respond to anyone. The other two men seemed to be obsessed with attacking each other, albeit gently, for the amusement of Golem. As one of them scored a little joke or tiny slight against the other, they would look towards Golem as though seeking approbation. Golem would return the inquiring look with one of total, detached, placidity. This seemed to satisfy the other two men completely. They remained, for the entire meal, in the best of humours.

As for the food, Golem had no need for it, so it merely picked, following the lead of the other two. Inadvertently, Golem understood that it was mimicking Max Schemler's behaviour; Max was notorious for picking rather than eating. And so Golem's first real human interaction passed by without incident and without raising any suspicions.

By the time Golem brought the Jaguar to the shtiebel it was after seven. Inside, the men were reluctantly finishing Ma'ariv, the evening prayer, and bidding a sad adieu to Max Schemler, the Rebbe's son. Max, in turn, promised to return soon, and left the basement house of prayer as though walking on winged heels. So, he thought, this is what it feels like.

The sight of the Jaguar waiting patiently a block away brought him down to earth. He had not been able, all through that day, to let go entirely of the fear that something at the office might go wrong. The fact that Golem had not called him on his tiny cell phone had been encouraging, but then maybe it had forgotten the number? Maybe the phone had confounded it? When he opened the passenger door and took in Golem's unperturbed face, all his fears vanished.

"Any problems?" asked Max as they pulled away, Golem driving with uncanny expertise.

"Problems?" replied Golem.

"Trouble. Problems," repeated Max.

Golem drew a breath, thinking. It took a few moments, as though organising its thoughts.

"Jocelyn Dubois' rental deal is going through, but there was a request from the bank for another inspection. The Toronto branch is being audited. There was a request from Hatcher and Hatcher for..."

"No!" Max interrupted angrily, covering his ears. "I cannot hear this anymore. That is finished for me, forever. Of that I am more convinced than ever. I meant, did you have any problems at the office convincing the people there that you were me?"

Again Golem chewed this over before replying.

"How would I know?"

Max grimaced, trying to calm himself. He breathed slowly.

"Did anyone comment on your behaviour? Did anyone say anything such as 'My, you're acting strange today, Max.'"

"No," replied Golem.

"There were no puzzled looks? No confusions? What did you do all day?"

Again, Golem organised its thoughts carefully.

"I looked out the window, at the mountain," said Golem evenly. "Whenever anyone came into the office, I did as you said and they left without saying anything. No, wait, some did say things…"

Max covered his forehead with his hand, feeling himself flush with anxiety.

"Oh no," said Max, shrinking from the inevitable. "What did they say?"

Golem searched its mind again before answering.

"One said, 'Thanks, Max.' Another said, 'Why didn't I think of that, Max? Great idea.' One woman said, 'Max, you are the best. I don't know why I didn't think of asking you sooner.' Then one man said…"

Max cut Golem off.

"That's fine. Fine. You don't have to go through your whole day."

"No," replied Golem.

They rode in silence for a few minutes and eventually entered the precincts of Hampstead.

"Simchat Torah," said Golem suddenly.

"What?" said Max, starting.

"You were thinking about something today. Simchat Torah. You were thinking how perfect it was, this thing, to be starting right now."

Max held his breath. What did this mean, he thought? Will it really know what I know? Will it read my thoughts, know what I am thinking?

"What do you know of my day, Golem?" asked Max quietly.

"I have an... an impression of what you were thinking. Now that impression is coming into focus. I believe that if you think of something, like you were thinking of how to drive this car, that I know it too," said Golem factually.

Well, thought Max, that's not so bad. It doesn't think, but if I think of something, it knows it too. Big deal. Max noticed them approaching his house. He crouched down on the floor, covering his head with his coat and was about to instruct Golem to back in, but he quickly saw that such instructions were no longer necessary. Golem skilfully backed the car into the drive and even activated the garage door. Once inside, Max kept Golem from getting out of the car.

"Remember," he said, whispering. "Ellen. Women are different than men. And Ellen is very much a woman. You must be careful to make no mistakes. Stay out of her way. Spend as much time as you can in the study. She will think this is normal. To any question you answer...?"

"Yes," replied Golem.

"I will be in the workshop if you need me. If you can bring me some food without anyone seeing you, that would be good. After tonight I'll organise things better. Do you understand?"

"And smile," replied Golem, and for a thin moment, Max entertained the notion that it was making a joke. However, it was clear that this was no conscious effort on the part of the creature.

As the garage door came down, Max slipped down the rear steps into the workshop and locked the door behind him. The chaise lounge was comfortable, but he would have to arrange things better. Eventually, perhaps, it would be necessary to rent a small room near the shtiebel. All would depend on how well Golem could keep up the pretense.

Apparently, it could keep it up rather well. Golem entered the rec room from the garage to find Max's youngest daughter stretched out on the floor watching the television. It carefully stepped over just as the girl turned over onto her back, leaving it straddling her waist. The girl looked up at it, and it looked back at her. For want of clear instructions, Golem thought for a moment and then smiled. It had been quite a while since the youngest daughter had seen her father smile or been this close to him or caught him in such an odd, awkward position.

"Hi, Daddy," she said, without thinking.

"Hi," said Golem, and as the girl turned back on her stomach, it continued stepping over her and proceeded up the stairs into the main hall.

Ellen had heard the garage open and the muffled voices of Golem and her youngest daughter in the rec room. As Golem appeared, she looked at it quizzically.

"What were you talking about?" she asked.

Golem straightened itself up, looked Ellen coolly in the eye, smiled and said, "Hi." It then headed for the stairs to the second floor. Ellen watched it leave, but as it started to climb the stairs she spoke.

"There's food in the kitchen."

Golem turned at the sound of her voice and, drawing on the day's events, replied, "Sushi."

Golem's serious aspect and the incongruity of its comment caught Ellen off guard, and she burst forth with a snort and giggle. Golem, stuck again for an appropriate response, merely smiled.

"Brisket. From Kosher Quality. You want some?"

Golem was eager to hide itself away in the study but clearly, something else was expected. It knew the kitchen and the rites of eating, and so decided to accept the invitation.

It knew which seat to sit at but when it looked down, the chair was piled high with newspapers. It took a seat that allowed it to face Ellen as she prepared a plate for him. Ellen looked over her shoulder and stopped for a moment when she noticed Golem was not in his usual place.

"Why are you sitting there?"

Golem motioned to the newspapers.

"Well, move them," she sighed.

Golem rose to follow her instructions, but she stopped it.

"Never mind. Leave them," she said, placing a dinner plate in front of it.

Golem noticed that Ellen did not join in the eating. It noticed too that she appeared dressed to go out and kept checking her watch. Ellen opened the fridge.

"Do you want some tomatoes?"

"Yes," replied Golem, observing Ellen as she placed the jar of Mrs. White's pickled green tomatoes on the table. It wasn't sure what to do with them but after a moment, Ellen opened the jar, removed one and sliced it onto a side plate. It ate a slice, with Ellen watching keenly.

"They're good, uh?"

The taste of the pickled tomatoes exploded in Golem's mouth like a contagion, a viral rush. Its tongue felt branded and alive with a craving for more.

"Yes."

There was the sound of something rumbling down the stairs, and Max's middle daughter burst into the kitchen. Immediately she spotted Golem sitting in her usual place.

"Mom, what's he doing in my place!" she cried, like the spoiled brat that she was.

Ellen placed a basket of sliced challah on the table.

"Ask him yourself," she said, checking her watch again.

Golem was already rising out of its seat, ready to abdicate when Ellen spoke up.

"Oh, for chrissake, sit down. She can sit anywhere."

The middle daughter, miffed but also puzzled by this sudden, new arrangement, flopped herself into her father's usual place.

"Fine," she smirked. "Then I'll take your place. That makes me the head of the family."

Golem turned its gaze to her and held her eyes for several long unblinking seconds. It then smiled broadly.

"Yes," it said.

The girl giggled at first, then, under the charm of Golem's smile, started to laugh with a full voice. Ellen clicked in from the foyer, puzzled again by the uncommon laughter around her kitchen table.

"I have to go. Glenda is picking me up for the museum opening."

"Yes," replied Golem, now fixing its gaze on Ellen.

The younger daughter bound up the stairs from the rec room, drawn by the sound of her sister's laughter. She, too, took in the new seating arrangements with surprise.

"I'm your new father," said the middle daughter, imitating Max Schemler's voice and cadence.

"Then I'm the mother," cried the youngest daughter, raising herself on tiptoe and stomping back and forth, a mimed phone pressed to her ear.

The real phone rang once. The lights of a car pulling up in front of the house could be glimpsed through the parlour windows. Ellen reluctantly pulled herself away from the uncommonly warm domestic scene playing out in her kitchen.

"That's Glenda. Girls, leave your father alone to finish. And not too late, it's a school night."

"I'm the father!" shouted the middle one. "I'll decide when I go to bed!"

Ellen leaned down towards Golem, noticing with a tiny flicker of satisfaction that her husband was raising his face to hers.

"I won't be late. Will you be up when I get back?"

"Yes," said Golem, whispering as Max had done in the Jaguar when they arrived.

This had the effect of shooting a shiver up Ellen's spine. As she straightened, she fixed Golem through narrowing, sparkling eyes as though trying to ascertain if he was putting her on or not. Golem went back to eating slowly, methodically.

When Ellen had been gone a couple of hours and the girls were engrossed in a television show, Golem took several food items out of the kitchen and stepped furtively down to the workshop. It tapped on the door lightly, and the door opened as though Max had been on the other side waiting. Golem watched as Max ate hungrily. Max noticed Golem watching him.

"How did it go up there?" he snapped, biting down on a piece of old Hebrew National salami.

"Go," repeated Golem.

"With her!" hissed Max, exasperated.

"She prepared a plate of food for me to eat. I sat in the wrong place. Then it was the correct place. Then, one girl came up and it was the wrong place. Then it was the right place."

Golem stopped as it noticed Max staring at him. It tried again.

"Ellen looked at me with a happy face. She asked if I would be up when she got back."

Max stared hard at Golem.

"You said no?" Max suggested cautiously.

Golem drew himself up straight, considering the question.

"I said yes."

Impulsively, Max dashed his food to the floor and started to pace the small room.

"You said yes?" he exploded.

"You said, 'Whatever Ellen says, I should say yes.' I have said yes to her already several times. Should I now say no?"

Max calmed himself, picking food off the floor.

"No! No, don't do that." Max paused, thinking. "Did she appear odd to you? Funny?"

"Funny?"

Golem was not able to understand the question. Max knew it and decided that no harm had been done.

"Make sure that when she comes home, you are in bed, lying on your side, eyes closed and making this sound..."

Max snored lightly and waited while Golem imitated him, perfectly as usual.

"If she tries to wake you ..." Max continued.

"Wake me," repeated Golem.

"Wake you. Or if she," Max squirmed, searching for the right words. "If she tries to put her hand on you. On your thing..."

"My thing?" said Golem, its face a question mark.

"The thing between your legs!" Max blurted out.

"My thing," said Golem, knowingly.

"Just keep your eyes shut and keep snoring, just like I showed you. After a while she will stop, and then she'll take some pills and she won't bother you again."

"It's no bother," said Golem evenly.

"Huh?" said Max, searching among the food for another scrap.

Suddenly the garage door opened. They could hear Ellen's car backing in. Max pushed Golem towards the door.

"Try to get to the study. Go, go!" he hissed, closing the door after Golem left.

Ellen was actually quite a good driver. She kept her eyes looking out the rear view window as she backed up and so had no problem spotting Golem standing at the back of the garage. Their eyes met, and Golem knew that it should not simply walk away and head to the study. It would have to talk to Ellen. There was no choice.

"Worried I'd scratch the car?" Ellen said, slipping her shapely legs out of her open car door. She hesitated a moment, pretending to reach for her handbag but actually sliding down low in her seat so that her skirt would ride up her legs.

Golem smiled.

"Yes," it said.

Ellen giggled and smiled back. Whatever had got into her Max, she liked it.

"I left early," she smirked, walking back towards Golem and taking his hand. She walked slowly, careful to show the toned, inside flesh of her calves.

Golem felt her firm, strong, well-formed hand and held it firmly. Ellen was caught short by the suddenly familiar, yet exciting, contact.

Her hormones, dormant of late, were suddenly perking up. She reached for the garage door button, leaning across Golem's chest, bringing her mouth near his. It smelled of the earth, warm and dark. Another shiver spiked its way up Ellen's spine.

Max's ear was pressed hard against the door of the workshop as he listened to the footsteps of Ellen and Golem. He was concerned that his wife would begin to suspect things were awry if Golem did not follow his instructions to the letter. On the other hand, it seemed to be doing fine – not exactly as he had anticipated, not precisely as he had wanted – was this the price of the plan he had put into play? Max tried to calm himself. He lay on the chaise lounge, but his mind was racing. He had to be sure.

Max crept lightly through the house, making his way up the rear staircase to the second floor and scurrying along the corridor to his study. Once inside, he moved to his bathroom and cracked open the door. He could see right through to the bedroom and Ellen's bathroom beyond.

Golem was sitting naked on the edge of the bed while behind it, Ellen, wrapped in a plush, white terrycloth robe, brushed her hair. She looked toward Golem.

"Lie down, honey," she said, her voice filled with bells and promises. "Would you like a massage?"

Ellen held up a bottle of massage oil, waving it so that its contents caught the light and shimmered. Golem turned to look, and then lay down on its back.

"Yes," it said.

Max, cursing inwardly, pulled the door closed till there was only the tiniest crack left, but one eye remained cemented to the scene. Ellen left the light on in her bathroom. The bedroom itself was dark, so Max saw everything in silhouette. Ellen stalked around to Golem's side of the bed, rolling the bottle of oil between her palms. Standing over the supine figure, she cocked her head and looked down, slowly taking in the entire length of the creature.

"Turn over," she said, her voice low and humble.

Golem turned over onto its stomach as Ellen dropped her robe on the floor. She was wearing matching underwear, lace-trimmed, French cut. Behind the door, Max took in her broad, lean back, her hips and thighs, full and firm. He had never seen his wife this way, and a feeling of shame worked its way into his guts. Shame, Max, shame!

Ellen uncorked the bottle and worked a quantity of the oil into her palms, warming it. She crawled onto the bed, straddling Golem's waist, settling herself down. Golem did not move.

"Are you feeling all right?" she asked, her voice small and girlish.

"Yes," replied Golem, quietly, almost whispering.

"I like you like this, Max," said Ellen, applying her hands to his shoulders, kneading strongly, the tennis-toned muscles in her forearms rippling.

It was a hallucinatory experience for Max. Every emotion came crashing through all at the same time. Shame was quickly displaced by guilt, larded with resentment, supplanted by anger, chilled by envy and then, burnt to a fine crisp by desire. Desire! As soon as Max recognised what he was feeling, he tried to stifle it but it was too late.

"Turn over," Ellen directed, and Golem complied. Ellen's eyes flitted over the form lying on the bed, stopping suddenly. "Oh!"

Ellen's eyes were fixed on Golem's now rampant genitalia. She picked up the bottle of oil, applied a spilling amount to her palms, and then reached down.

"I really like you like this, Maxie," she whispered, her hormones raging.

Max watched as the shadow of his desire found expression in Golem's physiology. Desire, desire. This was not what he had in mind.

Ellen did not bother to remove her underwear but merely pulled them to one side.

"I want to," she whispered. "Like this…"

"Yes," Golem whispered back.

With a cry and a deep, throbbing moan, Ellen settled herself on top of the creature. Max finally tore himself away. He would not provide the

Golem with the knowledge that would allow him to complete the act, he thought. I will deny her that, at least. Max hurried back down to the workshop; but even as he disappeared into the garage, the faint sounds of Ellen's satisfaction came to him, pulsating throughout the house and resounding as testimony, as the irrefutable evidence, of a healthy sexual consummation.

For its part, Golem knew about the act, but the received wisdom was partial. After this, what? He allowed Ellen to fill the missing pieces. Emboldened by his willingness to please her, and his seeming inexhaustible desire, Ellen took him through every move, every manoeuvre her heart had been incubating for the last unfulfilled decade. She would not stop. She didn't know or care what had brought on this change. She just thought, please, let this go on.

By the time the autumn sun was turning the night black sky a deeper blue, Ellen was, finally, sated. She had noticed that her partner had not flagged the entire night. Had not finished. There were questions, but not the kind she cared to have an answer to. In a few moments she was embracing the neck of Morpheus, her lips seeking a deeper dialogue with sleep.

It was morning now, and on the chaise lounge in the workshop Max Schemler dreamt of being upstairs in his shower, washing himself clean, cleansing his body. In Max's real shower, Golem acted out the same motions but under the sleepy, hungry eyes of Ellen. She had the desire to watch, just watch and try to figure out what had happened. She was barely able to stay awake while her husband seemed completely unfatigued by the night's activity. After a while Ellen crawled back into bed, pulling the covers over her head. She was fast asleep when Golem went downstairs with some fresh clothing for Max.

A couple of hours later, when Ellen pulled herself out of the clutches of the bed monster and made her way downstairs, she found her daughters around the kitchen table sipping cups of coffee and smoking her du Maurier cigarettes.

"Why aren't you in school?" she asked the two youngest.

"Professional day," replied one.

"I've got mid-terms," said the other. Both exchanged conspiratorial glances with the eldest, who kept checking Ellen's face.

Eventually Ellen felt herself falling under the girls' scrutiny. She settled herself down with a cup of coffee and lit a cigarette. Then the giggling started, infectiously, cutting and coy.

"What is with you?" asked Ellen shaking her head, trying hard to suppress a smile.

The two younger girls were leaning on each other with mirthful laughter. Generally speaking, they couldn't stand to be within ten feet of each other.

"What's up with Daddy? He was so weird last night," asked the eldest girl, blowing smoke through her nose, kicking the middle daughter under the table.

"Yeah. Why was he smiling so much?" asked the younger.

Ellen didn't answer but now gave up trying to hide her own smug smile. Her face practically split from contentment. The younger daughter howled and pointed.

"Now she's doing it!"

"Who are you and what have you done to our parents!" shouted the middle daughter, launching herself at Ellen, hugging her fiercely.

The eldest daughter pulled her sister off Ellen and pressed her mouth to Ellen's ear.

"Just tell me. I won't tell them," she whispered.

"No fair!" yelled the middle child, hurt at being cut out of the secret.

Ellen took a sip of coffee and looked at her eldest daughter, who looked so much like her. She hesitated, but the emotion, still bubbling deep in her belly, had to come out, had to be shared. So she brought her mouth close to her daughter's ear.

"Last night," she whispered, "after … he … he didn't get up to wash his hands."

The eldest daughter's mouth dropped open, and she backed away shrieking with surprise and joy. As she ran from the kitchen, the other two girls gave chase, demanding to share in the secret. As the sounds of their play filled the house, Ellen sat, sipping her coffee, smoking her cigarette, squeezing her thighs together.

I've won, she thought. It took ten years, but I've won.

And so every morning, Max would slip into the front passenger side of the Jaguar and crouch on the floor while Golem would take the wheel. Golem would let Max off at the shtiebel and drive on to the office, where it would sit, answer a few questions, smile, watch the sky light change the cityscape below, and then make the reverse journey at the day's end.

The shtiebel became a popular spot after Max began coming on a regular basis. Men who had known Rebbe Avigdor Schemler years before returned to look at him, sit next to him, and finally to engage him in conversation. Max decided his naked face was an affront to these regulars, so he let his beard grow. Naturally, Golem's face sprouted the same salt-and-pepper growth, but Max let his grow wildly, rarely combing it, while Golem's fell under the ministrations of Ellen, who combed and trimmed it while sitting on its lap.

"You are my little Rebbe," she said tugging his chin. "My horny little yeshiva *buchor.*"

Golem indulged her teasing.

"Yes," it said. "I am."

The day came, in early winter, when the late afternoon sky turned dark and the shtiebel glowed against the season's black and white. In the midst of arguing a fine point of Kabbala, one of the combatants turned to Max.

"And what is your opinion, Schemler?"

"Leave him out of this, Avram," cried an elderly Hassid. "He's the son, not the father!"

Max cleared his throat, drawing all to silence. It just so happened that Max did have an opinion. In fact, he had a rather unique interpretation which, when he managed to get it out, caused the room to explode in triumph and indignation. Men, roused from meditative stupor, grasped the situation in an instant and took sides. Alliances were formed and betrayed on the strength of a word misplaced. Battalions running on finely honed, intellectual horsepower were arrayed behind the ranks of the devout. Was this Hebron? Was this Toledo, Mainz, Cairo, Babylon? This was Montreal! This was Max Schemer's world and his birthright. Leaning back, watching the fray from the lofty position of instigator, Max thought that he loved this world. Not the warrior he, now. But the martyr.

Initially, Max had thought it a good idea to find a furnished room near the shtiebel where he could sleep, take his meals, perhaps bring in students to tutor, for his plan was not only to learn but to teach as well. He looked at a few rooms recommended by members of the shtiebel, but as soon as he saw them his thoughts wandered back to his house. Better, he thought, better I sit tight to keep an eye on things. Golem, after all, was not perfect. It made mistakes that, so far, had been lucky errors, but who knows? One day, Max's intervention might be needed.

He directed Golem to clean up the workshop, making it easier to live in but at the same time more cell-like, monastic. It suited Max Schemler to cast himself in the role of Rabbi Akiva, alone in his cave overlooking Kinneret, writing and thinking. Max would sit in his cell, under the house on Netherwood Crescent, under the city of Hampstead, and pray for the mindless, secular lives that passed over head.

And some nights, very late, when the sounds died down, Max would emerge from the workshop and spy on his family. He would watch Inchan as she ironed his shirts for Golem to wear the next day. He would observe her quick, practised movements and listen to her happy humming. He would slip up the stairs to his daughters' rooms, listening to them on the phone, peering through the open doors for a glimpse. He would often find them, sometimes the entire group, in the rec room, in front of the home theatre, watching, *en famille*, a PBS documentary, a rented movie or videotape from the family's past. And a knife would cut through Max's heart.

There it was, the picture he had once cherished. A family, sharing the same space, enjoying the same experience, chattering about it, discussing what they had seen, what they thought. And there, in the centre of it all, was Golem. Stupid, mute, smiling Golem, one hand held by Ellen, the other around the shoulders of a daughter. Once, he witnessed a little struggle between the daughters for the place next to Golem. Max had to turn away.

Back in his workshop, lying on the chaise lounge, Max Schemler had to sort out his emotions. What was the problem? It had all worked out exactly as he had wished. He was free! He had confounded his fate and conjured a better one out of thin air and dirt. That his wife and daughters preferred a compliant, smiling drone to a real flesh and blood husband and father did not surprise him. He knew for years what they wanted. It was what he was unwilling to give them! And so, and so. Still, still.

Calming himself, Max concluded that it was simply the nauseating tug of nostalgia that was clouding the scene. Golem was a thing, one cannot be jealous of a thing. His family preferred to be headed by a hollow creature? Well, what else was to be expected from such women, empty-headed as they were? It was senseless to harbour this anger towards that which he had created. He was above this.

Max Schemler was no longer of this earth. Max Schemler was a mind on the path to seeing the grand design, something even Rebbe Avigdor Schemler (may G-d gather him up) had been afraid to behold. He would succeed where his father had failed and vindicate that failure. Soothed by these thoughts, Max drifted off to sleep, while upstairs, sitting in the warm light of the rec room, surrounded by these women smelling sweetly of tea and honey cake and moisturiser, Golem was overwhelmed by impressions of anger and envy, and the face attached to this knowledge was its own.

It was an early spring that year, and by the end of March there was no snow on the ground, though it rained a lot. Max Schemler had settled into a routine that was leading him further and further away from his family and this world, and closer the next. Golem continued to perform well. Occasionally there was a hitch such as the time that Lewittes had come into the office with a direct question that Golem could not dismiss with a look or gesture. He tried to stare down the younger man, but it ended up with Golem sitting at his chair, staring at Lewittes standing at the door. When Metzger showed up, he took in the apparent showdown and asked what was going on.

"I'm not sure," muttered Lewittes, trying not to crack up. "But this time I'm not backing down."

Finally, after endless minutes, Golem tried his other prescribed response.

"Ask Metzger."

Lewittes finally broke into such gales of raucous laughter that the entire floor came running. Metzger tried to keep a straight face but finally snorted and cracked up, joining his colleague rolling around on the carpet. Golem merely changed its practised smile into something more human. Golem learned then, that it could appropriate behaviour from other people, not just from Max. In this way, its awkward fit in this world became more comfortable.

In the shtiebel, Max Schemler's spiritual evolution was taking its toll on his physical state. His beard had grown quite long, and he had let the rest of his personal grooming go. Previously, Max had visited his barber every week and his natural hirsuteness was, in this way, kept under control. Now his eyebrows had grown wild and bushy, hair pushed out in thickets from his ears, and that growing down from his nostrils joined his moustache in a continuous unkempt lawn. His back, once held straight and broad, was developing an unhealthy curve. He had lost a lot of weight, and there wasn't much fat on him to begin with.

Max Schemler of the Wilderton shtiebel had become an older, distorted version of Max Schemler, respected advocate of the city. Even his hands, his warrior hands, adept at any manual task, paled and became blue-grey, their smooth callouses giving way to an almost transparent, parchment quality.

He was making progress, however. Max had resurrected Avigdor Schemler's (may G-d have mercy on him and bless him!) afternoon Kabbala klatch, and learned men travelled from chaders and yeshivas on and off the island to listen, observe, and engage. Max's name was being uttered in Borough Park and Williamsburg, as well as Saint Eustache. There was a famous colloquium on the meaning of the Sabbath that lasted for over two days, with no conclusions, naturally, but a great deal of high-pitched shouting and the ritual give-and-thrust that is the Talmudic method of disputation. Match your mind against mine, Max would challenge internally, and together we will glimpse that which is invisible to all but those who dare seek it!

A few days later, on a Friday night, after the evening prayers, Golem arrived to pick up Max Schemler. It always parked one block away from the shtiebel so that no one would spot them together, let alone witness Max getting into a car on Shabbos. They had only driven for a few moments when Golem cleared its throat in a manner that was eerily familiar. Max cast a watery blue eye at his creation.

"That's Metzger. Pretty good," he said dryly. "Can you do Ed Sullivan too?"

Golem drove again for a few minutes in silence before trying again.

"I now understand about the Sabbath," it said evenly.

"Do you?" replied Max yawning. "What do you understand, my faithful servant?"

"It is part of the covenant," Golem said, using Max's reasonable voice.

"It is," replied Max, trying not to doze off.

"That which exists between G-d and man," said Golem.

Max turned his eyes to Golem's profile, which revealed nothing. Max's chest went a little cold as he considered the direction of the conversation.

"Stop talking, Golem," said Max firmly, thus ending the conversation.

Golem, however, was just beginning. It waited till dinner with Ellen and his daughters was completed and Ellen had gone to refresh her make-up for the evening ahead. Max gathered some food items and crept down to the workshop, where he found Max davening. Golem laid out the food in what it imagined was an attractive manner and addressed Max's curved, swaying back.

"Ellen wants to join the Calenders downtown for drinks."

Max continued his motions, but his mind was no longer on his devotion. He was, as the English say, all ears. And prickling.

"She wants to drive in the car, handle money. Perhaps she will talk about money as well. She wants to drink and tell stories. She will probably laugh, as she appears to enjoy laughing. She will smoke."

"Yes, Golem," replied Max, his back still turned against the creature.

"All of this is against the spirit and law of the Sabbath. If she does this, if I go with her, we will be contravening the covenant G-d made with man. We will be sinning. I do not wish to sin against G-d. I want to observe the Sabbath and participate in the covenant with G-d."

When the fierce red receded from Max's eyes and he was able to see again and to swallow the angry bile that had risen in his throat, he turned to confront Golem.

"I am affronted by your upstart request," said Max, struggling to control his indignation. "Golem, the covenant of which you speak, is between G-d and man. G-d and man!"

Golem stood dumbly, its face the picture of incomprehension.

"You!" Max exploded, pointing his pale, trembling finger at the stunned, unblinking creature, "Are not a man, you are a thing!"

Golem did not flinch, even as Max's enraged, acid spittle hit its face.

"I made you out of the earth and formed you with my own hands. I breathed *shem* into your corpse and gave you life."

Max snatched some dirt from the work table, shoving it under Golem's nose.

"You are a thing, and G-d does not have a covenant with things," thundered Max, closing it on the mute Golem. "You cannot participate in the covenant, and you may not observe the Sabbath."

Golem considered the impressions that Max had generated. It understood what Max was saying and yet …

"G-d created all creatures. He created everything. All must obey his laws. Not to observe the Sabbath would be a great sin," Golem said quietly.

Max's body started to heave with laughter, his face distorted by the contempt he now felt. He backed away, his fingertips at his lips as he indulged his cruel mirth.

"Really?" sneered Max Schemler in Golem's face. "I have another interpretation, Golem. Are you ready? Try this one: For Golem to observe the Sabbath would, in fact, *be* a sin! A travesty of the covenant between G-d and man. Why? Because Golem is not a man. Golem is a thing."

For a moment, Golem appeared stymied.

"G-d created all things, all creatures," Golem stammered.

Stepping close to the creature, Max cut him off without mercy.

"But I created you," whispered Max, ego and hatred leaking from his mouth. "I did!"

"To help you," replied Golem, as though seeing a larger picture in the confusion that was its mind.

"To help me," said Max, turning back to his evening meditations.

Golem took this as a sign of dismissal. It opened the door to the workshop. They both could hear Ellen call down from the main floor.

"Let's go, Max!"

Golem turned to watch Max, now rocking again over his sacred text.

"If I go out with her, on the Sabbath, I will sin," said Golem quietly. "I do not want to live with sin."

Max didn't bother to turn his head to look at the creature in the doorway.

"A thing," said Max coolly, "cannot sin."

From that night, things went from bad to worse for Golem. It could not let go of the idea that its existence was wrong and by not obeying the covenant, it was sinning. What Max did not understand, maybe we can say, did not want to understand, was that his own plunge into Torah had left moral impressions on his creation. Perhaps if Max has not put on the religious blinders with such eager devotion he might have seen what was happening. As it was, he had only to wait till the next Shabbos before he was delivered of a glimpse into the creature's mind.

Again, Golem waited till nightfall, till Ellen and the daughters were either sleeping or preparing for bed. It made its way down to the workshop with a slow, quiet purpose. Max was already sleeping on the chaise lounge when Golem entered. The creature did not bother to wake him or even close the door behind it. It merely stood over him and recited, as though from cue cards, the substance of its thoughts. With its first words, Max was wide awake, straining to hear but pretending to still be asleep.

"Free will or predestination," Golem began solemnly. "Both are reflections of His will. G-d made all things. He made the earth from which I came, and He made the dust from which you came. You made me, but G-d made you."

Max, feigning sleep, now realised, to his horror, that he had stopped breathing.

"So G-d made me too," said Golem. With that, the creature withdrew, leaving Max wide awake and trembling like a stunned carp on the butcher's block.

Ellen noticed the changes in Golem and tried hard to play them down. She lived in fear that for some reason, unknown to her, things were slipping back to the way they used to be. First, it was Golem's unwillingness to leave the house on the Sabbath. She had grown accustomed to their Friday evenings out and their Saturday shopping – imagine, a husband who smiled and said "yes" when asked to go shopping! It was frustrating that Golem refused to engage her when she questioned it about its growing discomfort. Finally, Ellen suggested the compromise; they would go out but she would drive and she would handle any money or charge cards.

This appeared to placate Golem for a while but then, only a few weeks later, it bucked.

"I'm being a hypocrite," it said, evenly, without bitterness. "It is a sin."

Trying to make light of the remark, Ellen slowly wrapped her handsome arms around Golem's neck, kissed it and said, "I would think that breaking the Sabbath would be the least of our sins lately, honey."

That was exactly the wrong thing to say. Golem began to suspect that their nightly exertions were not entirely kosher. Was all that a sin too, it wondered. And what about the missing part, the part that it had been denied? Was that the sin?

The creature withdrew somewhat both at home and at the office. When it was called in for meetings, it hardly ever sat but paced, its eyes fixed on a window, its entire being exuding the sense of discomfort. This did not escape Lewittes and Metzger.

Then, there was the time when Golem tried to enter the shtiebel in mid-afternoon. It was only Max's bladder that enabled him to avert what would have been a disaster. Coming out of the toilet, Max caught Golem before the creature had been able to take a seat inside. Hustling it out the door and into the street, Max ordered Golem home, forbidding it to ever enter any shul anywhere. Golem meekly obeyed.

Inchan Ferdinand had been used to working for Jewish families, and she knew the evolution of domestic help from employee to "one of the family." She herself had gone through the process a couple of times, and among her friends in the Filipino domestic business it was an old routine. Jewish people, she thought, were uncomfortable with the notion of servants. She didn't know why that was. As she read in her Bible, servants, maids, even concubines were part of the Hebrews' legacy.

Being "one of the family" was a convenient way for Jewish people to absolve themselves of the guilt associated with being able to afford to buy people's time. Buy their lives, actually. Inchan remembered the first time she was let go. Everything had been going very well with the family in the Town of Mount Royal. The husband was an architect, the mother a teacher, the two kids, sweet and good-natured. For a year, everything had gone very well indeed, until one day she had made the mistake of admitting that she had three kids of her own, back in Manila. Three kids. That she hadn't seen them in four years and that she had no plans to visit anytime soon. They were fine in the loving arms of her own mother, so there was no need. Besides, she supported two very large families with what she earned in Canada.

Within three weeks she was provided with impeccable, glowing references and asked to leave. Why? At first they would not say, but Inchan was not stupid. She figured it out.

In any case, she had no problem finding employment right away. She liked the Schemlers, and she especially liked Ellen because for years she had basically stayed out of her way and let her run the house as she saw fit. No one in the house ever questioned her decisions or methods. She had their complete trust. Inchan didn't kid herself about being part of the family, but if the family was more comfortable regarding her in that light, well, it was fine with her.

Lately, however, there had been some odd things. Like how Max and Ellen had rekindled their physical relationship after a scandalously long time. Like how Max Schemler's personality had changed, and for the better. Like how the children were home more often, how laughter was now heard around the kitchen table and how much more a family they all seemed. And how the door to the workshop, a door that had previously always been unlocked, was now always closed. And how Max had taken the household tool kit and moved it into the garage so that when she needed a hammer or screwdriver, she could get it without going into the workshop.

And how there was now the distinct, funky smell emanating from behind that locked door.

"Do you smell it, or am I going crazy?" she asked Ellen.

Ellen's curiosity had been piqued as well. Neither Golem nor Max had been as stealthy as they supposed they were. Ellen was aware that her husband was spending some small time in the workshop. She had assumed he was working on something, but when he reappeared his hands were clean, his clothes unruffled. What was he doing in there? And where was the extra key?

The locksmith from Martin's Swiss Shop had the door opened in about three minutes, but Ellen did not allow him to enter. Waiting till he left, she called Inchan and together they opened the door and turned on the light. The room was hazy with old-man smell. The summer chaise lounge was incongruously out of place. The work table was covered with religious texts and fringed with dirt, and there was a small pail filled with the remains of food from Ellen's table and fridge. Ellen opened several books, recognising them.

"At least he's not looking at pornography," she said, enjoying the mystery.

Ellen was putting it all together in her mind. Something, empathy, stirred in her heart. My G-d, she thought, so this is what he was doing. It was so important to him that he was hiding it from me. Poor little guy, she thought, down in the cellar with his books and his tallis.

"I'm going to have to let him know I've been in here," she said, her heart filling with warm emotions.

"Blame me. Tell him I was looking for a vice grip."

They were both startled by the garage door opening and the sound of Max's Jaguar backing in. It was the middle of the day, what was he doing home? Ellen shooed Inchan away, setting her face to register nothing but acceptance and love. She waited by the workshop door as Golem's footsteps came nearer. Ellen looked up just as Golem's sad face came into view. Golem froze.

"Oh, Max," cried Ellen, her arms out.

Ellen made them both drinks and sat Golem down in the rec room. She knew that somehow, some way, there was a compromise. The last few months had been a victory, but now she was willing to surrender a little. To keep what she had won, she was willing to back down a little.

"I want you to know how sorry I am, my love," she whispered, smoothing back Golem's hair and stroking its beard. "I know. I know now how much you've been torn, and I'm going to make it up to you. I'm thinking now of the both of us. I know there is a way we can both be happy. Will you let me try to make you happy?"

Golem was considering its options. It occurred to it that Ellen was not the woman that Max had warned it against, but what was Golem to do with this? Love. What was this love? Nothing Max had ever thought had ever given Golem an impression of this.

"We have made a home together," continued Ellen, perhaps carried away with the naked emotion of the moment. "We made our daughters and they love you, and I love you, very, very much."

Golem felt its ears ringing. Ellen pulled away slightly, gathering herself.

"A few months ago, you changed. After so long, Max, you changed," said Ellen the tears rising and then spilling out of her eyes. "And I thanked G-d for you. I thanked G-d for you because I knew that he had heard my prayers. And now I know that He brought you back to me because you found something in G-d that let you love me again."

Ellen's wet and crying face was not much like the southern face of Mount Royal, but Golem found it equally compelling. Because it was beautiful. An impression was being formed in Golem's mind.

"Would you come with me?" said Golem, rising and holding out its hand.

"Of course," replied Ellen, drying her eyes. "Just let me put on some make-up."

There were windows in the walls of the shtiebel but they were ground level and so caked with dirt that they were practically opaque. This suited the worshippers inside but momentarily confounded Golem's plans. To her credit, Ellen did not ask many questions. She assumed her husband was going to show her where he had been spending his free time.

Golem removed his overcoat and told Ellen to put it on. He tucked her hair up under her hat until she could have passed for a rebbitzin and then, taking her arm, led her with confident steps into the shtiebel.

No one challenged them as they entered. In fact, in the late afternoon, very few people were inside. Max was there, with a few acolytes and, as luck would have it, he was arguing with a man sitting behind him so that his face was clearly visible from the shadows beyond the entrance. The shadows, which was where Golem had brought Ellen. Golem stood in front of her, backing her into a corner so that anyone looking out would not see her.

Ellen was enjoying the subterfuge immensely. She was not unaware that women are generally not privy to the goings on in such a marginal house of prayer. From behind Golem's shoulder, her eyes roamed the small room, stopping on the greying, animated face of one old man with watery, blue eyes. He was in high dudgeon on some fine point of interpretation, his hands in front of him, shaping and moulding the funky air as though to give limpid form to abstractions. Ellen watched and watched until finally, the old man happened to look up, almost spotting her for a second, before returning to the intractable gentlemen in front of him.

That split second was all it took. Ellen's legs disappeared from under her as her sensibility was carried down, down into thick, unctuous blackness.

Ellen came to in the car. Golem had laid her out in the back seat and was driving towards the house. A strange uncontrollable fear seized Ellen. She did not stir and only glimpsed at Golem from the tiniest crack between her eyelids.

I should wait till the car stops, she thought, *and run. Just run and scream as loud as I can.*

She pressed her eyes tight against the after-image burnt onto her mind. The eyes were unmistakable. The face, though obscured by the beard and the pallor, was Max's. So who was driving the car?

Golem had not been insensitive to Ellen's situation. When she collapsed in the shtiebel, it used a strength it did not know it possessed to carry her quietly out and away. It sensed without knowing how, that Ellen was no longer insensate, and finding a quiet park off Fleet Road, it pulled over and switched off the engine. It turned to look at her lying on the rear seat, her eyes still closed.

"I had to show you, as I didn't think you would believe me. I didn't realise that you would react that way."

Ellen arched up to a sitting position, cramming herself against the door, noticing that the release was locked.

"Who was that?' she cried, putting up a brave front.

"That was Max Schemler," Golem replied slowly. It then smiled, hoping to disarm Ellen's mounting panic.

"Max Schemler, right," she snorted, one hand stealing across the door to the lock. Golem noticed and reached over, popping the door open. The cold evening air chilled Ellen immediately.

"Did you want to get out?" asked the creature. "Why don't you come around and sit in the front?"

Keeping her eye on Golem, Ellen slid out of the back and started to run. Once in the naked air, however, the ridiculousness of the situation stilled her thoughts for a moment. That and the idea that any number of people whom she knew could be watching her through any number of veiled windows right now. That and the image of the wizened, jaundiced face, her future, that creature staring at her from under the grey bushy eyebrows.

She walked back to the car cautiously and bent down, peering in at Golem sitting calmly behind the wheel. *How beautiful he is,* she thought. Golem smiled again, patting the seat beside it.

"If that was Max," Ellen said, addressing Golem through the open passenger window, " then who, may I ask, are you?"

As Golem walked her around the workshop, what at first seemed fantastical and absurd began to accrete the weight of truth. Golem showed her the opened bags of earth, the ritual passage in Max's red-bound Zohar, the Book of the Golem myth from Prague. It described how Max had set up everything, how he had instructed Golem to say yes to her and to smile.

And as the creature spoke, as though it had been evident for all that time, Ellen knew it was the truth. Perhaps she had known all along; known, that is, that something had changed and that the attentive father, the considerate husband, the indefatigable lover were all, in the end, impossible. No one that she knew had what she had. It was too good to be real.

Up in the kitchen, Golem made them a pot of tea. Ellen stared off into space, letting her mind steep in the bitterness. It wasn't true. He wasn't real. He felt nothing but contempt for her. Only a man who hated her could have turned such a creature loose on her. A creature.

Ellen raised her eyes to watch as Golem prepared the tea, loose tea in a teapot, with care and grace. Ellen's eyes fixed on Golem, searching for some sign that it wasn't real, that it was, as it had confessed, created out of a pile of dirt and a few mumbled prayers from a crumbling book. Her eyes bore into Golem, watching the hands, fine and strong, the thighs beneath the finely cut trousers, and the more she looked, the more a delicious and irresistible urge overtook her thoughts. Real? Golem was real, she thought. Like a heart attack.

"He forces me to sin," confessed Golem, setting the tea down on the table. "He knows that he is doing it, but he doesn't care."

"That's terrible," sympathised Ellen, still holding the face of her beloved creature with her eyes. "But, you don't think that we sin, I mean, what we do together…"

The Golem smiled at Ellen, its face so warm and familiar.

"No," it said, with a smile. "I know that is a mitzvah. It is what He wishes us to do."

"It is a mitzvah," Ellen agreed. She reached out to touch Golem's hand, tentatively at first, expecting – what? – but finding it warm, three-dimensional and comforting.

"He is jealous and quick to anger," the creature continued. "And that is when I knew for certain that I was correct and that he was wrong."

Ellen observed the Golem straighten up and square its shoulders. It had a growing, fierce light in its eyes.

"He dismissed every desire I had to be part of the covenant. He tried to convince me that I was a thing."

"Not a thing," said Ellen, both hands now grasping Golem's.

"His jealousy defeated him. I knew then I was correct," it said, looking down at Ellen, her eyes wide and black with wonder. "For how can one be jealous of a thing? One cannot be jealous of a thing. One is jealous of a rival."

Golem pressed Ellen's hands between its own, and the woman's chest flushed with heat, an ache forming in her belly. This, she was unwilling to give up.

"He has become a stranger to me, a dry old man. When I saw him, when I realised what that was, when I thought about lying next to that again ... while you ..." said Ellen, the saliva thick in her mouth. "You are everything."

Golem felt itself being stroked but noticed that Ellen's hands were not moving. It was inside it, unnerving, delicious.

"I considered that, perhaps, if my presence brought peace to this home, that he would go away. It is what he really wants. I know now he will not. It is his jealously and ..." Golem hesitated.

Ellen would not allow this reluctance.

"Tell me," she said, her voice now hard and demanding.

"He delights in your defeat," it said, raising its eyes to the woman.

"My defeat?"

"He thinks that every time we share each other, every time we fulfil that mitzvah, it is your defeat and his revenge. To him, you despoil yourself with a thing, you allow dirt into your body. And he laughs at your degradation."

Ellen steeled herself against her mounting anger. A line had just been crossed and doors had swung shut. She released Golem's hands and sat back in her chair, her eyes downcast.

"But I don't feel that," she started, before her tears began to flow. "When you showed me, G-d help me, it was a thought – I did feel that, but then I remembered and ... " she said, raising her wet face defiantly. "No! You are not a thing. He is a thing. He is inhuman!"

Golem stood and walked over to Ellen, kneeling down to take her into his arms, to comfort her.

"If he would just disappear," she moaned. "Just leave us alone."

"Yes," replied Golem evenly.

Ellen pulled back, taking Golem's face between her warm, smooth palms. She looked at him carefully, then pressed her mouth to the creature's, breathing in his breath hungrily, like someone drinking in air after almost drowning.

Perhaps Max Schemler had sensed something. Maybe when his eyes were flitting in the black shadows beyond the shtiebel doorway they caught a glimmer, the sudden horrified flash of recognition that fired there and was gone. Something needled, disturbed him deeply. He called his office and asked for himself. When he was informed that he was not there, he called a taxi, taking it into Hampstead a block from his house. From there he progressed on foot, sneaking around the rear of the house and letting himself in through the side garage door.

And what was he to make of this scene? Now it was Max who stood in the shadows watching, listening. They were speaking too intimately to make out, but their actions, Ellen's tears, Golem's comforting embrace, their gasping, famished kissing. It turned his stomach and piqued both his anger and curiosity.

He would forbid Golem from embracing Ellen ever again. No more kindness, no more empathy. From this day forth, the answer to every question would be no. Just like before. No. No. No. Let her hair grow white, let her head grow bald with wondering, why. Why? Why? Why?

Max watched as Golem pulled away from Ellen, craning its neck to look at the kitchen clock. It was saying something to her, indicating the time. Max withdrew into the shadows of the dark garage and waited. Within a few moments Golem appeared, the keys to the Jaguar in its hand.

"What did you tell her," he whispered quietly, stepping into the slash of light thrown from the stairwell.

Golem may have been surprised to find Max standing there but didn't show it.

"I told her I had an urge for some bagels. I was going to St. Viateur," it replied smoothly. "But I was actually going to pick you up."

Max stroked his beard, a smiling creasing his grey, ageing face.

"Then I suppose you should go," whispered Max, making way for Golem to pass. He watched as the creature entered the car and pushed the button to raise the garage door.

Golem walked automatically to remove the youngest daughter's bike from in front of the Jaguar. Max approached the driver's door just as Golem started the car. As the creature lowered the window, Max leaned in, that arching smile still bending his face.

"Pick up a half dozen white seeds for me," he said. "When you get back, we will have a little talk. OK?"

Golem nodded solemnly and put the car in drive, leaving Max in a faint cloud of exhaust.

They did not talk when Golem returned from the bagel bakery. The girls had been waiting, the Lewitteses dropped by with their kids, and a veritable party was thrown together.

In his dark workshop Max Schemler quietly seethed while up above the sounds of joy and laughter and human conversation filtered down. For some strange reason, Max was inflicted by the sounds of the cutlery on dinnerware, the cries of "Try the white fish" and "The herring is delicious!" and "Of course it's good, it's from Schwartz's!" His mind, recently so insensitive to the temptations of food and drink, roiled with the desire to taste, to drink, to consume. He entertained a feverish dream that it had been he who had gone to the bagel place, he who had stopped at Schwartz's deli, he who had picked the white fish from Kosher Quality. He saw himself in the golden light of the kitchen, surrounded by admiring, deferential people, his family and his friends, all smiling at him with deep affection and love. Love!

When Max woke, he was stuck to the chaise lounge by his sweat-soaked clothing. Wiping his brow, his hand came up dripping wet. He struggled to his feet, dizzy and confused, imagining himself lost and buried. He pounded on the door, hoarsely rasping, "Out! You let me out!" Finally, his senses cleared his panic, and his anger returned. He checked his watch and was surprised to find that it was almost four in the morning.

The creature had not come to see him, thought Max. I ordered it and it disobeyed me! We shall see, I'll fix it!.

Max crept out into the garage, heading for the rear steps. Every joint in his body ached and stung him. He found the door to his study wide open, the floor littered with fashion magazines, homework, travel brochures and family photographs. Even his desk was in disorder, cheques and money strewn over the surface. His anger welled in his throat like bile, nearly choking him. He slipped into the corridor leading to his bathroom, opened the door, and was assailed by the tearing, impassioned moans of Ellen.

Black, black swirled into Max's eyes as he cracked open the door between his walk-through closet and his bathroom. The opposite door was open and Max could see clearly into the bedroom, aglow with light. Ellen was on her knees, naked, facing where Max stood watching. Behind her, the creature, Golem, crouched, his arms around the nude, moaning woman, his crotch glued to her backside, following her writhing, sinuous movements as she murmured and whined, "Fuck me, fuck me..."

Max beheld the scene and a sour, salty liquid filled his mouth and throat. Against his will, his watery eyes beheld the unclean spectacle, the foul joining of flesh and thing. As his eyes travelled up his wife's body, he was unnerved to find that Ellen appeared to be staring directly at him. Impulsively, Max withdrew, uncertain if he had been seen, but soon his anger and curiosity drew him to the door to look again. Ellen's face was tilted up, the eyes fixed in Max's direction, yet she neither slowed her urgent movements nor showed any shame. She sees me, thought Max. She doesn't see me.

In a moment, it was no longer an issue for, as he continued to watch, a wave swept over Max Schemler, something rising deep in his flesh, twisting his guts as though G-d himself had grabbed his entrails. As the woman on the bed rolled back her head and cried out, as the whites of her eyes became visible under the heavy, lust-drunk lids, and before Max knew what was happening, a tearing pain knifed through his vitals and he emptied himself into his own, shabby pants, his stale seed giving off an odour that shamed him.

A split second later, with the relieved cry of a slave suddenly set free, Golem suddenly grabbed Ellen's hips between its two strong hands and drew her to it with mighty, slapping lunges until it too, emptied itself of its passion and with fading moans, moved slower and slower till both figures collapsed.

In the corridor, Max tried to move so as not to feel the gluey shame between his withered legs. The tears now poured out of him as he descended, down the rear stairs, down to the garage, down to his cave. He fell onto the floor, onto the dirt and dust and raked his face and beard with clawing, grasping hands as though to wipe from his mind the scene he had just witnessed and been an unwitting part of.

I will have to destroy it now, thought Max. I have blundered. I have given it the knowledge, and I will have to fix this once and for all. It will not be so bad. I will give her a divorce, cut them all free. Now that I've come so far, there is no question of turning back. I will find the appropriate passages and will the *shem* out of its filthy corpse. I will return it from where it came from and plant nettles in that soil. Enough!

In the morning, Max Schemler paced and worried himself, waiting for Golem to descend into the garage. It was late, morning prayers would not wait, and Max was anxious to begin the work of destroying his creation. He just needed to consult some texts, work out the progression. Finally Golem appeared, and Max threw himself on the creature, pounding its chest.

"How dare you make me wait!" he hissed, spittle wet on his lips.

Golem did not react at first, allowing Max to vent his anger.

"I was attending Ellen," replied Golem quietly. It then smiled at Max.

Max regarded the smile as an insolent smirk and slapped the creature's face so hard that he broke blood vessels in his pale, narrow fingers.

Golem did not appear to have felt anything. It simply walked towards the driver's door of the Jaguar.

"Give me the fucking keys!" hissed Max, snatching them away from Golem. "I'll drive. You crouch on the floor, on the dirt where you belong!"

Golem regarded Max curiously. If one had been observing the scene, one would have thought that Golem was looking at a specimen of some sort. Golem walked to the passenger's side and stepped in.

"On the floor, defiler!" spat Max, the bile rising again in his throat. "You think I don't know about you? You think I didn't see? You think you learned something last night?"

Max fired up the car and hit the garage door remote at the same time. He turned to Golem again.

"That was your end, do you hear me? That was your finish! Thing!" sneered Max, jamming the car into drive and accelerating, only to stomp hard on the brakes.

His youngest daughter's bike lay directly in his path, and for a brief moment, in his high anger, Max considered simply driving over it. He wrestled the shift selector back into park.

"Shit!" he cried, nearly tearing out the door release in his anger and haste.

Golem crouched on the floor, unable to see what the problem was. He had no idea that Max had not actually succeeded in placing the car in park but somewhere between neutral and drive. He did not notice the shift selector click into drive but he did hear the engine, still revving high under the automatic choke, take up the tension of the torque converter and feel the car jerk suddenly into motion.

Max grabbed the bicycle and, giving vent to his anger, was about to throw it across the front lawn, when he became aware of a change in the sound of the car's idling engine. He turned and found the Jaguar almost upon him. At that moment, fighting his own panic, Golem raised his head over the dashboard to find itself staring directly into Max's wide and terrified eyes.

So, consider Max Schemler's last moments of existence on this earth: a heavy, accelerating Jaguar sedan bearing down on him and, in the front window, the top half of his own face, the eyes marked with a strange, unspeakable expression of vindication, watching, as this last joke, this last jest of G-d is played out. Then, blessed nothing.

And imagine the scene from the front row: a withered, jaundiced middle-aged man in a shabby overcoat, a girl's pink bicycle raised as though to be thrown, the head turned toward the car closing in, the mouth opened in surprise, the eyes bleeding defeat, and Golem, receiving it all, in an instant, everything. Then, finally, nothing.

As soon as the car hit, Golem had grabbed the shift selector, jamming it into park. There was no sound, no cry, no reaction from any corner. Getting out, Golem walked to the front of the car to find Max Schemler lying face down, his head folded under his chest, his neck broken. The bicycle had somehow ended up under the Jaguar's front wheel, effectively stopping it even before Golem had.

Golem felt the hair on the back of his neck prickle and, looking up toward the house, found Ellen at the bedroom window looking down, her hand clamped over her mouth.

In the sub-basement workroom, Ellen watched quietly as Golem laid Max Schemler's body out on the table. Golem closed Max's eyes and the open mouth.

"No one saw anything," reasoned Golem. "If they had, the phone would be ringing, the authorities would be here already."

Ellen spoke in a fearful monotone.

"The hedges," she said softly. "People can't see over the hedges. It's still early."

Golem busied himself removing Max Schemler's clothing. Ellen recoiled both at Golem's actions and at the soiled, foul smell that emanated from the corpse. Golem noticed and explained, almost as an apology.

"It was hard for him to wash here. He had to wait till everyone was sleeping, and then he could only use the laundry sink. After a while, I think he just didn't bother."

Ellen continued to watch and then, as though stirring out of a dream, questioned Golem.

"What are you doing to him?"

"We have to decide. We have to decide what we want to do, Ellen," said Golem evenly as he continued his work.

"What do we have to decide?" replied Ellen, an angry edge crowding her voice. "I have a dead man in my house, and I have a man who is not really a man telling me I have to decide. What is there to decide? We have to call someone. You have to go somewhere. G-d!" she shouted, the tears flowing again.

Golem had Max Schemler half undressed now, the body bathed in the unhealthy light from the fluorescent fixture overhead. Golem stood back, pressed his palms together, considering. He then turned to Ellen, taking her shoulders in his hands.

"There is another thing we can do," he said holding Ellen's eyes with his own. "We can go on. We can continue living our lives. This was … you see there is free will and there is predetermination and …"

"What are you saying?" cried Ellen, confused and lost in her fear.

Golem calmed her, taking the seriousness out of his voice and assuming the crooning of a lover. He indicated Max Schemler's body.

"This was *beshert*, Ellen. Of this, I am certain. This was meant to be and how we deal with this decides both our futures."

Ellen withdrew from Golem's grasp and circled round the work table.

"This was meant to be? This had to happen?" she said, her voicing rising in tone. "Max, there is a body lying in my house! This is a body! What do you suggest, burying it in the garden? Going on like nothing has happened?"

Golem relaxed his shoulders. He approached, taking Ellen into his arms again.

"There is a way. I won't tell you. I can't explain, but if you trust me, if you believe that we can go on being happy together, then there is a way to make all of this disappear."

"What are you going to do?" asked Ellen, cautiously warming up to the idea.

Golem led her gently to the workshop door.

"I cannot tell you. I can only do this if you agree to try to carry on. To try to carry on being happy. Do you?" Golem asked, searching Ellen's eyes.

She was looking at Max Schemler's corpse, looking at what it had become. She was repulsed by it. She looked at Golem, putting her hand on the side of his face, feeling the warm wrinkles, the perfect flesh. She turned and walked slowly up the steps to the garage.

"Do what you have to do," she said quietly.

When he could no longer hear her footsteps, when he was certain she was somewhere far removed from the cellar, Golem turned to Max Schemler. Slowly, reciting the *Kaddish* from memory, Golem removed the rest of Max's clothing.

"*Yisgadal, vi'yiskadash....*"

Magnified and sanctified. Magnified and sanctified at last.

When the body of Max Isidor Schemler, son of Rebbe Avigdor Schemler (may their names be writ large in the book of the Lord), lay pale and lightly blue under the faintly pulsing fluorescent light above the table, Golem raised himself onto the work table, moving on his hands and knees till he was straddling the corpse. He brought his face down, till it was quite close to Max's. The two profiles formed a queer tableau: Max as a fun house mirror, reflecting and distorting the beautiful face of Golem as it hovered.

"You made me from the earth as He made you from the dust," Golem said, incanting. "Return to him, now, through me."

Golem turned himself over and began to lie down on top of Max Schemler's body, absorbing it like a shadow eclipsing the moon.

"Return to the dust that is me. Come into my being and be me," uttered Golem, settling back and obliterating any sign, all evidence of he who had been Max Schemler, son of Avigdor Schemler, may their names be bound up in the book of light.

Later that day, Ellen and Golem took stock of the situation.

"He has become so much a part of the shtiebel life that if he suddenly stopped coming …" said Golem.

"They would be concerned. Suspicious," sighed Ellen. "You have to keep going, at least for a while."

"And the office? I can't simply stop showing up," reasoned Golem.

"So, you go to shul in the morning. Stay till lunch say, twelve, then get downtown. Arrange as many meetings as possible for lunch time. Take care of business till five or so, then you're home free."

Golem worked it all out in its his mind.

"And then, do I go back to the shtiebel?"

Ellen snorted, rising up to sit in Golem's lap.

"Oh no. You come straight home. The idea is to give them the impression, slowly, slowly, that work is becoming important and that you can no longer spend the whole day *shnoring*… they'll get the idea," Ellen said confidently.

"Slowly, slowly," repeated Golem burying his face in the nape of Ellen's neck.

"Do you feel bad, Ellen?" asked Golem after a few moments.

Ellen nuzzled her lover a little before answering.

"I did. I don't now," she murmured. She rose, taking Golem's hand. "Come with me, I want to check something." Ellen led Golem up to their bedroom.

The first week was nerve-wracking. Ellen adjusted Golem's look to match somewhat more closely that of Max at the time of his death. Still, that first morning at the shtiebel Golem felt the hot glare of many suspicious eyes. It looked like Max Schemler, they thought; it even sounds like Max Schemler, and yet…

Golem was smart enough not to exchange more than light pleasantries with the regulars and let it slip that there were big important problems at the office.

"We are doing work for the Congress," he let drop. "Got to beat up on some former Nazi slave-labour companies."

The Brethren nodded in admiration, giving the tacit license for Golem to absent himself. He could barely wait for twelve noon to come. He bolted for the office and arrived in time for an important meeting with the Singh Brothers. They were expanding into West Africa and needed some advice.

Nerves had never been a problem for Golem. He simply didn't know enough to be frightened of anything. Something had changed, however, and he often felt himself gripped by anxiety. What was the poison pill he had swallowed along with Max?

Each day that followed presented its own worries and reasons to be nervous and yet, whenever Golem assumed that the worst was at hand, discovery would be evaded, disaster avoided. Then the week ended, and both Ellen and Golem sighed with relief and sought each other in the night.

Ellen put Golem's less-than-stellar bedroom performance down to stress and anxiety. What did she expect, anyway? Poor little guy. Just to be held was more than enough. Just to have an embracing body, an arm around her made her feel that they could pull it off.

The first week at the shtiebel Golem had been deaf to the give- and-take of Talmudic discourse that buzzed around him and his eye rarely left the clock on the wall as the hour hand faltered and trembled toward the time when he could leave.

The second week, he entered the shtiebel still anxious, but he calmed as he sat down, shrouded from the other's eyes by his talis. He discovered, mysteriously, that he could recite the morning prayers flawlessly, and with a convincing, old-school, shtetl Yiddish cadence. As the morning disputations commenced, as the curious stepped forward with challenging questions, Golem sat still, watching and listening. And when the clock bade him depart, he did, but the air of the shtiebel went with him. He often found himself rolling a particularly tricky bit of Midrash interpretation around and around in his head, even as Metzger droned on about business.

By the end of the second week, a violent argument broke out in the shtiebel regarding whether or not there was a specific admonition in the Torah against women lying together. Arguments and counter-arguments flew thick and fast, fired with righteous fury and intellectual indignation, which Golem found absorbing. By the time he raised his eyes to look at the clock, it was past two in the afternoon. Tearing himself away, he made it to the office, breathless, only to find that his absence had scarcely been noted.

The next morning, eager to find out how the disagreement had been resolved, one arrogant pisher yeshivnik sneered, "Answers are for those who ask questions, Schemler. Nothing here is for free."

This time, another captivating but far more subtle line of discourse was contested, and at one point a probing question lit a match in Golem's mind and before he could stop himself he offered a tentative theory. The entire shtiebel stilled and went silent as Golem's voice, faint at first, then more full-voiced, posited an opinion that was both fresh and insightful. The silence was pregnant. The pisher yeshiva-putz leaned down and said quite loudly, "Welcome back, Rebbe Schemler!" The entire shtiebel cheered and clapped, breaking into one of those pounding, wordless Hassidic songs, a tune without words that expressed, better than any lyrics, the exalted cry of a soul filled with joy.

That day, Golem never made it to the office. I've got news for you, he never got there the day after nor the day after that nor the day after that.

Finally, his law office partners called him at home to request a meeting. The next morning, sitting anxiously in the conference pit in his office, Golem wondered to himself how he was going to resolve this problem. He pressed his fingers together as he waited for his partners to gather. He noticed that much of the hair on his hands had disappeared and that the skin of his fingers had grown quite pale. Even his nails, once rounded and hard, were flatter, softer.

Lewittes and Metzger entered, with kind smiles and empathetic concern. They explained everything, how they knew about Max's deathbed promise to his father, Avigdor Schemler (may G-d take him up and give him peace). They revealed that they knew where Max was spending his days, and they said they understood how the practise of law no longer appealed to him.

Lewittes spread out documents before Golem, listing the firm's assets and Max's personal holdings. It was an enormous sum, thought Golem. Princely.

"So you see," said Metzger, putting his hand on Golem's shoulder. "You've succeeded, Max. You've done it. There is no reason for you to be worried about what happens here."

"Not to say you won't be missed," chuckled Lewittes. "The Singh brothers are jumping out of their pants at the possibility of your retirement. But, you have to admit, Max, your heart just isn't in it."

"No," said Golem, the numbers on the documents still spinning in his head.

"No," repeated Metzger with finality. "You have earned this, Max. If anyone has. Why tear yourself in two?"

Metzger held out his heavy, deep black Mont Blanc fountain pen, indicating the places where Max's signature was required. Golem took the pen and was momentarily transported by the weight and perfect balance of the instrument.

"Study, Max," said Lewittes. "You have a chance that some of us, many of us, have often dreamed for ourselves. G-d willing, in a few years, maybe I can keep my promise too."

The signature came out of Golem from somewhere deep inside of him. A single breath, a thought and the black, thin ribbon that sealed his fate.

"Don't let us down, Max. I mean, Rebbe Schemler," said Metzger, offering his hand.

Golem looked around at the smiling men, the pen still defying gravity in the palm of his hand.

"No," he said, taking Metzger's hand in both his own. "No, I won't."

Lewittes hugged Max tightly.

"Yasher koyach, Max. Yasher koyach."

Ellen was waiting for him when he returned, a head of steam building, waiting to explode. As soon as Golem entered she was on him, her sharp, medium-height heels chewing up the floor as she paced from side to side, blocking him in, forcing him down in his chair at the kitchen table.

"Did you think I wouldn't find out?" she hissed, her dark eyes flashing. "What happened to you?

Golem did not answer her but laid out the documents he had signed. Ellen stopped in her tracks as she scanned the acts of dissolution, the disclaimer against any further recourse, the stipend agreement, and her face went another shade of white. It was a shade Golem had not seen before.

"They cheated you!" Ellen cried, her lower lip wet and trembling. "You signed this? Max, they cheated you!"

"But it is so much money," pleaded Golem, confused and hurt. "How much more money do we need?"

Ellen smashed both fists down onto Golem's shoulders, and then collapsed into a chair.

"That's not the point, Max!" she shrilled. "Max would never have signed this. Why did *you*, Max!"

Ellen clamped her hand to her forehead as though to stop the world from spinning. When her eyes fixed on Golem, fixed on the smile he assumed to show his empathy, Ellen merely shook her head with stunned disgust.

"My G-d, what is happening to me … I'm going insane," she muttered, staring again at the documents before her, which described the rest of her life in bullet points of diminishing returns.

She calmed herself, sitting back in her chair to gaze with wonder and contempt at the creature before her.

"What has happened to you, Max?" she cried. "Look at you. Look! You're starting to look like him. You're beginning to smell like him."

As the nausea rose in her guts, she pushed back from the table, lowering her head towards her lap. It was no good, nothing was going to stop this.

"What have I done?" she said, as she ran to the guest bathroom.

Golem sat still, listening to the sounds of Ellen being sick, his ears still ringing, stinging from the sharp, cutting insults and accusations. He It had a sudden longing to be back in the shtiebel, back in the cosy, close embrace of men with something other than money on their minds.

And so they grew apart, slowly, inexorably. Ellen tried to get the acts of dissolution revoked, but Metzger and Lewittes had created legal documents that were iron-clad. There was little wiggle room but finally, to avoid anything scandalous, they agreed to increase Max Schemler's monthly stipend to a level that Ellen could live with.

Golem was now spending all his time at the and over a short time forgot practically everything else. His three daughters became once more estranged from their pale, ghost-like, humourless father. Ellen sealed herself off hermetically from Max and his world, plunging once more into what gentile society could offer by way of diversion. Perversely, her estrangement from Max only elevated her status in her crowd. To have what she had, and then to lose it, cast her as a tragic heroine. She was free now, they assured her, to take a lover, to reach for any kind of happiness available to her. She owed it to herself, after suffering such a fall with that monster, that religious hysteric.

One last Shabbos, Max arrived home in the evening to find Ellen preparing to go out. Having lit the candles, Max sat quietly in the kitchen, his siddur opened, his kippa on his now balding white head, swaying slowly as he intoned the Sabbath Kiddush. He could hear Ellen's footsteps as she clipped to and fro, fussy, adjusting. Soon the cadence of her steps changed, became repetitive and circular in nature. After a few moments, she appeared in the kitchen doorway.

"My car keys," she said evenly, barely able to bring her eyes to look at Max.

Max did not reply. Ellen let out a long-suffering sigh.

"Fine," she muttered as she stomped off. In a moment she returned, her purse open and empty.

"That's enough, Max" she said, her voice crisp and rising in tone. "I let you live in your little world, you let me live in mine. Give me back everything you took. I have to go out now!"

Without looking up, Max said quietly and slowly, "It is Shabbos. It is a sin to go out on Shabbos. To spend money. To drive a car. To talk gossip. I will not allow sin to exist in this house."

Ellen threw her purse at Max, hitting him solidly in the face, knocking off his kippa, knocking over the Shabbos candelabra. She glared at him, her legs planted against retaliation, her fists clenched. Max merely retrieved his skullcap, righted the candles and re-lit them, intoning the Shabbos prayer.

"I will walk out of this house! I will walk out of this house into the street if I have to!" she shouted, the windows rattling at the force of her voice. "I will not be a prisoner of you, Max. Of a thing like you!"

Max started, stung by her anger, her choice of words. He closed his siddur, rising slowly. Ellen cringed slightly as she saw Max's ashen, emotionless face, the eyes hooded by shadows thrown by his unkempt brows. As he approached her, Ellen, in her anger and frustration, began to cry, her still-clenched fists rising up under her chin like a child trying to comfort herself.

"Who do you think you are, doing this to me?" she whimpered. "Who do you think you are?"

Max took Ellen by the shoulders, forcing her down into her chair. He peered out of the blackness that were his eyes and spoke to her out of the blackness that was his voice.

"I'm your husband."

Das ende.

GLOSSARY OF YIDDISH TERMS AND WORDS

Aliyah — Literally, Hebrew for "going up." The modern meaning refers to temporary or permanent immigration to Israel.

Angeshparte natur — Stubborn or obstinate nature.

Beshert — Pre-ordained; meant to be.

Bubby and Zaydie — Grandmother and Grandfather. An interesting sociological phenomenon is present in this description of these pishers. Max's friends were all pretty much self-made men. Certainly they stood on the shoulders of fathers who made enough money to send their kids to McGill, but they were not wealthy. The "pishers" comment refers to people in Cote St. Luc, Montreal's other Jewish enclave, who are living off their father's or, in some cases, grandfather's wealth. The fathers were also self-made of the previous generation and regarded their children, rightly or wrongly, as remedial in life at best and not to be trusted with money. This hereditary/economic family structure ensured the emasculation and infantilization of a generation of adults. Their own parents didn't trust them enough to tie their shoes and so handed out houses, vacations and living stipends until their children were well into their fifties and sixties. The actual wealth was bequeathed to the grandchildren. And so a generation of grandchildren have grown up eventually controlling the family wealth and having to take care of their spoiled and ageing parents.

Buchor	Boy
Goniff	Literally, thief. In this context, an affectionate term for a child.
Goylem	Golem, the Yiddish version of the word, sometimes used as a rough term of affection for a troublesome boy in pre-war Eastern Europe.
Greiven	Stuffed chicken skin; stuffed derma.
Kabbalah/ Kabbalist	The Zohar, or Kabbalah, book of Jewish mysticism. A person who studies the Kabbalah
Kaddish	The prayer for the dead.
Kiddush	The prayer over wine to welcome in the Sabbath or holiday. Also, the prayer before the snack to celebrate a happy social event such as a bris (circumcision) or bar/bat mitzvah.
Kippa	Skullcap; yarmulke.
Lubavitchers	Members of the Lubavitch sect, a Hassidic or Orthodox group of Jewish people who anticipate the coming of the Messiah with good deeds, songs, dance and fervent prayer.

Ma'ariv	Evening prayers
Naches	Joy; sometimes parental joy in the accomplishments of a child. Always joy at any accomplishment of a grandchild.
Pisher	Literally, one who pees himself. Referring to grown men who are still childish in their demeanour, behaviour and ability to realise their ambitions.
Putz	Literally, penis or prick.
Shem	The life force
Shmaltz	Fat.
Shmear	Literally, to spread, referring to the butter on bread; in this case, a freely given bribe.
Shnorring	Freeloading. Ellen is not using the term correctly, an indication of the degree to which she has been assimilated. This is common among the bourgeoisie of enclaves like Hampstead. They enjoy dropping Yiddish words into everyday conversation, but sometimes the actual meaning of the words and the proper pronunciation are lost or confused.
Shtiebel	Literally, a house, but in this context, a neighbourhood prayer room. In Montreal, usually a room in a house, the basement of a duplex, even an old store front in a strip mall donated

by a sympathetic Jewish owner. Generally, these houses are self-run, there is no permanent rabbi. However, because the men who attend make it part of their daily routine, there is a territorial imperative regarding who sits where, who leads the prayers and who gets to talk. The territory notwithstanding, men go to shtiebels because they tend to be less formal, more purely religious without the social niceties and superficial obligations one finds in organised synagogues. Often, men attend them simply because they are close to where they live.

Shul	Synagogue.
Siddur	Daily prayer book.
Tamavate	Meaning stupid, dumb.
Treif	Not kosher, usually referring to food.
Yahrzeit	The anniversary of a death, usually observed by a visit to the cemetery and the lighting of a twenty-four hour yahrzeit candle.
Yashir koyach	May your strength endure. What one says to a Jewish man who has just completed a Torah reading during daily prayers or any other religious reading.
Yiches	Bloodlines; heritage.

ABOUT THE AUTHOR

J. Jacob Potashnik spent his youth working with his photographer dad, travelling whenever he could and working as a prep chef in restaurant and hotel kitchens but decided he didn't have the back for it. Instead, he studied communications and cinema and moved into film and television. He co-wrote the WGC Award-winning feature film *Stardom* with Denys Arcand. In addition to screenwriting, he works as a producer, script consultant and educator. Writing in prose has been his lifelong compulsion.

Jacob lives in his boyhood home in Montreal with his wife, Pascale Landry, PhD.

Made in the USA
Charleston, SC
27 February 2017